Dear Reader,

My first sight of an ancient warrior's treasure inspired *Fearless*. I had little thought, making my first visit to London since student days, how a story would spring to life out of a thousand-year-old treasure hoard on display in the British Museum.

Perhaps I should have guessed. The treasure itself was discovered as the result of a woman's particular vision. This woman, Mrs. Pretty, was convinced the mounds of earth on her lands at Sutton Hoo hid the treasure of kings—she was right.

Many precious objects were buried with the Sutton Hoo warrior king around 625 AD, but it was the battle helm that caught my interest. Rich with symbols of forgotten power, it had a mask to protect the wearer's face—and a story was born.

A helmet of this type, which both proclaimed and concealed identity, was meant for someone with a heart as brave as a king's, who yet hid their face. The idea invaded my story and the helmet became Judith's.

Treasure of a very different sort sparks *Untamed*, my next story of King Alfred's time—a man's heavy torc, or neck ring, made of eight strands of twisted gold. Such torcs are British—"Celtic"—like the warrior who wears it in my story. Macsen, burdened by secrets, is both blessed and cursed with as much mysterious power as the symbolic gold. Only one woman can match his dangerous power with her own, and heal the bitter pain of his past. I hope you'll join me for their story.

Helen Kirkman

Praise for Helen Kirkman

"Dark Ages? In Helen Kirkman's hands, they shine."
—*USA TODAY* bestselling author Margaret Moore

A Fragile Trust

"Kirkman's lyrically descriptive prose sustains
an unusual emotional intensity. This one generates
that rare urge to read it straight through."
—*Romantic Times BOOKclub*

"*A Fragile Trust* tells the story of a love so powerful that
readers will never forget it…absolutely awe-inspiring
and sure to be one of the best historicals of 2005!"
—*Cataromance.com*

A Moment's Madness

"This debut novel is rich with textural details of an
ancient time, retelling with flair the age-old story
of love trumping vengeance."
—*Romantic Times BOOKclub*

"*A Moment's Madness* is a mesmerizing tale and I was
loath to put it down until the very last page was turned."
—*ARomanceReview.com*

Forbidden

"Very graphic and sensual, this tale is well-told and
fast-paced from start to finish."
—*Old Book Barn Gazette*

"*Forbidden* will hold your attention from the
vivid opening to the climax."
—*Romantic Times BOOKclub*

Embers

"The lush backdrop and intrigue-laden plot
make for good reading."
—*Romantic Times BOOKclub*

HELEN KIRKMAN

Fearless

HQN™

HQN™

ISBN 13: 978-0-373-77119-6
ISBN 10:   0-373-77119-3

FEARLESS

This edition published by arrangement with Harlequin Books S.A.

® and TM are trademarks of the publisher. Trademarks indicated with
® are registered in the United States Patent and Trademark Office, the
Canadian Trade Marks Office and in other countries.

www.HQNBooks.com

Printed in U.S.A.

For Barbara and Peter Clendon—
for their generous and unfailing support of romance writers,
for sponsoring the "Clendon Award" and for giving
me encouragement when it was needed.
Thank you.

Also by Helen Kirkman

Destiny
A Fragile Trust
A Moment's Madness
Forbidden
Embers

And coming soon from HQN Books
Untamed

N

Viking forces control
all of England north of
the River Thames

Saxon warriors fiercely
defend their king in
the last free land...
Wessex.

NORTHUMBRIA

THE WELSH

MERCIA

EAST
ANGLIA

Sutton Hoo

River Thames

London

Derne

WESSEX

KENT

Stathwic

Winchester

CORNWALL

England 875AD

(Author's Note: Stathwic and Derne are fictitious localities)

1

Kent, England—*the South Coast*, A.D. 875

THE MAN WOULD REFUSE HER.

Judith saw it in the dangerous face with its fiercely carved lines, in the implacable gaze. She read the limitless determination, a will as strong as hers...*pain*. No. That was a mistake. There was nothing in the green eyes of the foreign mercenary but the dark ruthlessness, complete as the fluid strength in his body when he turned. Strength and power and something harshly contained

The desperation inside her, the anger, broke—

"Then you will cause death." She would stop him. She watched his broad back; expensive blue linen stretched tight over moving flexible muscle, the tangled gold coil of his hair flooding across it.

A woman's words fell unheeded in a hall packed with warriors. But she caught his attention, so completely he did not notice that someone in that room full of hardened men was trying to kill him.

But Judith's gaze caught it, the death she had summoned by

her furious words. It was here, in the sudden bright flash of un-sheathed steel.

He did not see. No one saw. Not one arrogant, mood-proud warrior in the crowded hall moved, even though the carved blade poised behind the mercenary's shoulder caught the narrow beams of the sun.

"No——" She wanted to scream the warning at his oblivious face. But her brain could not find words fast enough in the tiny fractured instant of time that remained.

The green-grey eyes locked on hers suddenly narrowed, but it was too late. No one could prevent his death.

Except her.

One had the courage or one did not. One's life had a purpose or it was empty for all eternity. Useless. Useless...

"*No——*" This time the sound was full throated and shocking. She thought the trained warrior in him realised not exactly what was happening, but danger. She saw the thick muscles under the blue linen bunch, rearrange themselves into a tight line of power. But for all his fine strength, he would be too late.

Judith had no sense of making a decision. She only knew that her body was moving towards the wall of coloured linen, the expanse of vulnerable unprotected flesh beneath it. The dark shadow behind him lunged for its target, off balance now, because of her scream. She brushed past a turning, bright-blue shoulder and hit the murderer full on.

The impact smacked through her, jarring bone, harder than it should have been, like hitting a wall. But the whole of her weight thudded home. There was a moment of recoil in the assassin's movement, a moment beyond time, full of the pounding of blood in her ears and the wild beating of her heart. The black shadow wavered, but then it collected itself. Not a shadow but a solid body of muscle and bone, more than that, hard as stone.

He was frighteningly strong.

She struck out, knowing the knife was still somewhere, twelve inches of fire-hardened steel. She saw it, trapping the high sunbeams. The light through the open window blinded her eyes. She hit out again, the tough years of training making her faster than he expected, forcing him back. But the creature had hold of her. So strong. She tasted fear. She twisted in his grip, knowledge and primitive terrified instinct. Her muscles bunched, the way her brother had taught her, as though she were back in childhood wrestling with Berg in some nursery fight.

She always won.

But Berg had never used all of his strength against her, the way this man did. He would crush the life out of her. She hacked at his feet with the sharpness of leather heels. He cursed. Foreign. She hacked again, harder, heard a grunt, felt the involuntary shift in his weight, got an arm free. If she could use an elbow—

She must have taken his balance after all. He collapsed, hitting the rush-strewn, wood-planked floor with a sickening crack. Gone. But so was she. Falling. She tried to roll under the impact and half succeeded. But she still lost her breath, felt the hard thud of seasoned oakwood jar the side of her hip, her shoulder, her head. She gasped, the pain shooting through her. It felt sharp enough to cripple. She forced movement, twisting over, scrabbling for purchase like a drunk under the mead-bench.

Outside the harsh rasp of her own breath, she could hear the beating swell of disturbed voices around them, see a forest of feet. Not his. Someone grabbed her from behind. The fear blossomed. And the anger. She hit out, backwards. There was a suppressed grunt of pain.

"Murderer..." she yelled. Her voice cracked. *Deliberate, cold-blooded killer.* The knowledge hammered inside her throbbing head. Unacceptable. An offence against all the right order of the world.

She could not move. She could not understand exactly how he held her, but she was helpless.

"Nithing." The accusation of cowardice, of utter and unredeemable lack of worth, struck round the crowded hall.

There was silence, no movement, nothing. Just the sense of being held. Trapped. And the sharp pain.

She became aware of his heat, of the unforgiving closeness, of the long stark lines of his body on the wooden floor with hers. Of the sharpness of his breathing. She could hear it in the stillness. The sound of it mingled with hers. And then the background noise began again, the hissing roar of dozens of voices like the sea, like the dizziness behind her eyes. The hall was full. Someone would help her. Someone...

"Nithing." It was a breath of sound.

"Nay." The foreign voice cut across the noise, slicing through the swirling currents with the strength and accuracy of the forged-steel blade. "Not an entirely worthless life. Not if you saved it."

"I—" A different voice, even though the flat accent was the same. Not the murderer's voice. Deeper. Her eyes focused.

She saw the bright-blue cloth first, even before his hand where it curved round her rib cage, stopping movement. The bright gold swing of his hair touched her shoulder.

"You…" The burning heat from his body struck through her, the feel of a man, not the anonymous barrier of the assassin hard and frozen as stone, but the close human contact of male skin burning through the linen. Not the assassin with the knife, but the man who had refused the desperate boon she had asked of him. The murder victim.

Alive.

She felt his warmth and the dizziness beat through her mind. She was shaking, now that it was over, trembling like a child.

"The man was an assassin. A murderer—"

"He is dealt with."

Dealt with. "I thought you were dead. I thought he would kill you. He had the *seax* blade and you did not see. You—"

He said something. She did not know what. The sound of it breathed against her hair and her face. Warm against her cold skin.

His deep voice was harsh, like his strained breathing, and then it became steady. It was like an act of will even though she could feel the laboured movement of his ribs against her back. Such control. It negated everything that had happened in those few desperate moments when he had been attacked. It blocked off all the primitive, gut-wrenching turmoil of that deadly struggle. It covered much more. There was fire beneath that ruthless covering, something depthless. She had thought it was pain. Anger?

Whatever it might be was blotted out, obliterated. No. Paved over. She could feel the hot power inside him. He said something soothing. She wondered at the control he had over whatever it was he felt.

What lived in his mind?

She had to know.

She had to be aware of everything this dangerous creature thought because she had to get him to do what she wanted, what had to be done to prevent more bloodshed, killing. That was why she had come here to the port at Stathwic. She had to understand because she had to manipulate him. That was her reason. There could be no other. She could not allow it.

She swallowed pain, feeling the stark heat of him. It touched her as though it could burn away everything, even the cold emptiness inside her.

Her head lay against his heart. She felt its harsh beat like the echo of her own, still too fast, strained, so at variance with his ruthless control.

Such control was not in her, however much she tried.

How did she combat that kind of power?

"Hush…"

They were so close, she and the ruthless mercenary, close as a single being. She let him touch her.

He held her very, very still, as though he knew that was what her abused body craved, as though he could sense that the slightest movement would set the aching in her head to raw pain. She lay quiescent in the unsafe embrace of the stranger and he never moved. Oh, that carefully wielded power. She envied it beyond anything on middle earth. It had a deadly attraction to her. Perilous.

She kept her bruised flesh still and his voice touched her, the unguessable depths in him hidden. She let the voice hold her. She felt the sound of it and the fine steadiness and the power that went fathoms deep.

So perilous.

The heated touch of his body against hers was as intimate as a lover's embrace. That was what it must be like, to be held by a lover, this dangerous closeness. Touching. The deep timbre of his voice seemed inside her own mind.

But she could not understand the words he said.

They were foreign. *He* was foreign. He called himself a merchant, but he was a warrior. He was not an inhabitant of this English land, neither Saxon nor Angle nor Briton, but a foreigner, a man from the grey, flat, windswept country at the mouth of the River Rhine. From the turbulent, ill-starred merchant city of Dorestad. A Frisian. If even half the tales were true, he was a pirate. He hid what he thought. Pirates were slayers for hire. He was dangerous—

"Lady!" A new voice, English, sharp with alarm, male, jolted her thoughts. Hunferth, her escort. But sharper still was another voice, female.

"Princess…"

The fine title hung in the air. The smallest frisson of movement passed through the strong body that held her, a reaction as deep and elemental as the strained heartbeat, the rapid breath. It was just as suddenly and as mercilessly controlled.

She could have imagined it.

The two anxious figures from her retinue shoved through the forest of feet, one pair of heavy leather boots, followed closely by delicate finely worked shoes.

"Princess," said Mildred, her maid and companion, her voice emphasising the word, insistent. The title grated. It no longer had any meaning. Mildred knew that.

"Lady," said her male escort more circumspectly. His boots shifted.

The Frisian murmured something incomprehensible against her hair and the disordered edge of her head veil. It sounded throaty, like music. Indecent. She felt the shivering movement of tight muscle against her flesh. It could have been sudden amusement. Unexpected. Unsettling as whatever foreign words he had said.

She had to get inside his mind. That was her mission. Whatever it took. She shifted. Her small weight brushed against heavier flesh. The reaction was instant, heated, intensely male.

She went still. Then she straightened her aching head slowly, trying not to touch him, as though that movement could unlock her thoughts from the fog of disturbing sensation, strangeness. Heat. Her hair spilled over an expanse of blue linen, over an arm ring of red-gold, over the mercenary's hair, scarce two shades darker than her own. She watched the thick mass of pale flaxen waves spread out, mingling with deeper gold, sinfully tangled like a lover getting out of bed.

"Princess?" Mildred was staring at her. There was no regret for the use of that lethal, long-dead word. Her maid was angry underneath the bland face of courtesy, no, frightened. She was looking at the gold-ringed hand.

Judith's gaze followed the other woman's. She saw what her maid saw, what Hunferth, who was both her own man and King Alfred's representative, would see. Beneath the heavy circle of gold shaped like entwined dragon's heads, the man's hand spread out against the shadowy green of her tunic. His thick fingers touched the underside of her breast. His touch was heavy, his palm bent only slightly to accommodate the curve of her body. The tightness of his hold showed clearly the rounded outward thrust of her hidden flesh.

The indecent hand never moved. That was how he had caught her when she fell and that was how he held her, the man who was a confirmed pirate, hard against his body, the warmth of his chest against her back, one heavy, finely shaped leg entangled with the length of hers. And his hand… He would be able to feel her heart beating.

The unsettling heat struck through her, deep in some part that should be hidden, that should never see the light of day, that she had never acknowledged. Something that fascinated, that was so hot it could overcome everything else that existed in the world or inside her, even the emptiness and the black despair. Something that could touch who she was with no defence—

"Let me go." There was a packed hall full of people staring at her, at a woman lying in a man's arms like a *hor-cwen,* a brazen whore scenting the possibility of extra payment.

"I must get up."

"Then take your time." That dangerous accent—

"Lady…"

"Princess…."

"No. Let me stand." Every movement, each struggling breath, pressed her flesh tight to his. She could not cope with that, with him, or the thought of illicit warmth. Not at this moment. Later. Later when she could breathe. She pulled against the shocking palm, against the fingers decorated with yet more gold. For one appalled moment she thought he would not unhand her and then the strong grip relaxed, the warm fluid body moved.

Her knees nearly gave way. The weakness in her limbs and the pain in her head were beyond her expectation. She could not stand up on her own. She bit her lip. He pulled her to her feet. Hunferth started talking. He sounded agitated, stark with shock. But even agitated words were something. She tried to collect her thoughts, her volatile senses. She and Hunferth had been sent here for this one reason only. If they could keep their quarry talking. If she had a moment to gather her wits, to try again. She could still turn this to advantage.

She had saved his life. The consciousness floated in her aching brain. The man was in her debt.

It was low to make use of that, not precisely honourable. But then she thought she was quite probably beyond honour.

She watched the Frisian but she saw another face, fair beyond reckoning, twenty-seven winters old, a king's face burdened with the world's fate. Her heart contracted with the unending pain and then she was seeing someone else, not fair, his familiar beloved looks scarred and ruined beyond healing, her own brother, and behind him was the messenger who had come out of East Anglia. The man who had nearly died, who would never be whole again. Such things had to be stopped.

She would stop them.

Mildred took her arm. If she stood quite still and leaned on Mildred, she would not fall over. Simple, really. She could manage this. She would let Hunferth, who was officially the King's man, begin and…. Then she saw the assassin's body, the slash of blood at his neck.

She had not done that.

"You killed him."

The conversation between Hunferth and the Frisian stopped. The Frisian looked at her.

"Aye."

A single word, and there it was, the deep fire that had been hidden. It was anger, anger beyond reason or what was fit. But behind it was something else, something worse, something she recognised to the depths of her soul.

It was desolation. Despair.

She took a step forward. She knew what she saw in the Frisian stranger's eyes. There was no mistake, none possible. She was not sure that it was calculation or the demands of her mission or even a king's fate that drove her. She only knew she could not turn away. It was like a fated connection, stronger than any tie that could belong to this life, more real.

But Mildred, out of fear or anger or both, pulled her back. The small jolt, traveling up her arm and through her shoulder and her neck into the aching mass of her head, was too much. She tried to keep moving, but Hunferth got in the way.

Then she could no longer see the Frisian, or the mirror of despair, if such a thing existed. She could see nothing. Only blankness, the black deadly emptiness that would swamp everything. It was so familiar and it had so much power. The power to break the strong connection. It could have been her own personal pit of hell.

It took her.

"THEN WHO IS SHE?" The man's voice was unfamiliar, English. She lay still in the dreaming darkness and listened.

"Judith." That was the convicted pirate. Her breath caught in the heady blackness of pain. He could not pronounce her name.

"Judith? What sort of a name is that?" demanded the English voice.

"A remark like that could make you sound like a heathen." The pirate sounded very close. His voice was strong, unmoved, undisturbed. She was shivering. She knew what his closeness was like. She knew what the unmoving façade hid. Mayhap. If she had not dreamed it. If she was not dreaming now. She lay still, because the slightest movement brought on the pain.

"Was there not a Judith in the Bible?" An educated pirate. A contradiction. That was what he was, fire and shadow, ferocity under restraint, a frightening contradiction. "You should be telling me. A princess among her people. Was she not?"

"A princess?" asked the other man. She must have moved, because the pain struck at her. She could not move again, could not open her eyes. Weakness. But just for this moment in the dreaming blackness she did not want to face…things. There was a pause. It stretched out. It should have been part of the blank darkness, but it was highly charged, aware. She thought she could sense his frightening warmth. Then his companion went on speaking.

"…and you carried her in here like a sack of onions and threw everyone else out?"

Sack?

She forced herself to hold still.

"Einhard?" pursued the voice.

That was him, the one who had refused what was so desperately needed. She had almost forgotten he had a name, *Einhard*. She did not want to think of him with a name. Or with despair....

"There is a man of God here," said Einhard. "Besides," he allowed a pause, deliberate, as highly aware as the preceding stretch of silence had been. "I do as I will."

Not terrible despair, that was not what lived behind his carefully constructed façade. It was just the anger, the unfathomable anger beyond the bounds of what was right, an inward focus that seemed absolute. Selfishness— She held still, even though the heavy air crawled over her skin. She was sure she had not moved again.

She had to deal with what was, not fancies. She had to gain what she wanted. The consequences, if she did not, were something she was not prepared to face.

She had to listen while they thought she was still unconscious. She had to fathom what went on in the head of the man called Einhard, merchant...Frisian shipmaster...*pirate*. She would take him and his unfathomable anger and he would do what had to be done, what she wanted. No one else had either his knowledge or his skill. That was what she would take.

"No one on this earth does entirely as they will," said the man of God. There was the consciousness of sudden movement, very close. The rustle of fabric. His clothing? *Bed linen?* Was that where she was? Taken to a chamber apart? A bedchamber.

By the foreign pirate. And his man of God.

"Hold still," said the English voice, directed to Einhard. But she felt the faint shift in his weight, as though he were stretched out beside her, in the bed—

"Almost done."

She was in his bed.

There was a faint sound, like pain, ruthlessly suppressed.

"And this lady, this Judith, what is your connection to her?"

Judith held her breath. She sought for stillness, the same merciless power of control she had seen in her self-seeking adversary. He would think her asleep. He must.

"My connection to her? I thought that was known."

The shivers coursed over her skin.

"Hold still." The man of God's voice was sharp, anxious. But this time the movement did not stop. It continued, inexorable, sensed on the edge of perception. He turned towards her, until he was facing. She guessed it, knew it through the strained edge of hearing, through the skin-tingling awareness of touch denied. Through the edge of heat.

Fire.

She could feel the answering flame spring to life inside her, a counterpart, just as it had happened in the hall when she had felt his hand touching her heart.

She bit down on the feeling. Nothing touched her heart now. No one, no man. Except the true king and his just cause.

Certainly not this man with his strong will given to selfishness.

"My connection to this woman—" The deep foreign voice spoke directly to her. She could feel his gaze on her skin, on her closed eyelids, as though he knew she could hear him, as though he could see inside her head, to her thoughts, to the darkness. "My connection, *our* connection, is that she moved to save my life—" the heat passed over her in dizzying waves "—and I killed someone for her."

She moved. Just one tiny betraying tightening of shaking

muscle. The man of God could not have seen it because his reply was directed to Einhard, just as before. But she knew the pirate had seen, guessed, *sensed*. She knew—

"You both acted in defence," said the other voice heavily, tinged with regret even for a murderer's death. "She saved your life and the assassin would have killed her for it. You had no choice—"

"Choice." The single word was uncontrolled. It must come from the hidden place far beyond the reach of that merciless power over feeling.

"You did what you had to do. There can be no dispute...." The priest had missed it. He thought only of the moral blame attached to killing. He did not understand. There was something else besides that, something that burned the man Einhard with a heat that was far greater. *Helletrega.* The thought came into her head unbidden. The tortures of hell.

"You will have to rest this arm for—"

"No. I am leaving with the first light tomorrow."

Leaving.

"What? But why?" It could have been her own furious question, her own burst of alarm. *Leaving?* "You cannot," said the priest. "You planned to stay. You said—" Then an abrupt movement cut off. "Because—"

"Because." The single word stopped whatever the priest would have said, cut it off because *she* would hear it.

There was silence, laden with a power that could catch fire out of the air.

"And the lady," said the priest, at last. "This princess..." The word jolted her dizzied thoughts.

"Princess?" The word was bitter, unexpectedly so, as though

it touched on the volcano inside him. She could feel his movement, inches away from her, the power of him; she could almost feel the heat of his skin. Then he said, "She is East Anglian."

That was all. Just those two words, *East Anglian,* and the world seemed to stop. No one spoke. No need. *East Anglia.*

That was where it had all begun, the Viking invasion that had swept away every English land except Wessex. The terror had begun in her home, in the place where she had been born, where her ancestors had lived and were buried still in their great silent mounds rich with treasure.

That was where the terror went on, where Earl Guthrum and his Danish troops waited and planned how to bring the last free kingdom of Wessex to its knees. Perhaps with a land army, perhaps by sea.

By the sea....

She heard the mercenary pirate breathe. "East Anglia is gone. Wessex will fall the same way. There can be no other outcome. They know that, the Saxons."

"*No.*"

Her voice came out with the same uncontrolled force he had used when speaking of choice. She sat up. They were staring at each other. His eyes, bright against his sunbronzed face, were the colour of a summer storm on the ocean. The man who was a priest made noises of astonishment, words probably. She did not hear them.

The pirate was not surprised at all.

He watched her.

She sat up straight in his bed and said, "Wessex will not fall." The words came out distinctly, every syllable and every pause achingly clear. Something flitted across the stormy eyes, so fast she could not catch at its meaning.

"That is what you believe."

His voice held no expression. Statement or question? The pain in her head wracked her. She held upright in the tangled mess of the bed linen. She stared at him. Her eyes were dazzled by a wealth of skin, by the blue valleys and the bright-gold power of moving muscle, the heavy curve of a shoulder, the end-less length of an arm, tight pads of flesh over the flaring shape of a rib cage. All moving. Shadows forming over firelit bright-ness in the curtained enclosure of his bed. She thought he was naked.

The priest steadied the candle flames and she understood.

"You are hurt." The unanswered questions about Wessex were pushed back. Her gaze fixed on the ugly reddened line of a cut high on the opposite arm. The priest had been cleaning it. There were stitches. "The assassin…."

"Aye." He stretched out, full length, leaning back against the linen-covered bolster. He was half lying, half sitting, one dark-trousered knee drawn up, his forearm resting on it. She could see the tight line of his belly, the starkly curving muscles of his chest scattered with dark-gold hairs. Power. Such power. But living flesh. Vulnerable. The appalling, fear-filled moments in the great hall played out through her head.

"He hit you after all, with that knife. I did not know." He had held her in stillness and comfort, bleeding. He had made sure she was safe. *I killed someone for her….*

"I did not know. You did not speak."

The fine gold skin moved over tight muscle. "It is naught."

"He will live, lady," cut in the priest. "It was you who frightened us with your swoon."

"Nay, not me. I am well enough."

"This is Tatwin," said the pirate. "He knows healing. He is a lay brother now in training to take holy orders, by which means the Saxons have lost one more clever thane."

A thane. A nobleman then, and a warrior. She transferred her gaze from the stormy-eyed pirate with the lethal body to the other man. He was well-favoured enough, strongly made. She thought he could be formidable. He did not have raging fires trapped inside.

"Then you are God's thane," she said.

"At least someone still understands what belief means."

The stiffening of each separate muscle under the golden skin was undisguisable.

"See to her." The tone was blank, indifferent.

Judith did not take insolence from a dubious foreign merchant. She was still that much of a princess.

"Lady?" began the priest.

She bit the anger down. Control. Anything to delay the moment. Anything to keep her close to her less-than-scrupulous quarry. She allowed the monk in training to examine her head and feed her some vile-tasting draught. It settled the queasy feeling in her belly but made the dizziness in her head stronger. She wondered whether there was wine in it. But all through that competent examination, she was aware of nothing but the man stretched out next to her in the great bed. Of what she must do and what she must persuade him to. She must....

The priest fussed. She tried to make plans in the disquieting lightness of her head. She felt the movement the man called Ein-hard made, the shifting of his heavy weight against the mattress. He would get up. He would go.

"I am well now," she said. The monk made pacifying noises.

Einhard stood. She caught the flash of bared skin in the can-dle flames.

"You need rest, lady."

She would lose him.

"No. It is not necessary."

The fall of fine white linen. His shirt.

"We will have your maid fetched. She should have been here. Einhard? She…"

She could see his hand, the linen bunched in it. The hard glit-ter of gold at his bare wrist as his arm moved.

"*Einhard.*" It was not the monk in training who spoke, cutting the candle-lit air with the sharpness of glass. It was her.

He stopped, the crushed linen in his hand. Her heart beat as though she were someone running a race, as though she were someone drowning. He would hear it.

"Lady?"

She could not find the words. She had never begged. She had never abased herself to crawl after anyone in all of her life.

"Princess?"

"I have no need of my maid," she said. She held the storm-dark eyes with her own. "Not yet. There is…. There is a mat-ter I would speak to you of." She glanced at God's thane. "Alone."

She thought the Frisian would not do it. She thought he would not grant her even that much. She sat straight. She swallowed the remnants of pain, the dislocating dizziness that remained. She willed a clear head. "Please."

He made her wait, the insolent bastard. He made her wait until the sweat started on her skin and her heart beat so hard. Then he sent God's thane, his friend, away. He did not call for her maid.

They were alone.

2

SHE THOUGHT HE WOULD COVER his nakedness, that at least he would slide the shirt over his head.

He did not. He sat on the bed and watched her. It was not decent. *He* was indecent with his half-bare body and his flaunting muscles and his dark foreign voice. Nervousness nearly choked her. Not fear, not fear alone. It was something else.

She sat in his bed, staring at him, willing herself not to get up and yell abuse at him and his fine bronzed flesh, his silent, carefully contained depths.

He moved his knee. He laced his fingers round it. The thick muscle of his thigh compressed against the dark fabric of the linen trousers.

She could not do this.

"I have something to ask you." She had to fight to make her voice work. It came out strangely. She wanted it to sound sweet, cajoling, even remotely pleasing.

It didn't.

The storm-green gaze was fixed on her. He did not move his head. He did not speak.

"Einhard." Her breathing stuttered out of rhythm. The small sound it made was embarrassingly obvious. He never moved.

Whoreson.

She began again.

"I—" Her voice stopped altogether.

"You want something from me."

That did it. The anger came back. His eyes were hot, hot as his golden skin. Fury swamped all the other feelings, the fear and the dizziness and the pain and all the breathless awareness of who he was and his naked body. He was not some trapped and wounded creature, desperate with the pain of it like her. He scorned such things. He scorned everything. He scorned her.

He was a trader at heart. He expected her to ask her favours. Beg.

She smiled. "Who was the assassin?"

Her query hit its mark. First blood to her. His face changed. She had thought it was harsh before. Now it was deadly. The strength pared down to the finely wrought bones. He had expected her request for his aid, her acknowledgement of his flaunted power.

"Bad debt?" she enquired. *Merchant.* If he needed money—

He shrugged. The heavy shoulders moved under the lissom skin. Denial? But she had caught him in something that...

"Do you think it was a bad debt, princess?" He turned towards her. "It is not a debt." The narrowed eyes glittered. The flickering light cascaded over blood-thick muscle like fire. He said something, dark and incomprehensible. She thought again how foreign he was, foreign, and beneath that fiercely held exterior, completely uncontrolled. The strange word reverberated in her ears, a portent of darkness. It sounded like *fehida…faihitho,* something close to English because their heritage was alike, but something unknown.

"What do you mean?" She ought to draw back, move away from all that dangerous power in case whatever restraint of will it was that held him back was broken. Broken, like belief.

At least someone still understands what belief means…. Despair.

"Tell me."

She touched him. Her fingertips and the small curve of her palm came to rest on heated skin, on thick muscle like cords.

He had to say whatever it was, regardless of what she thought or even of what she wanted. He had to speak the thing buried inside him. Things buried were lethal, she knew that.

"Tell me."

The burning eyes watched her, but she thought he did not see her, that he saw nothing in this firelit room. Only another place. Another person? Someone who moved him beyond endurance? Her hand tightened on the hot skin, the frighteningly strong muscle.

"Tell me," she asked again. The third time might release enchantments. She watched his eyes, the many thoughts that crossed them. *Find the words.*

"The word?" he said, as though she had spoken. The myriad lights flickered in his eyes, as though he could not focus on the Wessex bower, on her. "The word in English is *fæhth.*"

Her heart froze. *Feud.* Blood feud. They were lethal, such terrible matters of honour, of vengeance, destructive of everything that lived and breathed. A fight to the death that might burn and smoulder and burn again, through generations.

"I see you understand me."

"Aye." How could she not? There was no one living who had not been brought up to avenge wrongs, either to oneself or to a kinsman. She understood the necessity of that, the obligation. But its justification, its reason for being, was essentially inward looking, a contest of brute strength. The king in his great palace at Winchester wanted to limit the scope of feuding. The king wanted people to live.

The king at Winchester had his back to the wall. The world had moved past contests of honour. The world was mad. There was chaos not forty miles from the door of this room.

"I understand that——" she began. The dark eyes watched her. The candlelight played restlessly across their depths, across the stark face. "I understand there are some matters...." Something flared in the eyes. "Matters of honour, perhaps."

She kept hold of one lethal undamaged arm, her hand intimate against his flesh, skin to skin. She wanted to keep his gaze, so that there would be some light in the dark but it was so hard. She tried the next step. She felt afraid, afraid of making a fatal mistake, afraid far beyond the scope of what she must gain from him.

She lost his gaze.

"Such matters seem important." She fought for better words. She watched the imprint of her hand on his skin. She would lose him entirely, in a way beyond her comprehension. She could no longer see his eyes, only the deep goldness of fine flesh under her fingers, and on the damaged arm, the linen band over broken reddened skin high up near his shoulder.

The knife wound. The assassin.

"Such things only perpetuate destruction. Destruction without purpose that achieves nothing." Her fingers curled round his living flesh. "When there is so much else that—"

She stopped speaking. He had not moved, not one finely balanced muscle.

"What else?" he said.

"The future," she burst out passionately, the words suddenly finding her in a flood, all that was locked in her grieving heart. "Not just one person's good, or even one kindred's, but a country's future, a whole people. People who will be hurt or killed or dispossessed or sold off into slavery if no one protects them, if no one stands up against an army that will take everything they have."

"The kingdom of the West Saxons, Wessex and the threat of a Viking army?"

"What else? Hunferth told you. He tried to explain." Her fingers dug into his flesh. "*I* told you—"

"That you would ask something of me."

"Yes, but—" She tried to hold on to his arm, to the strange connection that had burned between them, to what was in his mind. He could not be entirely without honour. She did not believe it.

"You will ask me in return for saving my life." His voice mocked her. "Is that it?"

Trader.

Yet he had known from the start that she wanted to ask him something. He had expected it when she had begun instead with the dangerous subject of the assassin. She had sought the barbed and potent connection between them, called it forth because of its frightening power.

Used it?

"Yes," she said, goaded. He was playing with fire, with lives. So many lives. Out of selfishness and greed and perhaps out of the prosecution of some endless feud. He was not a man trapped in torment, a man with thoughts.

Stupid, selfish dolt.

She lost control.

"Let me explain how things are. You are here in Wessex with your ships and your men because of piracy. Because you attacked and crippled or sank four trading vessels laden with amber and furs and with silk from Byzantium, and no one knows what you did with the cargoes. You are here because your violent gree—" She cut it off and attempted the impossible control.

"You are here because your *trading* methods have so angered Rorik the earl of Dorestad that you can no longer go back there, to your home. It was Wessex that gave you shelter when Rorik's ships were so close behind you they might have caught you if it had not been for the edge of a storm and the intervention of the port reeve here at Stathwic." She fought to steady her voice. Her skin touched his.

"Wessex continues to give you shelter even though Rorik wants to take you back to face justice—even though Rorik is a powerful enemy to make and a Viking, and Wessex already has its share of Viking enemies on its own shores." She could feel the solid tightness of his arm, the warmth. A connection that was not there, did not exist.

"You are a man under threat of death for more reasons than one. I think you owe more than me. I think you owe something in return to the land and to the king that saved your hide."

"Saved me from the Viking Rorik's wrath? Rorik's men would not have caught me."

Arrogant peasant. *Pirate.* Why had she ever thought there was anything above greed and selfishness in him?

She took a breath. It seared her lungs but even the small sharp hurt held its own strength. Her mind felt suddenly and utterly clear. She had lost track of the nature of her mission, just for one moment under the spell of his eyes and the touch of his burning skin. She had lost what was important. But not now.

"You mean Rorik's men, Danish sailors, experts, would not have caught you because of the skill and the value of your seamanship?" Then so be it.

She did not let go of his arm. The words came out of the air. "No one disputes your skill with ships or your knowledge. That is what I want. That is what Wessex wants, and the king."

"I will not give it."

"Will you not? Over the border," she said, "in East Anglia—" She could say the name. She did not flinch under its bale-filled power. She watched him from the warmth of his bed. "In East Anglia, at Cambridge, there is a base for Earl Guthrum's invasion army. But farther round, out on the coast, is a harbour, not far from the Wessex border, not forty miles from here. It is just a small base. Sometimes ships sail south from there, towards Wessex, and if the coastal defences cannot match them they raid and plunder and rip people from their homes and sell them into bondage. That is how things are."

Fine tremors ran through her flesh where it joined his. He would feel it. She kept speaking.

"But things are changing. Someone brought a message." She

swallowed. She had seen the messenger. She had seen what had been done to him.

"They broke his arm when he escaped. It was shattered. That man will be a cripple all of his life but that did not stop him. He was true to the oath he had given the king." *You would not understand it, but I would serve to that extent if I could, if God would allow my courage. There is nothing else in my life.* She did not say it. He would think she was a woman crazed.

"Earl Guthrum thinks of an invasion by sea. He will test out the strength of the defences set against him." Her hand slid across the solid mass of his arm. The movement was deliberate. Enough to arouse the black-edged fire. "The coastline of Wessex is long, hard to defend. There are too few ships, too few shipmen of skill."

"Yes."

She felt the warmth of his skin. Her hand glided over it, slowly. He did not withdraw from her touch. They shared the same bed. Neither of them had moved.

"If nothing is done, this kingdom will fall to the Vikings like all the other English kingdoms, East Anglia, Mercia, Northumbria. There will be nothing left."

She breathed. They were so close, connection and division. She felt the size of his body in the gathering dark. She saw the shadows and the light across his naked skin. Risk. "You know what it means to see Viking raiding, to have the horror of it repeated year after year." Her breath faltered. The air in the curtained space of the bed held light and darkness, moving shadows. The man who shared the shadows said nothing. He never moved. She took the last step on faith.

"We both know. We have seen, you and I, what despair is. We understand the taste. I come from East Anglia. You come from Dorestad, once Frisian, now in Rorik the Viking's hands."

It was there in his eyes, the knowledge that could never be changed, or disguised, or truly told to anyone else who had not lived it. The knowledge of pain and destruction and of loss without boundaries. It did not matter that he was a pirate and a thief of material goods. She knew he understood. Better than God's thane had. He had said the necessary words himself. *She is East Anglian.*

The shadows held them, and the rippling motes of light.

"I want to stop it," she said. "I want to stop all the destruction. That is what Alfred the king of Wessex wants. You have the key, the knowledge he needs, the way to build more ships, better ships, the way to man them, to sail them, to provide a defence." The words spilled out of her into the waiting shadow and light, into his silence. He would know. He would see.

"The work is half there already." She thought of the half-built ships farther round the Kentish coast at Derne. "But it needs more. A few weeks of your time in return for the protection you have been given in Wessex, in return for your life. That is all." Her words, the sound of her voice, the knowledge filled the air. "That is the only payment—"

"Payment? Payment for—you?"

She stopped, her hand still joined to his flesh. The moving air stilled, suspended. The candle flames burned. She could see their thin smoke. Her throat was suddenly dry. Her skin felt hot as the golden, smoking flame.

Payment. "I meant—" But he had already understood the true meaning behind her words, all the pain. He knew.

"If payment is what you seek, lady, I will give it to you. Out of amber, was it not? And out of furs and Byzantine silk."

"No...." The shadows gathered, the shadows in the chamber and the shadows forty miles away, across the border, waiting for death and maiming and suffering without mercy. His arm moved under her touch, muscle and heavy bone and the fine warm covering of skin. Strength. Pirate's strength.

She sought his eyes. She sought everything that should be there, everything locked in his head, in his mind. He *knew*.

"It is not some merchant's payment I ask, not mere riches." She kept his arm. The dark intimacy of the small chamber pressed on her. "I want you."

The air choked her. The light flared in his eyes, burning her. She was sharply and intensely aware of the touch of his skin. It was like pain. Her whole body seemed to tighten in response. She could feel the sudden surge of burning need, elemental, primitive, uncontrolled. She was aware of his earthy attraction, of his heated flesh and the masculine shape of his body, of its dark promise. Intense and power-laden and to be desired beyond knowledge. Open and bound by nothing, like sin.

But beyond that she was aware of the power of his mind, of what lived in it.

She wanted that.

The hot flesh moved, the living skin sliding against hers. The intimacy of it was shocking, blinding sensation, leaving her own flesh shivering, fire and ice together, heated desire and fear.

But it was only the shadow, the flame-streaked shadow of another intimacy, far greater. He understood her thoughts. Because of Dorestad, because he had lost his home, because he had seen what despair was. He was the living bridge to the emptiness inside her. The one who could share the darkness. Her heart leaped. She would never find that understanding again from another living being. Never.

She heard his voice, the foreignness of its shape nothing compared to the intimacy of the touch of his breath on her skin. She felt the smooth slide of his hair. She turned her face, seeking him. Then nothing.

Nothing.

Her hand touched air.

"Einhard..."

She watched his face, the blazing heat in it, in his storm-cloud eyes. And then the sense of his words became real.

"...I have told you, once. I have told that importunate king's thane, Hunferth. Would you have me tell it to you again?"

The dark Frisian voice cut like a whiplash. She fell back, as though the blow had been physical. She made a faint sound. Pain.

"Judith!"

She was bent double in his bed, like someone maimed, like a coward, like the *nithing* she had called him across a crowded hall.

"Judith—"

Like something worthless. Hurt. She straightened up. The Frisian was staring at her with his bright, bright eyes. Despite his ruthless control, despite his mockery, she could see the depthless emotion that was kept hidden. The feeling she had thought was despair. She could see the anger. Bitterness. All the fury of the world. Pity? No....

"Then say it, man of Dorestad. Say you will not lift one finger to help a desperate kingdom even though you have the power, even though that kingdom has saved you."

"I think you overprize what power I have." The hardness in his voice was deliberate, an act of strong will that covered every feeling, so powerful. Self-will. It had to be.

"Aye." She looked at the burning eyes. They were nothing. "I think I overprize you and what you will do for honour. Or even for reward."

"Reward? What reward would you offer me?"

The dark intimacy of the chamber enclosed them, the heavy air, the dancing light. He never moved. They no longer touched. But she was utterly aware that she was in his bed, that her head-veil was lost, that her hair spilled in waves over her shoulders. She realised for the first time that the neck of her gown was un-laced, whether by the dispassionate hand of the monk, or by his burning fingers she did not know. There was nothing beyond the way he looked at her and the fire.

Such fire.

"You do not know what honour is. You would take what you want and give nothing." There was no air left to breathe in the confining space of the bower, the space between them.

"Aye. I will take what I want."

The pull, the physical awareness of him was overwhelming, the dangerous highly charged meaning of their words. She stood up. The dizziness and the ache in her head pounded. Her dress was untied, beltless. She could feel his gaze, her own louche state of undress, her louche thoughts. She forced herself to stand straight.

"You think you can have whatever you desire. You think you are a great merchant. A trader. But you have nothing." Her voice found the deadly, inadmissible words. "You cannot even go back to Dorestad and if you did, it is not your home. Not anymore. You have lost it to a Viking ruler."

The lethally fine body moved. She watched the play of muscle and her flesh shivered. She moved towards the door, keeping him in sight, and the loose material of her gown rustled against her skin. His gaze followed her. His beautifully shaped mouth curved.

"As I understand, it was not lost at all. It was sold off by King Lothar, the fair head of the fighting nobility, for a profit. That was what one might call a deal. Trading."

She bit her lip. The bitterly smooth accusation was true. The hard-pressed king of the Frankish empire had given the great river port of Dorestad to Rorik because it was indefensible. The inhabitants had not mattered. At least East Anglia had been able to fight for itself. The uncomfortable thoughts ran through her mind but she was too angry.

"Perhaps you thought you could have helped him with the deal? Perhaps then Rorik would not be pursuing you for piracy. Or perhaps you just think that you can get anything you want. But you will not."

She turned towards the door. She gathered her skirts. She had no shoes. Her bare feet scuffed the rushes. She felt sick. She did not show it. Not by the deviation of one hair's breadth from her course. He did not try to stop her. She undid the door. The iron of the latch was cold against her hand, against heated flesh, burning with the fire he had made her feel.

"You will never get what you want," she said. "Because you have sold your soul to do it."

She shut the door.

"YOU SHOULD REST," said Mildred.

"The man is a peasant," snarled the lady Judith, exiled princess of East Anglia, unofficial representative of the Wessex king. "Nothing but a cheapster, a hawker of tawdry baubles and bits of tatty old fur."

Her maid indicated a soft bed with bright blue hangings. Judith turned her head away.

"The bed has fresh linen. They have given us a fine chamber."

"*Amber* for goodness' sake."

"Linen?" said Mildred hopefully.

"Doubtless. If there is a profit in it."

"No, lady. The bed."

Bed.

"I am not lying down in another bed. I have had my fill of lying in beds." *His.* "No more beds." With curtains and flickering candlelight and a sense of intimacy that was—

"Aargh!"

"Lady? You are not well."

"I am perfectly well."

"That monk left you another posset of herbs. He said—"

"Falseness. It was all falseness."

"Did he?" asked Mildred uneasily. "Will you drink it?"

It tasted foul. But mayhap it did have wine in it. Her empty belly glowed. The warmth, quite a different warmth from— At least it made her head feel better. Somewhat giddy, but better. Much better— This was the answer, the thing that would stop the pain.

"Fetch me some mead."

"Mead? Are you sure you should have…. Very well then." Mildred poured. "A small—"

Judith took the silver-chased flask out of her companion's hand and served it herself.

Definitely better.

Mildred tried to twitch the glass goblet out of her fingers. But she was up to tricks like that. She was up to anything. The glow, which had somehow moved from her stomach into her head, assured her of it. The huckster and peddler of second-rate goods would regret the day he was born. The day he had ever dared to set his sea-green eyes on her. *Touch* her and make suggestions about payment that—

"Do you know what I would do if I met that assassin again?"

Mildred looked at her. "The man is dead, for his sins, lady."

The glass goblet nearly spun out of her hand. She caught it. Nothing wrong with her reactions. She pushed the weakness aside.

"I would stand there and hold the man's cloak for him, that is what I would do. I would step aside to give him elbow room. I would assist him with his aim. I would make sure the blade went in right to the hilt. Somewhere permanent." She took a rather dizzying breath. "Preferably irrevocable." There was nothing wrong with her diction.

"I would do it myself."

"Do what, lady?"

"Kill him."

"The assassin? You did help—"

"Not the benighted assassin." Could Mildred not keep up with the suddenly dazzling clarity of her thoughts? "The Frisian. The crack-brain from Dorestad." She took another sip. It was remarkably restorative.

"Oh."

Sometimes Mildred simply did not appreciate the finer points of an argument.

"Did you know," she said, waving her empty goblet, "that Frisia is so flat and grey and damp they have to sit on mounds of earth to stop their feet getting wet?" She poured herself another glass. It was generous. "Trips," she said. "Mounds of earth."

"Terpen," corrected Mildred unexpectedly. "But that is only in some places and the land itself is very fertile." Then she added, "Anyway, I thought that was what people said about water and East Anglia."

"Hah. East Anglia is not that low-lying. At least, not all of it. We raise horses." We *did* raise horses. Once. Before— Heaven preserve her from a West Saxon maidservant enamoured of geography. She beat down the terrible ache of loss.

"They have cattle in Frisia," offered Mildred.

"*Cattle.* What they have are pirates. Unscrupulous ones." She swigged more mead. "He thinks he has won. He thinks he can sit there with no clothes on and—"

"No clothes?"

"Well, trousers," amended Judith reluctantly. *Just because he is like fire. Just because he has skin that glows like—* She swallowed. "He believes," she said, "that he can sit there wearing trousers and dictate his terms, and everyone will do what he wants." She tipped the flask. The mead splashed. "Even the men of Wessex who have risked reprisals from Rorik the Viking in order to save his worthless neck are supposed to do what he wants."

"Judith…it is not your fault if he refused. The king will not blame you. Or the lord Hunferth."

Alfred, the king of Wessex. She thought of his face the last time she had seen it, not serene and wearing a crown and taking due homage, not flushed with the fitting joy of the feast. But in the middle of a war-council at Winchester, watching and planning and deciding how to defend a coastline that stretched for more than a hundred miles.

Deciding. Always deciding. Making choices that were impossible. Because there were too few men, too few resources, too much open land. Knowing what the consequences of the smallest failure would be. Taking the burden. Always.

She wanted to do something that would help. She wanted to take one small and vital part of the burden away from someone who did not deserve its full weight, but who never turned from the path he had been given.

She had begged to come on this mission. She had used the fact that Hunferth was a vague kinsman by marriage and could stand in for her brother who was not here. She had used any argument she could think of. She had let Hunferth take the credit, believe he was in charge. But this was her chance. They would not let her fight, even though she trained for it and had done so both openly and secretly all of her life. This mission was the one thing she could do. Redemption....

Judith stared at the dregs of mead in the bottom of the fine glass.

She had given her loyalty when she had come to this land and Wessex had offered her protection, just the way it had been offered to the Frisian.

She wanted to pay her debt, as anyone would who had honour. The courageous and overburdened king had everything she could give. Even though she could not swear a warrior's oath.

He had her heart even though she had never said the words. Even though she was only a woman. *Because* she was a woman.

A woman.

She thought of the fire in the small dark room. Flickering light and fire and burning heat. *What reward would you offer me?* The flame in his eyes. She put the glass down.

"Fetch me my red dress."

"The red dress? You were going to bed."

Bed. "There will be feasting tonight, will there not? The Frisians will celebrate their narrow escape, the fact that we beat off Rorik for them, the fact that no one managed to kill their beloved leader. I want to help them celebrate. Of course I want my red— No, not that. The silk. The one dyed with grains from the East. Vermillion."

"The *silk?*"

"And the rose-scented oil. You can rub it into my skin. And the kohl for my eyes I got from—well, never mind. It is in the Maplewood box. No, the *Maplewood*." But it was little wonder Mildred did not recognise it. No one had seen it. No one knew she had it. The scandalous collection had its roots years ago, when she had been a girl. A silly, vain, ignorant little princess who fancied her chances at attracting a prince. She had decided at the age of thirteen that she would choose her own life-mate. They were going to live happily.

"Hurry. Thank you. Yes, and that cream." That was new—

"That cream? The—"

"Red," said Judith hardily. It had pressed cherry juice in it. "Lip dye." She refused to blush. Perhaps one could also rub a little on the cheekbones? It was embarrassing to own cosmetics when you were supposed to be above using such things. Or when you were uncomfortably ignorant of what to do. "And the rags and the curling tongs. Heat them."

All the saints… Where did she start?

Forty concentrated minutes later, a surprisingly skilled Mildred held up the polished sheet of bronze. It showed a reflection Judith had never seen.

"Do you think, lady," ventured her maid and companion, "that it is quite suitable for a—"

Virgin? Judith tugged on the scandalously loose lacing at her breast. Something was going to fall out. She stopped pulling. She tossed her head. A thin and fluttering excuse for a head veil did little to conceal from predatory masculine eyes an abundance of light flaxen hair. Unbound. Artfully curled by the use of the heated tongs and the damp linen rags. Gold clinked at her wrists and glittered round her exposed neck. She pulled her girdle as tight as it would go.

The face worried her. Mildred had a deft and cunning touch. It was not overdone. At least, she did not think so. But the flecked grey eyes that looked back at her were not hers. They were darker, touched by something indefinable, a secret knowledge that had not been there before and was now ineradicable, like a mark from the stranger because she had lain in his arms, touched him, known—

"You tell me."

"Lady?" faltered Mildred; Mildred who obviously knew far more about the art of seducing men than she had ever let on.

"You have been wed, have you not? Twice? The first one divorced and the second one buried?"

"Yes, but—"

If that kind of history was not racy, Judith did not know what was.

"Then I need your expertise."

Mildred's eyes rounded. "My—"

"Expertise." She fluffed out a fat curl and tried arching a tweezered eyebrow. What if the kohl came off her lashes?

Mildred's jaw dropped.

"Expertise," she snapped, turning her back on the mirror. "At least you have bedded a man. That is more than I ever got round to." *Yet.* But she would not let it go that far. She was not stupid. She was not some half-brained fool to be trapped by darkly dangerous spells of carnal love, her life made subject to a man. There was too much to be done.

She had long given up dreams of wedding. It was dangerous, vulnerable. And neither was she the kind of luxurious sybarite to fall under the lure of licentious and illicit loving.

It would bring ruin. It would trap her and she would not be able to bear that.

She was free. *Alone....*

Judith shut her mind to the feel of another human being's closeness. Male. Heated. Alive.

She picked up the mead flask. It was already empty. Her bruised skull throbbed. She felt horribly, desperately, terrifyingly exposed. She stood up. The silk dress slid over her skin. She wore no shift underneath so that there was nothing to stop the thin fabric clinging to her form, so that it would outline each hollow and curve. It was like being clad in a whisper of cool breath, in nothing, just air on her body, a shadow. She would walk like this into a great hall packed with men far gone in *sym-belgal,* the wanton lust of feasting. Foreigners shouting in their strange voices.

But there was only one voice in her head, like deep earth, dark wine. Her hand shook on the silver-chased flask. She put it down. The firelight reflected off the golden ring on her finger, the cunningly wrought shape of a boar, a royal device, belonging to a dead royal house.

She thought of the massing of the Viking troops forty miles away. She thought of the king. She let go of the flask. The ring flashed. The boar was a symbol of courage, courage that was eternal.

"You can explain to me on the way to the hall how it is done." She set her hand to the door latch. Cold. Memory came back to her, such memory. The heat that came from touch. Burning eyes. Gold skin.

"Explain what?" squeaked Mildred.

"How to seduce a man."

3

MILDRED'S DISJOINTED RAMBLINGS were no help at all. They consisted largely of speculation on what Judith's brother would do if he learned the Awful Truth of his sister's depraved plans.

Judith had no need to speculate on what Berg would do. She knew. She ground her teeth.

"...finds out about such reckless and lascivious wantonness..."

"He is not going to find out," said Judith through clenched teeth. "Not unless someone is foolish enough to tell him." And she could bet her last silver penny it would not be Einhard the seeker after profit.

"It is not right. It is wicked licence, looseness of behaviour that..."

"For the last time," she yelled. "It is not going to come to *forlicgan*." There was a silence fit to stun. Mildred looked round while the appalling word resonated into every last indigo shadow. Fornication. Sexual intercourse.

She and Mildred were alone in the darkness, surely? Judith

bit her lip and tasted cherries. It was not going well. The headache hovered behind her eyes like a raven waiting for the corpse. She tried to force her brain to think. The cold air whipped at her dress, the loosely laced material no barrier at all. She had not realised it was so cold. So far, seduction seemed to consist of freezing your most personal assets off.

She resisted the impulse to tug the neckline of her dress higher. She wished she had brought her cloak. She began walking across the black courtyard that separated her bower from the lighted hall belonging to the small and rich colony of Frisians who traded through the Kentish port of Stathwic.

"It is mad," muttered Mildred, trailing dutifully behind. "Sin."

Sin. The wind came from the east, from the swan-road, the sea. She could smell the clean tang of it, like a promise, full of power and wild. Einhard.... Suddenly her skin was no longer cold. It was burning. Burning up, like her.

"This Frisian," began Mildred. "You know he has already buried one wife? They say...."

Married. Married and his wife had died. "The man is a pirate, nothing more." *Nothing.* "I am doing this because I will not see Wessex destroyed by a ship-army without a fight."

"Fighting. Fighting is for warriors, not well-born maidens."

Judith stiffened, the old fury, the soul-destroying frustration, boiling up inside her.

"I want to do something. Help people—"

"They should never have given you that name."

"That—"

"Your name."

Judith. The sound echoed inside her head, mangled in an outlandish Frisian accent. Judith. The daring maid of the Bible.

The saviour of her people.

It was a sin indeed to think of herself in the same breath as a courageous woman and a saint. But the true Judith had triumphed over Holofernes, her enemy, and a foreigner.

She had defeated him in his bed, pure maiden though she was. She had saved her people from their enemies because she had kept faith.

Surely Judith might look down and give her courage.

"I know what I am doing." The torchlight hit them. The bright, fire-heated air of the hall poured out through the opened doors. The sounds of people, shouted words, singing, the scent of wood smoke and roasted meat, the higher and sweeter note of the mead and the ale that could inflame sense. Noise. Such noise. She stood still and the wind clawed at her.

This was how it began. Holofernes had sent for his chief thanes and they feasted, and the wine was poured and he urged the guests on the benches to disport themselves. All the proud warriors sat in their seats and he drenched his troops with wine. And Judith…Judith….

"We do not have to go in there. Judith? Do not go on. Turn back before it is too late. No one can expect you to do such a thing as this. Come back. You would be safe, safe and whole."

Safe and whole. There was no safety in this world, not unless it was fought for.

She stepped forward. The guards at the door leaned back on their spears. She passed through.

He wanted her.

She could see it.

He was also ale-sotted. The fool.

Judith swallowed more mead. It was amazingly pleasant. Not that she particularly craved drink. It was just that she did not particularly feel like eating and the smooth liquid had a way of sliding down her hot throat like the honey it was made from.

She stood up. The Frisian's eyes followed her, perhaps caught by the movement of the brilliant, indecently laced dress. Perhaps by the glitter of inadequately clothed flesh. Her skin flushed. She picked up her glass. It was intricately made, gleaming green like light through a forest.

It was empty.

She had a seat at the high table, as befitted her lost rank. The din of male voices bounced off the heavy oak beams, off the smoky thatch above her head, the wooden walls. Hunferth selected a roast pigeon from the table still littered with fine dishes. The great hounds lying below the trestle boards gnawed on venison bones. Einhard merely drank.

Like her, as though their movements and their decisions, even their thoughts, were linked like flame and shadow.

She reached across for the nearest flask. She could do this. Einhard saw her move. She thought every half-drunk predatory warrior in the hall saw her. Yet through that living heated wall of male attention, of wine-stoked lust, she was aware only of the fair-haired Frisian. He watched her. She felt his hot heavy-lidded gaze, even though she looked down at the flask and she could not see his eyes. The shared awareness was like something physical.

Was that what seduction was? Like a burning cord that bound two people, man and woman, even though they did not speak, even though distance, the press of a rowdy dangerous multitude came between them?

She grasped the flagon.

"Lady, should you not retire and rest? You cannot be well."

It was the future monk. Her hand tightened.

"No, I am quite well." It was almost true. The headache simmered somewhere beyond the reach of her unsteady senses. There was only a strange dizziness, not unpleasant, rather like floating, and the heady, sense-filling awareness. "You need not worry." She smiled. She had a killer smile. Seductive. She had practised it in front of the mirror until her face ached. It was—

His heavy hand closed over hers, fast as a striking snake. She remembered that the monk used to be a warrior. Einhard's friend.

"You should rest."

"I do not need—" She could not move her hand.

"Princess." Warriors were arrogant as *hellthanes,* all of them. They thought no one could match them. Her arm flexed. She would—

"Lady? Is all well?" She looked up and saw Hunferth was on his feet, watching. Gold glittered off his hands, the sign of a man of consequence and authority. King Alfred's own representative. And here she was, struggling with a monk for the possession of a mead flask and wearing a crimson dress fit for Jezebel, her body full of frightening, unfamiliar heat.

"Everything is quite well, thank you."

She did not have to be told the glittering-eyed Frisian had seen everything. She did not even have to turn round. She could feel his gaze, molten fire down the thin skin of her neck, her scarcely clothed back.

She dredged up the smile.

"I was just—" What? Pursuing a plan involving deceit, drunkenness and Mildred's sinful debauchery?

She widened the smile.

"I came to bid you good-night," said Hunferth. Ladies were supposed to retire before the feasting became too raucous. But there was one thing about ladies: they had superior wits. Hers were completely unfuddled. She had thought, in her heart of hearts, that the mead might have soaked her wits, too. But now she knew she had total control. She set down the mead flask.

"You are right," she conceded, all meekness. Her plan was perfectly in place. However deeply the pirate had drunk, he would have to retire at some point and she had lingered so long, that it had to be soon. If he did not simply fall under the mead-bench, he would make his way to his chamber. And when he did, she would be there. Waiting. The more he was fool enough to drink, the better. *Medu-gal.* Drunken lust. Her breath hitched.

"I am tired," she said and stretched. Even Hunferth's eyes bulged. She twisted her body. The silk clung to her breasts, to the deep valley between her legs. She did not turn towards the man who was at once quarry and terrifying hunter. No need. The knowledge of him was in her bones, hot under her skin, tingling.

"No need to escort me," she said to Hunferth. She began to walk, dry-mouthed and stiff-backed, towards the doors. She signalled the desperate-looking Mildred to accompany her so that the men would not need to do so. She had to walk the whole length of the crowded hall. She kept her head, despite the heavy pounding of her heart. She was very dignified. She made a brave and beautiful picture despite the dress; even though the pirate, in the midst of his roistering men, did not look, but kept on drinking, deeper and harder than she had, shouting with *medu-gal.*

Holofernes, all unknowing of his fate. He had laughed and he had roared and he had yelled, bold and flushed with mead. He had stormed and raised such a din that all the sons of men could hear him.

Oblivious.

But she knew that Einhard was aware of everything, of the steps she took through the ale-stained rushes, of the men who made way for her and the men who called out to catch her gaze. Of the pale fall of her hair under the fluttering scrap of embroidered veil, of the hard-won gold that adorned her person. Of the swirling movement of the thin vermillion skirts round her legs, the glimpse of her ankle when she raised the folds of silk.

"Wæs hal."

The clear voice, soul-deep, carried the length of the hall. The foreign accent was as strong as ever, as yet unmarred by such heavy drinking. But the expression he chose was peculiarly and intensely English, a greeting or a farewell at once commonplace and imbued with a thousand subtle meanings.

Her feet hesitated, caught by the first clumsy, uncontrolled movement she had made in the length of that endless walk through the ranks of men.

She did not turn. She did not look on the fierce, mead-flushed face, the bright eyes. But the awareness between the two of them snapped tight, tighter than a bowstring with the arrow notched for flight. Just as dangerous. Her breath caught. Even though she was separated from him by all of the heated, teeming room and everything she did was a deception.

He did not wish her well.

Her heart stuttered. It was false. He had determined that because there was nothing in him, nothing but greed and selfishness and an empty black pit.

Empty. The emptiness that took deadly hold inside a person, like a wound that would never heal.

Wæs hal. She did not say the words in reply. She did not mean them and he would not have heard. Already the Frisian voices clashed across the English hall, shouting out to each other in their baseless arrogance. Laughing. Filled with lust. He joined them. She heard his voice loudest of all.

Light-minded fool, purposeless waster.

There was nothing between them.

The guards snapped to attention at the door. Outside was black night, dark as the emptiness that lived inside her. Night that disguised a thousand things.

Across the border in East Anglia, Earl Guthrum would be watching the blackness, waiting, calculating all in his clever mind, risk and reward, weakness and strength.

The guards clashed weapons.

She knew what she had to do. Her body moved, light caught her dress, her skin, the turn of her throat, the open slender wealth of her cleavage. The cold hit her.

THE SMALL CHAMBER WAS EMPTY. No one there except the dead, who should be left in peace by those who honoured the ways of God.

Einhard went in.

The assassin's corpse had been placed on the wall bench. The light of the single torch cast shadow and fire in a narrow pool, the smoke and the heat and the smell of pitch bitter as a hell-flame in the confined space.

They had laid the man out decently under linen and covered his face.

He should have been left out on the hard ground under the stars, in the blackness, for the lank wolf and the white-tailed eagle. The feeders on carrion for a creature who preyed on those who had no help.

His fist clenched. The bones ached. He took the torch from the iron bracket on the wall. He brought the flickering pool of flame down over the silent form. He uncovered the head, his fingers twisting in the blank square of linen, jerking it away to expose the dead face.

The thin scrap of cloth pitched into the staleness of the rushes at his feet. Shadows danced over the colourless features, shadows and hell's fire. He brought the torch lower. The flame could have scorched the skin. The fire moved across the blood-less flesh, like a mockery of life. But there was nothing. Nothing he could reach out to in the emptiness. *Naught.*

Something moved behind him. He turned. The blade tight in his hand caught the light.

"Einhard? I thought I saw you come in here. I thought that—" The words, inane, harmless, well-meant, stopped on a rush of breath that was spine-chilling in the small space of the death-room. His face must have shown something, an exposed glimpse of the lethalness inside.

Tatwin, whom the woman had called God's thane, the only friend he had known since he was six winters old, stepped back.

"What would you do? Why are you here now? Would you violate the dead?"

"If could get me what I wanted." The blade he had snatched up from its place beside the corpse was rock steady in his hand, the weapon that had belonged to Skar's man, the blade that had been meant to take his life and had so nearly taken the woman's.

Light turned the grey steel molten. The copper inlay of the single rune burned red. The torch flame showed him what it was—*kenaz.* He nearly dropped the knife. But the blade stayed caught in his hand. The rune blazed in the light, *kenaz,* the torch, the fire within, the creativity that shaped things.

His heart stopped. It was the sign that might lead to a child.

Or to the death of one. His hand slipped.

"Look out—" There was a rustle of fast movement in the shadows. But he was faster. His fingers had already closed tight over the smooth hilt, the bright fall of steel arrested by competent muscles trained in fighting, by a will trained by hell. His mind kicked into action, assessing even while the inner part of him reeled.

Kenaz. The *child.*

The knife was fine, beautifully weighted, highly functional. He did not need to touch the sharpness. The metal of the hilt was warm against his palm, gold laid over silver, too ornate for a hired killer. It was, had been, someone's prize possession.

"Einhard—" The sound of Tatwin's voice registered at a vast distance. The rune glittered, its shape foreign, Danish not Frisian, the connecting stroke slanting upwards, not down.

He stood with the blade in one hand and the flaring torch in the other, while the pain in his heart would kill him and his thoughts raced, stretching out to grasp the meaning. Bright or dark? The transforming fire, or the flame of the funeral pyre? His sight ached and sweat touched his skin but there was no indication, just as there had been no clue in the dead man. The locked rage inside him notched higher. The answer had to be there, in the knife, in the dead man's face, in his clothing. Meaning. The shape of it streamed past him in the shadows.

His eyes burned and the pain from the cut on his arm stole sense. Even the mead in the crowded hall would not deaden that. Just as it would not deaden the other pain.

Behind him in the shadowed chamber, Tatwin made a wordless sound.

He shifted the torch. Hurt stabbed through severed muscle. The blank face of the corpse, unsighted, still, without life's breath, held nothing he could see. Nothing. All life, all possibility gone. He set the torch back in its holder.

"*Einhard*—"

"It was my hand that took the life from him." His words sounded harsh, stretched, unreal.

"I know that but—"

"God's pity," he yelled. "If I could somehow have held back. If I had struck less hard. If I had not..." His voice stopped. The shouted oath rang in the air.

Tatwin moved, as though he would close the small distance between them.

"Your life hung in the balance, as did the woman's."

The woman. She had thrown herself at the assassin like a fury, as though she were possessed by the kind of blank single mind-edness that possessed him. She had a whiplash strength that would not stop. Yet it had been light compared to the heavy, hard-edged weight of the dead man. So light. He had tried to kill her, the East Anglian princess. It could have been her slight form lying here in all its brightly-flaunted beauty. *Her.*

He walked away, blind, seeking the shuttered window by instinct. Away from the corpse, away from the flickering light and the heat of the flame.

It made no difference. The fire burned him.

"That is the way things happen." Tatwin's voice followed him, as though it could bridge the void. "There was no time. There never is. There was precious little choice. Einhard—"

Little choice. The man had been prepared, wearing body armour, the steel links of chain mail hidden under his clothing, and so Einhard had struck at the unprotected neck. Too well, with too much force because of the girl and the scent of death. Tatwin, at least, understood what a fight was like, the speed of it, and for every last skill learned and every ounce of will, the ultimate lack of control over the outcome.

Tatwin knew everything.

"I wanted—" *To find the truth. I wanted to take it.* The black emptiness cut off his voice. He turned back, his free hand clutching the rough wooden edge of the window frame so hard it bit into flesh. Tatwin was still speaking.

"…such things happen. It might not have been a clean death in battle, but no one could blame you for what you did. I understand your anger and see now the regret you feel. I understand…"

He clenched his fist on the roughness of the wood. The pain jarred through his arm, raw and merciless. Tatwin kept speaking. He spoke as a priest might, as a friend of very long standing. A friend. Tatwin did not see. God's thane had no idea what lived inside him, the blackness and the rage, the anger that did not die. The ugliness inside him was not a thing that should be hidden, not even from a man prepared to believe the best. Particularly not from that man.

"You think I regret killing Skar's man?"

"You must. You have never sought wanton death. I know you—" The voice, certain with the gloss of shared years stopped. Then, "Cuthbert's bones," said the English priest. "Your only regret is that the man could not speak before he died. You thought you would get information out of him, even now when there is no hope, you came to—" Tatwin's voice died. But his head was up. He was a rough fighter. They both were. It was like a bond. Had been. "That is the truth. You will regret no deed. Not anymore."

Tatwin did not move. The air became unbreathable.

"No."

"Then you should." The voice hardened like quenched steel. It was the rough fighter who looked back. "It should finish, this blood feud, this *quest*. There is no hope left in it." The words struck like an accusation. "Will you not give it up?"

"No. I will not." The truth was that he could not. But Tatwin would not understand that. Tatwin had not married, owed a nine-year debt to someone who had died, so long before her time. A promise.

Tatwin had never had a child.

Einhard let go of the wood, straightened the aching, battle-hard mass of his fist.

"There is no turning back." He pushed forward. But Tatwin stayed. For one moment he thought the other man would try to detain him. Every muscle tensed.

"Einhard—I am saying this for your sake. Because I have known you all my life and now I no longer do. The person who would try to wrest secrets from the dead is not the man I knew."

It was not the bitter accuser who spoke, but the friend, the friend of childhood, the friend of an adult life spent in the dangers of a rebellious land occupied by the Vikings. Someone who would watch your back.

"Let it go. Do not do this."

He stood up, through the pain. The fire and the shadow caught at him, caught Tatwin's abrupt movement, the dead man's exposed face, the burning rune. Kenaz which might mean death or a child.

"Nay. There is nothing I would not do."

He watched Tatwin's face close off. The isolation broke over him like a black wave with the power to kill all in its path. Like the pain, physical and of the mind.

No way back.

He made himself walk. Tatwin's voice followed him.

"One death cannot change another," said the man who was his friend. "Do not think it."

Death. The flame of the funeral pyre.

THE SERVANTS HAD LIT A SINGLE lamp in his borrowed chamber. The moonlight and the wind streamed in through the open shutters, silver light mixed with the gold. The brightness of it shimmered against his eyes, so unsteady he stumbled, the appalling weakness no longer possible to disguise. But it did not matter. There was no one left to see. No one who touched him.

No one except that other soul who was lost, who was out there, somewhere. Waiting to be found. Waiting in desperate longing and fear. Waiting to be brought home. Waiting for *him,* perhaps hating him now for taking so long.

And the only clue to the trail lost with Skar's man. *Death.*

One death cannot change another—

His child was not dead.

He touched the wall with his good hand.

His son, that other small soul who was part of him, lived.

The skin of his palm slipped on the rough planking. The borrowed room was empty. Not the room. The emptiness was inside him.

He moved. He had known that what he did, what Tatwin had called his ruthless quest, would cut him off from others. He had accepted that because it was necessary.

For the first time, the completeness of the isolation hit him.

He shut his eyes. But then he saw the woman's face, the raw beauty of it, not as she had been in the scarlet dress in the crowded hall, but as she had been in the silence of this chamber, in the shared bed. Her eyes pools of fire and her slender body burning his, burning with a life and a bright purpose he did not share. Could not.

His other hand clenched over the hilt of the rune blade.

You have sold your soul....

He felt like a madman, like some crazed berserker fighting

on in a battle fury long after the sane had abandoned the field, lost to reason and reality, a creature locked in a savage hell that existed only in his mind.

Suppose it was so, that what everyone else believed was true? Suppose his son, not yet eight winters old, was dead.

He could not face that thought. He would not. He was locked into his crazed single-mindedness, unreachable. The East Anglian woman's bitter words echoed in his head.

You have sold your soul…You will never get what you want because you have sold your soul to do it.

Her face filled his mind, her eyes. Her heated skin. His own skin burned like the onset of fever and the pain in his arm clawed at him.

We have seen, you and I, what despair is. We understand the taste….

Despair. The only sin with no forgiveness, because it cut off belief. He could no longer grapple with belief. He was not worth it. There was nothing but the creature he had become and the knowledge of the thing he had failed in.

Perhaps that was what hell was, the knowledge that there was nothing left. For the first time since Thieto's disappearance, the pain broke him, its power impossible to stop. He sank down. The instant of despair was complete, but it did not matter. There was no one near.

The isolation closed over his head, unbreakable by another living being, emptiness without a boundary. Black, the darkness real, stronger than the light in the room. He caught at the frame of the door, but his injured arm could not hold it. He fell. The pain hit him. Like the darkness.

Just as the blackness closed over his head, something in the light-filled chamber moved.

4

"WHAT IN HOLY GOD'S NAME are you doing?"

The black voice stopped Judith's feet, so that she stood, poised on the edge of the circle of light. Her heart beat hard. It was impossible to speak, to move a single cramped muscle. Breathe. She held still, her gaze fixed, trapped by the fierce creature lying where it had fallen on the ground, black shadow and fire. Feral muscle.

"What are you doing?"

A wild animal, wounded, lethal. This was the man she had come here to trap.

"I—"

He had a knife.

"What?"

I came here to seduce you.

She could see his face now. His eyes glittered. Like a man who had fever.

Like someone who had slipped beyond the confines of this world to somewhere quite other.

"Why are you here?" he said.

She was silent. She could not say into the brittle tension of the air the stupidity of what she had thought to do. What she had planned had been the impulse of a moment, a moment born of anger and frustration and the madness inside her head, assisted by a reckless indulgence in mead. As wilful and illusory as something out of an adventure tale for children. But this was reality. It held no mercy.

She watched the dark curve of his body in the light-filled room. It was the most dangerous thing she had ever seen. Her first mindless, terrified impulse was to step back, escape. He was so quick, so strong——

"Why?"

He did not move.

Her mind filled with the way he had stood in the lamplight, with the suddenly bloodless lines of his face, the sliding fall, the horrifying downward rush of movement that she had been able to do nothing about, that she had wanted to stop. That he had not been able to stop.

He had not moved to stand up.

Do not go on.

That was what Mildred had said. Do not persist in madness. She kept her ground. She took a breath of warm, smoke-scented air.

"I came to find you."

The dense muscle shifted. She thought her heart stopped. *Turn back before it is too late.*

She could turn aside. A person could always turn aside.

She took a step into the light. He moved. One sharp flex of muscle, the flash of gold.

Incised steel.

She nearly broke, stepped backwards and fled. He saw it. As though he could read her mind, all of her thought-hoard, all that she was.

When he moved again, it was to gather the solid weight of shadowed muscle. The knife was still in his hand.

"You should not be here. Princess."

Princess. The boar-shaped ring dug into her fisted hand.

She took the next step, the one that took her farther into the bright circle of light. She was of the house of King Edmund. She did not step back.

"Why?" she said in her turn.

But the creature, the man-shape, did not answer. No need. The answer was there in the silent line of strength, in the vicious tightness of each muscle.

You should not be here.

She watched him, then said, "I do as I will." He understood. He caught the echo of his own mood-proud words. Sharp mind, even behind the fevered brightness of his eyes, behind the strength like that of a wounded wolf.

"God's thane would take issue with that."

"Aye."

He did not move again and she knelt down near him in the rushes. It brought them close. She could see the torchlight play its colour over his blanched skin, redden the brightness of the unsheathed blade in his competent fingers. She caught the golden sweetness of mead on his breath. She knew the force of it was in his blood.

It was in hers.

She was mad.

She moved slowly, the way you would if you did not want to startle a savage beast. He was like a black firelit shadow in the rushes, darkness stretched out in endless supple lines on the floor. He lay as he had fallen, his back against the bare wooden planking of the wall. His hand was closed over the gilded knife hilt.

He watched her settle herself on the floor. His bright gaze covered the way she sat among the dusty rushes, the way her fingers arranged the thin silk of her skirts to mask the curve of her legs, the way the boar-shaped ring on her finger caught the light.

He sought the shape of the thoughts in her head.

As she tried to divine the shape of his.

The next step, if she took it, would not be physical at all.

"Can you not tell me what it is?"

She did not know whether he would speak. She thought at least he would look away because the light hid nothing. There was no concealment. She had seen what no man would ever want any person still alive to see of him. She had seen the shape of defeat.

He did not look away, bend his neck, turn. He watched her, without moving one muscle of that heavy, shadowed, body. The pure power of will was the most merciless thing she had ever seen.

"No." That was all he said. The finality in the short, foreign-accented word was complete, like a door slammed shut. She could not guess what animated his mind. She could see nothing, only the blank closed wall of his will, the feral glitter of his eyes.

I am sorry.

The damning thought, the swamping feeling behind it, came out of nothing, out of everything, out of the terrible pressure round her heart, so powerful that she wanted to give form to the words burning through her mind. But she could not. No one could say those words to that kind of ruthlessness.

He moved with terrifying suddenness.

The rough planking dug at her back and the torchlight hissed with burning wax over wood. Her hands clenched.

"You should go."

"Why?"

"There is nothing for you here."

"No." Nothing but agony and bitter secrets. She took a breath. "That is why I am staying." Her words made his eyes narrow. Clever answer on her part. She had lost her wits.

"You are afraid."

She held her head still, the way he had. She did not move.

"Yes."

He threw the knife.

She saw the muscle contract in his arm and the straight savage movement as he threw. The *seax* blade spun aside, cleaving through the musty rushes. Harmless. So that he was unarmed. The last gesture she expected. She thought—she recognised what the knife was.

"The assassin's blade—the man who wanted to kill you…" She leaned forward, craning to see. His voice followed her.

"Aye. That is all there is of the man who would have done murder. No soul. Just one Danish blade."

"Danish? The man was Frisian."

"*What?*"

His skin was hot. The touch of his loose hair cool as a shadow, like remembered silk. She felt his weight. His hand was closed round her arm, above the elbow. She could not move. The dragon's gold at his wrist caught the light.

"What do you mean? Why do you say that?"

"Because I heard his voice before he died. Before you stopped him from killing me," she added levelly, so that there could be no mistake. "I do not speak your language. I do not know what he said."

She took a small breath in the silence. She sensed his heat.

"My guess is that he cursed me and my entire existence." She forced herself to keep speaking. "Mayhap he also cursed the lives of all of my kin."

There was a small sound. His head bent. His hair rustled over her skin.

"He wished to curse you and all of your kin?"

"So I believe."

He said something in Frisian. She did not ask what it was. He was probably in agreement with the last thoughts of the man who had tried to kill him. He shifted just a little. The colour had come back to his face, but it was hectic, burning.

"And what makes you believe he said all this in Frisian?"

"Because of his accent. I am…familiar with Danish. This man did not speak it. The shape of his voice, the sound it made, was like yours."

"Like mine."

"Yes. He was like you."

His breathing was sharp, shallow. She could sense the effort through the rapid movement of his chest.

His hand clasped her arm. She could feel the curving grip

of each separate finger. It did not hurt. She could feel his closeness.

"Would you swear to what you have said?"

She felt the movement of his body against hers, the sleek glide of heavy muscle. It was intimate, already familiar even though the depths of him were unknown.

"Aye." That was all she said, as though the weight of a single word from her matched the same from him, as though nothing more were needed between them. Her dizzied senses felt light from his touching. Giddy with his nearness and the shape of his body. She was exhausted from all that had happened to her, from the pain that still plagued her, from the shock and all that had come after. He moved so steadily, the only steady thing in the universe. Yet she had felt the pain that ran through him.

"I believe I am right in what I say. You spoke to me in your own tongue when you..." She hesitated. *Comforted me.* "You spoke to me in Frisian when you held me in your arms in the great hall. You spoke it again just now."

You held me in your arms. She was leaning against his body. It was like the way he had held her after the assassin had tried to kill both of them. She had lain in just such a way and known his closeness, felt the clean male lines, the burning heat.

She had known that heat for her own, so intensely alive. She could see the harsh lines of his face, the flushed skin. "What I say is true."

She could see the overbrightness of his eyes. Feverish.

"True? Why did you come here? To me?"

Truth. She thought she might not have admitted it, even then. But then he said, "Princess?" and the word did not hold mockery. It held everything, the empty wasteland and the bright flicker of all that had once been. It was real. As real as the concealed depths she had seen in him and never expected.

His heat burned her.

What she had seen of him. Reality. Truth.

She had to tell him the truth. All of it. That she was a fool. That, despite her protestations, she had had too much to drink. That he was right when he said she should never have come here. She had to say it and then it would be over. Finished. She would not fall into the dangerous depths with him, the consuming flames that ignited desire. She would be where she should be. Alone.

Yet she wanted the flames. She wanted them for what they were. For the fire in his eyes and the hot hard touch of his body.

It appalled her. She tried to cut off the surge of feeling. But the knowledge had flared up in her eyes, deep and primitive as the fire in him, like a counterpart. He recognised it. The awareness burned in his overbright eyes, in the touch of his skin.

It was wrong. She had to stop it. But her body trembled against his and he would feel that. He would know.

"I came here for you, but—" Her words choked. His eyes burned with all the unsaid things, all the things locked away in his head. She could feel the tension in his body, the harsh strength.

I acted wrongly. I thought you were nothing. I meant only to use you. I wanted to set a trap. He looked at her as though he would take the thoughts out of her head. He looked at her as though he knew, and yet he could not. Did not.

She struggled for speech, through the dizziness in her senses, in her mind.

"I came here for…"

"For me?" His hands moved on her body. She was intensely and utterly aware of him. Of the way her flesh tightened in unstoppable response. Of the rustling slide of the silken dress across the surface of her skin already sensitized by inappropriate desire. Of the shivering movement where he touched her, the erotic thinness of the dress. Of the bright colour that was painted on her face to make it more beautiful, to trap him. Her skin burned. Her breasts felt heated and swollen against the loosened neckline of vermillion silk, already half exposed, aching even though he had not yet touched them. Not yet.

"Is that what you would say? That you came here for me?" The drugging touch of his fingers traced her skin, strong as the darkest enchantment, intensely arousing. She watched his burning gaze, the hidden bitterness. The power. Her thoughts moved like lead though her body felt light, floating.

"I came here because…" Her painstakingly curled hair spilled over the bright dress in waves that were artful, a creation that was calculated, artificial. She had to tell him the truth. Her thoughts spun. She did not know that she had moved but she must have. Her body must have turned, seeking the steadiness of his because she touched the hot subtle lines of him. The thin silk, already warmed by the burning heat of her body, pressed against his flesh.

"Because of what?"

She could feel his hidden harshness, the measure of his strength. So much greater than hers. Despite all the deadly despair she had been a secret and unwilling witness to, he would never help her in what she wanted. Whatever she had seen in that black moment, whatever she had believed, he was still dangerous.

"Because of what, Judith?"

She looked into the burning eyes, the black depths underneath them that she could not fathom, that no one could fathom because he would not let them. She made the last effort. His strength was like a wall of steel and over it the bright volatile recklessness that she recognised to the depths of her soul. It was in her, shared like the fire of their touching.

"I came here to seduce you."

Something flared in his gaze, brief, cut off. Too brutally suppressed for her to fathom. Anger, perhaps. Perhaps the pain. Certainly strength and the driving recklessness. It beat through his blood into hers.

"Then do so," he said.

The recklessness bit through her, the wildness, all the bitterness that had been tamped down and corded for six years. All the burning desperation and the terrible steadfastness of purpose that was the difference between living and dying.

All the pain— That was shared. Shared and real, though she could not bear to think of it. *Shared*. She touched him. There was a moment when time seemed suspended, when either of them might have drawn back. She held him.

His mouth came down on hers.

He was like black fire. So hot. A man's desire. Her silk-clad body moved and her painted face turned to his. Something unfurled inside her like the brush of wonder, like madness, like fear and newness and the terrifying power of the unknown. She touched his skin. Her heart beat out of time and her fingertips rested on the stark rise of his cheekbone and the rough line of his jaw. She felt his heat.

She stayed still, fascinated, afraid, her hand on his hot skin. His mouth firmed over hers. He would have tasted the cherries rubbed into her lips, the sweet shared aftermath of mead.

Her fear. No, not that. Desire.

Match and counterpart. Intimate as the living touch of breath.

She had not known how it would be. Mildred had told her nothing of that. It was like catching a flame, sudden, a thing beyond controlling. She felt the shock that ripped through his body, deep inside, and the piercing intensity of the feeling, the fierce power of her own response. The rush of it scorched her skin, turning her body molten so that when he tightened his arms round her there was no resistance; she sought the closeness, the touch of his body through the thin barrier of her silk dress, the feel of his mouth, and after the first stunned moment her lips moved against his.

That was all she offered. Because she had no idea what to do, how a woman kissed a bed-friend. But she heard his breath catch, a heated, uncontrolled reaction that could have been her own. That was how it was, not her childish, empty, coldly-imagined trick of seduction, but this. Reality. As uncompromising as the terrible sight of his pain.

She touched a person who was real. She felt the sharp tightness of his breath, the movement of muscle, the way his heart beat. She felt the smooth hot glide of his mouth against her burning lips. The touch of his tongue. He leaned over her, pressing her back against the wall, moving closer, the shadow of his body blocking out the room, filling sight, filling the hot, desperate sense of touch until there was only him and the nearness of him and the bright edge of passion. The warmth of his lips on hers urging her on for she knew not what, only that she was desperate and faint with longing. She could not match this. She did not know how. She felt him hesitate. But her fingers dug into him, fastening on all that dark feral strength because her mind and her body were wild with need, helpless.

His body moved against hers and she gasped. The sound and the tightness of her breath made her lips open wider under his but he did not stop kissing her. The touch of his mouth deepened, as though the dark hunger only increased, as though the passionate, dizzying touching of his mouth to hers had only just begun. Her heart beat like a wounded animal's but she did not draw back. His hand moved round, seeking her face, cupping the shape of her cheekbone, caressing the thin skin, the loose tantalising curls of her hair. She felt the slide of his tongue inside her mouth.

Her body stiffened, hard against his. But there was no room in the confined space between the barrier of the wall and the dark mass of his muscled strength. The movement brought her closer, so that the contact of their bodies became deeper and more intimate. She made a small breathless sound but there was no hesitation this time. His mouth held her, his mouth and the slow erotic touch of his tongue inside her. She could not move away. That was how he kissed her, openmouthed and indecent. Hot and smooth as the touch of silk. As though there were no shame. As though he touched her for gladness. For the fierce carnal pleasure of the way it felt. For the heat.

It was like tipping over into another world, a secret world that ran parallel with the familiar shapes of every day, a world that was hidden and intimate. She had always shunned that world. Because it was dangerous and had the power to destroy.

She could not pull away from the danger, not now.

The heat born from the touch of mouth on mouth melted through her, through tightened muscle and tingling skin until it unfurled deep inside her and her body moved, restlessly seeking the man who already held her close. Wanting the blinding sense of his nearness and the heady spell of pleasure, wanting the greater pleasure that lay ahead in the shadows, in the tight, heavy, mysterious shape of his body. She pushed closer.

She felt the sudden harshness in him, in his breath, the deep, almost rough movement of his mouth, the fierce unslaked desire in the way he held her. She felt the danger close over her head.

His hands skimmed her body and she writhed under his touch. His mouth slid from hers to fasten its heat on the naked skin of her neck, the delicate cords of her throat, the thin vulnerable hollow at its base. She felt his tongue. Her body jerked, her hips tight against his so that she could feel him, desire-hard. The unfamiliarity should have made her pull back, but the feel of that alien hardness against her softer flesh, the mysterious, erotic line of that dense other shape drew her. The danger drew her. The unexpected excitement.

Her body sought his, moved with his movement, pressed against the fierce masculine heat and the need inside her was beyond knowledge or control. She knew she would not be able to bear it. Her breath came in gasps. She was shaking. The whisper of his hair and the warmth of his mouth slid over her naked skin, across her throat, down to the shadowed valley between her breasts. She moved, but the closeness of him was sense-dizzying. The loose lacing of her dress would be no barrier at all.

She felt the moment when he pushed the material aside. She

felt the sinful lightness of the crimson silk slide across the aching hardened tightness of her nipple. She shuddered, clinging to him, the reaction uncontrollable. By the time he took her in his mouth, she was sobbing for breath.

He picked her up. The swinging movement left her giddy, light-headed and faint. She knew that in some other lifetime she had courted light-headed madness by drinking too much and too recklessly, that the injury to her head was not paid for, but she could do nothing about that. It was too late. She was in too deep, far too deep. Deep in the wild and dangerous intoxication of him.

She could feel cushioned softness under her spine, not the rough floor, but cool linen, the rich covers drawn back. He must have carried her to the bed. *His bed.*

"This is where I lay with you today." Her voice sounded strange, hoarse, not her voice at all. Just as she was not herself.

She watched him kneeling on the bed.

"Aye. This is where we lay together, as we will again. Now."

She could not read his eyes, fire and shadow. *Flickering candlelight and the blue smoke. Voices. Herself speaking with such passion, and his refusal. Yet the fire of passion had been there, inside him. She had known it. She knew it now.*

"Now…" Her voice trailed off. She watched his hand at the heavy buckle of his belt and her body burned.

Now.

He undid the buckle.

"It is what you intended, is it not? What you want."

Yes. No. *It was not part of my plan. Not this…this madness.*

But she could not say the words, not in the low hoarse voice that did not belong to her. She lay still in her crimson dress, un-laced to show her skin and the shadowed curve of her breast. She watched him with her carefully painted eyes. She saw him pull the fine tunic over his head. The shape of his body was already intimately familiar to her, the thick muscle and the dark shadows, the brilliant skin with its light dusting of dark-gold hair. The supple turn of his movement...

She lay back against the thick mattress, against the smooth linen already warmed from the touch of her body, softness and a comfort. But the warmth did not touch her skin. She was shivering too hard, even though she was burning up, burning because of him.

"Judith—"

She did not say *no*. She no longer could. Because she did want him, desperately. Not want, need. She needed the heat of his touch because it might fill the emptiness. For both of them. She knew the shadows in his eyes as he knew hers.

She reached out, touching him on the bare skin of his undamaged arm. She held him as she had once before in this bed.

Such fine hot skin.

She wanted him because she was mad.

Her hand shook so hard she could not disguise it. It could not matter. Her unsteady gaze fastened on his face. He was frowning. She expected him to come to her, but he did not move.

So she leaned towards him. The open neckline of her dress gaped. The aromatic oil that Mildred had so grudgingly rubbed into her skin gleamed in the light, releasing scent from her heated skin.

She could see the fire in his eyes.

"What I want," she began, but the hoarse voice that was hers gave out and the words eluded her, spiralling like the blue smoke from the candle flames beside the bed, formless as her desperation. Her hand was resting on his arm. She did not move it. She looked up to prove she was in control, because he would feel the fine tremors that ran through her heated flesh. He would feel that through his skin. She put her head back until the artfully curled hair cascaded over her shoulders. Her painted face smiled.

He watched her hand on his arm. She could have thought he was suddenly indifferent, cold inside. But the dangerous brightness in his eyes was visible to her below the thick brown lashes.

"What I wanted—"

"Seduction."

She did not say, yes. But she moved towards him.

5

THE MOVEMENT WAS INSANE, the choice of a reckless fool. Judith leaned forward until she touched the hard shadowed body of the pirate, until they lay side by side in the bed and the naked skin of her exposed breast pressed against the tight hot flesh of his chest. Her mouth came down on his. There was nothing. For one stretched endless moment there was nothing. Just the touch of lips and skin and his tightly-held, unmoving warmth.

Panic rose up inside her, mixing with the wild heat as though it were part of it, as though the reckless strength in her passion was the reverse side of fear. Her fear of defeat, of failing in what she had set out to carry through—to turn him to her will, to make him do what needed to be done to prevent disaster. And underneath, the deeply hidden fear, the fear of her own desperate emptiness.

She slid her mouth across his, moved her provocatively reddened lips. But she did not know what to do. Not the way he did. There was a breathless moment of forced stillness while he seemed to absorb all that she was. Then he reached out. The tension was so stretched inside her that she flinched. He touched her face, as he had before, his hand caressing her skin. Why had she not thought to do that to him? She was so ignorant. Useless at seduction. His mouth moved against hers and the kiss began.

But it was not like before. This kiss was hard, its sensuality more harshly edged, demanding. At a level where she did not know how to follow. Yet she had to. She expected his hands on her body like before, touching her in a way that would lift her miraculously back to the breathless heights. Where she wanted to be. She wanted… But she did not know what she wanted, even though she had told him she did, almost taunted him with it.

He held her head. Nothing more. Just held her head so that the kiss went on and she…

She was mad. She knew it now, utterly and fully mad.

She felt desperate. She touched his body. His naked skin. It was hot under her fingers, smooth and heavy and finely turned, the muscles thick with tension. But he never moved. The touch of his skin burned. It burned her the way his mouth did, but her fingers on his flesh trembled and were clumsy and she did not know how to—

The trembling was right through her, unstoppable. She made a small sound. The kind of sound made by someone lost, trapped in pain. But she did not know, in the harsh-edged place he had taken her to, whether he would stop. Or whether she wanted him to.

He stopped the kiss.

She bit down on her swollen, painted lower lip. Her body went tight, and the desperation raged through her veins. Her hands moved over his flesh, down across the taut skin of his belly, the solid mass of his hips. She was shaking. So badly. He would see it, feel it. She watched the solid fire-gilded shape of him against the crushed linen of the bed. She did not know what to do but she could not stop. She touched the shadowed thickness, the heavy blood-gorged jut of his sex.

He caught her hand, so fast, imprisoning it, taking her clumsiness, the full measure of her madness and her folly and her desperation. She gasped, the sound harsh and ugly and without grace. She wanted to fight, strike out at him, but she could not. There was no point. She could already feel the emptiness taking her back, familiar, her proper element. It was where she belonged, not in a world of human touching or shared heat, not even in its bitter seductive shadow.

She felt his arms close round her. She felt his warmth. Not the flames of bitter seduction, not the fever of what she had done or tried to do with him, not the harsh-edged fire he had shown her at the end. Just his solidness in the spiralling dark. Just his warmth.

She fought to control her breath, the unrelieved tension inside her. Her body stirred, restless, still driven in a way she did not understand.

"Hush." His arm across her body was like iron. "Stay still." The deep voice was controlled, as uncompromising as the arm that held her.

She tried to speak, to say something, anything that was coherent, to assert the same measure of control. But only the small lame sound she had made before came out of her mouth. Her head spun as though the mead and the stress and the pain were taking their payment all at once. Her body arched.

"Stay still." He shifted her weight, drawing her closer into the heavy solidness of him. "Stay still and even this will pass." She lay quiescent, while her mind picked out the sharp thread of amusement under the bitter control. She tried speaking again but it proved to be incoherent. He stopped her moving.

"It is over," he said. "Let it go." That last sounded so bleak she wanted to argue but there was not a single useful thought in her head.

THE SEDUCTRESS WAS SHAKING. Einhard held her, motionless, while he fought down the fast harshness of his breath, the surge of his blood, the anger, and embedded behind it the depthless white-burning heat of desire, unrelieved, stark as the rage, dangerous. How could she not have known the madness inside his head at this moment?

This moment. She had deliberately chosen it. She had seen…what? Weakness.

Her chance?

He pushed aside the black wave that held pain and anger and all the despair he had given way to. Such things remained hidden, locked away, or they would drown him. He watched the sole witness to the black demons. She lay still, breathing as hard as him.

She was trembling.

He waited. There was nothing else to be done. Except throw her out into the gutter where she belonged. But the hellcat wench did not belong there. She was a— He caught back the movement, the savage tension. Controlled it.

He lay still. Her shaking stopped. He felt through burning

half-clothed flesh the moment the small tremors in her slender body ceased. She was pressed hard against him, the scent of her warmed skin in his blood. The silk dress, fit for seduction gaped.

Still he waited.

She turned her head. Her eyes, in the shadows of the great borrowed bed, seemed not grey but black. She stared at his face. Her gaze took in the sharp movement of his chest as he took breath to speak. The breath nearly choked him, but his control was in place. He was sure of it.

"What in the name of all the saints did you think you were doing?" He bit off the words as she shrank back against the over-stuffed bolster with its ridiculous tassels as though he would compound his folly by strangling her. His hands clenched. The untied dress sagged open.

Stupid woman. Running around in a whore's clothes and talking about seduction. Had she not worked out what the end result was? Her hands clenched and the baffled rage slipped. What did she think he would do? Use his strength on a slender girl? He took a breath. Her slight body shivered again in the thin silk. An expanse of delicate flesh escaped its inadequate sheath. Firelight raced over her skin. He ripped the top cover off the bed and threw it at her.

"I said what did you think you were doing?" He shouted it, his voice out of control. He thought she would flinch again. She was fragile— She caught the cover, snatching it out of the air in full flight with a deftness a warrior would envy. Her small, finely sculpted muscles flexed. The silk swung across her bare breast. She glared at him.

"I told you," she muttered.

"Seduction?"

Her head came up. Her hand paused on the wealth of wool he had flung at her.

"Even so."

His gaze took in the fall of crushed and dishevelled silk, the gleam of her carefully oiled skin still pliant and heated from his touching. The power sprang between them, potent and unfinished. Her eyes told him her awareness, even her hidden fear. But she did not scrabble at the expanse of wool to cover herself. She took her time over every deliberate movement.

Stupid, idiotic, *dangerous* wench.

"So that was why you came here dressed as a—" Fortunately the word came out in Frisian because his insane, fever-filled head would not get round the English equivalent. But she must have understood it. The mutinous face set.

"I am not a whore."

"No," he bellowed, and the inexplicable folly, the witless magnitude of her deception came out. "You are worse than that. I would say that you are damned well a virgin."

She gave a little gasp. Then the red-stained, maddening, cherry-scented lips tightened.

"It must be the first time a man has ever complained about that," she spat.

"First time?" he said. "You would be regretting a first time right now if I had not stopped."

"Really? Do you count yourself that poor a lover?"

Control. "I do not believe you had much to make a comparison with. Unlike me."

She bit her lip. "Aye. You seem to know enough about whoring. You were acting no better. I do not see that you can count your behaviour just now as so much finer than mine."

"Hiding in my room? Offering seduction?" The colour in her brilliantly painted face rose. "You came here wearing a dress that—" Scarcely laced at the neck, no shift beneath. At least she had the disaster covered. Most of it. A slash of red material escaped the wool.

It was not a whore's dress however she had chosen to wear it. The tabby woven silk was dyed to that particular shade by the use of bizarre black bugs from the East, sold under the description of "grains" because it sounded better to rich clients. Vermillion. That silk had cost someone a fat purse of silver coins. He could calculate exactly how much the purse would have weighed. He was a merchant after all, as she so frequently pointed out.

And she was some godforsaken princess, even when whoring around with her clothes undone and her face painted and offering the devil knew what.

She was a maid. When he had forced the initiative on her she had had no idea what to do. Under the haze of mead-soaked lust and deception, he had tasted fear. She was a virgin. She had as good as admitted it in words.

"Why?" he said again. "What sort of game did you think you were playing?"

Her face flushed scarlet, the fine brilliance of her skin and the glitter of her eyes beyond what any art could achieve. "You know why. I told you."

He swore inside his head as the full realisation hit his mead-soaked brain. "The future of the country? The Vikings not forty miles from this door? A few weeks of my time which is supposed to fend off a seaborne invasion by an army like Earl Guthrum's?"

"Yes."

He watched the straightness of her back. Not just fear, but courage, the high-hearted kind that led to disaster. "And you cannot see the folly of that?" The potential for damage. "You thought you would change my mind by a little feminine persuasion?" From an ignorant virgin. He could still remember her shaking, taste her fright. She had no idea how much he had drunk, of the savage black fire that burned him, that burned him still. She had no idea of anything.

"Something like that," she said, her head at the angle that screamed princess from birth.

Stupid, *stupid* woman. What he could have done— "Who put you up to such a witless trick?" The high colour deepened in her face.

"No one."

"Hunferth." The man was a tough little bastard for all his courtier's smiles and his pandering to the lady's rank. Speaking of *pandering,* "If he forced you to do such a thing——" He had a sudden vision of ripping Hunferth's grinning face off.

"No! It was not Hunferth. I would not— He would not *dare.*"

Rank and position. "Who then? Not that foolhardy idiot who still thinks he can hold on to Wessex. Is the new king so desperate for allies he will use women to get them?"

"No." The high colour drained from her face, like the life-giving flow of a stream suddenly dammed off. The reckless king of Wessex had no idea then—

"The king," she snapped, "would not use any woman in the

kingdom's service. He…he thinks as any honourable man would. And yet I—" The brilliant colour flickered like a flame, lighting the fine bones of her face.

"It was my decision." The light voice firmed. "I can be as loyal as any man." The slender hands that had caught the wool he had thrown at her clenched. "I might be a woman, I might be feeble, I might be despicable compared to a warrior but I can still keep faith— I can fight."

She looked so small wrapped in the heavy bedcover, for all her determination, totally and criminally young. He doubted whether she had more than twenty winters. Six less than him. He could remember being that young. If he cast his mind back he might remember feeling much of what she felt. But he could not cast his mind back. It was impossible.

"So you would fight for a lost cause? For someone who will ultimately fail you?"

"It is not a lost cause," she said. "And before you speak so disparagingly of failure, try doing something." Her breath heaved. "Something that is not motivated by profit or the benefit it will bring to you. Try doing something that takes all of your skill and all of your time and all of your thought, something that needs courage and daring and high spirit. Accept a burden that takes all of the strength that you have and always demands more. All of your heart. That is what the new king of Wessex does." Bright colour flooded her skin.

"I would help him."

She looked at him with her beautiful vivid face and the heat flushing the skin he had just touched. "There is nothing I would

not do for the king of Wessex. But you? You would not understand."

"No." The familiar blackness pulled at him. There was nothing else in him. He noted the moment she realised.

"You will not deviate one hair's breadth from your course."

"No." He turned away from her beauty because it was not for
him. Her voice followed him.

"Whether there is hope or no hope makes no difference in
the end. That much I think you do understand."

He stood up. *No hope.* The darkness was there, all round
him, waiting. The torch flame mocked him. *Hope or none.* He
thought the blackness would steal sense, the blackness and the
pain and the fire that burned through his aching flesh like fever.

"Einhard…"

The woman. He passed his hand across his face to clear sight.

"Wait. You are not well."

He moved away, but she caught at his undamaged arm when
he was unbalanced, dragging him back to the bed, the movement enough to send the pain jarring through him.

"Wait." She held on to him.

"Leave it." It was impossible to keep the savagery out of his
voice. "Just go. There is nothing here for you. Go while you can,
before someone misses you and guesses your tricks."

"I cannot go. Not yet. I cannot leave you. Not—"

He watched her slender hand on his flesh. The way it had
begun.

"I would help you."

"What? The way you would help your honourable king? Or
is it more persuasion?"

"No. I—" The pounding against the wooden panels of the door, fast and urgent, stopped her words. *Before someone misses you.* She was not so stupid, or so reckless, the virgin princess.

"Persuasion?" he inquired. "Or coercion?"

"No! I swear. It is just Mildred, my maid and companion. I told her..."

"What? Where she should come to find you? When?"

Again the colour had leached out of her face, leaving only the thin bones. She looked exhausted, pushed, so small he could have flattened her with one hand. "Yes," she said. "I told her all that, how to find me, how to...find you. I wanted to..." she swallowed "...trap you before a witness, one I could control, so that you would be glad enough to take the payment Hunferth has already offered you for your ships." She stared at him, fear, defiance and that terrible courage. "I arranged it all." The pounding on the wooden panels got louder. She turned her head. Her eyes narrowed, as though some lightning-fast decision had been made, incalculable as anything she had done and just as resolute.

"I will not do it."

"What?"

"Not now. Mildred will tell no one if I ask her not to. I give you my word." She did not let go of his arm. The oak door swayed back on its hinges.

It was the idiotic maid. Behind her was Hunferth and four men, presumably more of the sainted West Saxon king's loyal companions. They were armed. He had no weapon. The assassin's knife lay at the other end of the chamber.

The lady Judith must have believed that she had gained what she wanted.

"Hunferth?" Her cold breath touched his shoulder. She followed it up by swearing. It was a sound of disbelief. Then she said quite clearly, "I cannot let them do it."

She was coiled in the bed with him, her hand on his arm, the brilliant dress hanging off her scented body and her hair cascading over her shoulders.

"Princess," said Hunferth. The tone was polite enough, but the cold, hard-faced warrior came through the courtier's gloss. It was probably the first time she had seen it. "Lady?" His gaze flickered over the scarcely clad girl. The four men behind him blocked the doorway, falling over each other to see. Their commander did not gesture them back.

The bright colour was hot under her thin skin.

Hunferth took a step into the room. The men behind him followed, their eyes riveted on the half-naked woman like hunting dogs on the kill. Hunferth, resting the sword, merely waited it out.

Bastard.

"My lord?" Judith looked across the width of the chamber at Hunferth and four men.

"My lady," said Hunferth heavily. The idiotic maid wrung her trembling fingers as though she washed her hands of this. "I was charged with overseeing your welfare by the *king.*" Einhard heard the sharp hiss of her breath, like a knife wound. Hunferth's eyes flickered. "The king," he repeated, the emphasis smooth, deliberate as a sword thrust. "He would not—"

Einhard felt the thin fingers grip at his arm. The tremor of her body passed through his skin.

"I am a princess of East Anglia. My welfare is my own concern."

She had caught the blow, deflected it despite the pain. Hunferth was on shaky ground dealing with two foreigners.

The Wessex man's feet moved, a fighter's stance, no quarter to be given. He gestured the king's men closer. As though he could need them with a maid for any purpose beyond humiliation. Einhard moved. It made Hunferth's attention fasten on him. The four king's men shifted. He saw Hunferth's hand tighten in frustrated longing on a silver-plated sword hilt.

Judith dragged at his arm. "It will be all right," she whispered, as though she thought he needed protection. "I have said this will come to nothing and I will see that it is so." She kept her head up. "There is naught that you need do."

That last was brutally true. The defence the lady had used was a two-edged weapon. She had miscalculated both her plans and her worth. She thought like a princess but the land she gained her rank and her standing from was politically dead. For all her fierce pride, she had to be of less practical value than him. Einhard highly doubted that Hunferth, much as he wished it, would be stupid enough to lay a hand on him. He was surrounded by a colony of rich Frisian traders and if there was one thing Wessex was desperate for, it was money. He had three ships of his own in the harbour. Loaded.

He had his own goals to pursue.

Hunferth, like a goaded bear, turned his attention back to the only victim he could touch. "When this becomes known, lady, even a princess must feel the effects."

The calculation had obviously been made. Hunferth, fighter and politician, was going to have to sacrifice a useless princess from a dead land. He straightened, making the best of a messy job. He was right. Honour had no place. "What the prince your brother will think, what will be said, what your future prospects will be, the lord king's disappointment—"

Loyalty and faith.

Mad recklessness. And deep courage, the kind that had saved his life.

"Disappointment?" Einhard's voice lashed through the flow. Hunferth started. So did Judith. "You are mistaken."

Hunferth took a step forward as though propelled. There was a general shifting of blades.

The mead-sotted virgin clung to Einhard's arm in a death grip.

He watched Hunferth. "I permit you to be the first to congratulate me on my forthcoming marriage."

Judith's curse touched his skin.

"Marriage? To you?" spluttered Hunferth. "To a ship-trader?" he added, forgetting which side policy had driven him to take. "You would treat with the prince her brother for her hand?"

Exiled prince. "Happily," returned Einhard. "As you so kindly pointed out, I am a merchant. I could buy and sell him." Judith's fingers dug into his flesh. He smiled. "Was there anything else you wanted to ask?"

Deyr.

He knew what that meant. *Die. He dies.* He knew the Vikings were talking about his father because they had said his name. Einhard. And then they had said, *he will die.*

Thieto kept very still. He took up so little room in the bottom of the dragon-ship that they hardly noticed him. The furs covered most of his body making him warm. He could see the stars.

His father would come for him. He knew that as well as he knew his own skin. His father never let anything go. That was why he was such a good merchant. Better than Skar.

He watched Skar the Viking roar with laughter. He howled, grasping his sword hilt and then slapping his great meaty hand against his great meaty leg. Thieto shivered, despite the warmth.

Deyr and then something about a place, no, a river, the river *Deben*. He tried to hear. The river. They did not know he could understand bits of Danish now. He listened, as hard as he could, but the words, slurred with ale, hard to hear, swirled over his head. Now they were telling each other ghost stories, enjoying themselves hugely. He heard the word *draugar,* the kind of spirits that haunted burial grounds.

He did not like ghost tales, even though sailors were supposed to. His father had not minded that; he had teased him and said it was all right. His father could make anything all right because—

He would not think about his father anymore, not just now.

Theito looked back at the stars, but their shapes were blurred and the light of the torch beside the mast hurt his eyes so that he could not see. He suddenly knew, as he sometimes did, that his father was thinking about him. Perhaps he was even watching torchlight, too. Perhaps he had followed him in his ships all the way to England and he was already somewhere quite near.

Thieto dragged the furs tighter against the night air. His father would come. He wished it was soon. He was taking so long.

But they had said *deyr.*

The timbers shifted beneath him as the longship rocked gently on the tide in the hidden inlet. He had not gone ashore much on this journey and the Vikings watched him. There were so many of them. More men than his father had.

They wanted to kill his father.

He had to escape.

"YOU HAVE TO GET UP."

"No." The morning light sliced across Judith's eyes.

"But it is already late. You must…" began Mildred's anxious voice from somewhere far away. Judith groaned and clutched her bedcovers like a shield.

"Not yet. I have something to do first."

"Something else? What?"

Judith thought about how much her head hurt, about what she had done last night. "Die," she said.

"I will fetch the leech."

"No." She thought a bit more. More pieces of last night came into focus. Hot skin. A tight body made entirely for pleasure. Clever hands and carnal knowledge. Such pleasure, both addictive and wildly terrifying. The heat of his mouth. His voice.

Then Hunferth. Hunferth and four gaping faces while she was rolling about in bed with a carnal lover. Hunferth talking about the king—

"I never want to see him again," she said clearly.

"Who, lady. The leech?"

"That…that *Frisian*." She banged her fist. It sent shock waves right up her arm and her neck into her head.

"Oh," said Mildred nervously. "That is a shame. He—he sent for you."

"What? Who sent for me? That…that *Frisian?*"

"He is your husband-to-be," said Mildred by way of excuse.

"Saint Athelbert's bones." The hundred-year-old name of her martyred ancestor, the East Anglian king, reverberated round the chamber.

Mildred swallowed. "I am sorry. It is all my fault. I did not mean Hunferth to find you… I should never have allowed…"

"It was not your fault." They had had this out last night and it was hardly possible to blame Mildred for letting herself be constrained by Hunferth. Judith pushed a set of unraveling curls out of her face. The fault was hers and hers alone. It had been her brilliant mead-soaked idea. She crawled out of bed. She had to put this right.

"I will teach him to send for me." *Husband*. If there was one thing clear out of all this in her aching ale-sick head, it was that she was not going to wed a hot-mouthed pirate.

6

JUDITH FOUND HIM at the water's edge, counting his moth-eaten goods as they were carried off the largest ship. Further proceeds of piracy, doubtless. He was marking a tally stick. The only consolation was that he looked like hell.

"I am not going to marry you," she said, since there was no point in wrapping up a mess like this in clean linen.

He glanced up. "Princess," he said. He finished marking the stick with a rather sharp-looking knife. He paused, possibly working out something beyond the size of his profit in his dim-witted brain. Then he passed the tally stick to someone who looked like a cutpurse, or possibly a murderer. He sheathed the knife in the leather scabbard that hung at one exotically lean hip. "Shall we take a walk?" He took her arm. "Sweeting."

The murderer with the tally stick grinned.

"I am not going to——" His grip was rather firm. They began walking. The sheer size of him blocked out the small cold wind from the sea. She had forgotten how large he was. The embossed leather scabbard swung as he walked.

"I have to tell you…" She stuttered. Her betrothed's hair stirred with the breeze, sunlight sieved through honey.

"Yes?"

She wished she did not know what he looked like with half his clothes missing.

"I came here to tell you that I am not going to wed you," she stated hardily. Of course, he would make her apologise first. His boots crushed the shell pathway.

This was going to be appalling—

"Not?"

"No," she snapped. "And another thing," while she thought of it, "I do not appreciate being *sent* for as though you were send-ing for a—"

"A wife-to-be?"

"I was going to say as though you were sending for a bale of your overpriced merchandise."

He made some movement, because the sun flashed off the gilded knife hilt.

"Overpriced?" he said. "Has someone been undercutting me? That last load of fish oil was below cost, not to mention the—the fish blubber. I am going to complain to the port reeve."

"Fish? That's revolting."

"Ah, but that is what you are marrying into. I will have you skinning fish in midocean one-handed before next Martinmas is over. It is fine work. You will love it."

She contemplated skinning something else. Slowly.

"I am trying to tell you," she began again through gritted

teeth. *What?* That last night her wits had been addled from a blow on the head? That she had been gloriously and culpably drink-sotted and so had he? That inside she had been filled with the terrible desperation that ate at her soul? That she had been mad?

But her decisions were her own. They had to be faced.

"Last night was——" She was suddenly aware of the warmth of his hand, of the strong clean lines of his body. Of all the dark mystery she had touched. He turned, the sun at his back. The knife swung at his hip, the light slid over the movement of the fine tunic, the tight dark trousers. She was intensely, frighteningly aware of his maleness. He stood still.

"Last night was what?"

"A mistake." She came to a halt beside him on the white path. She wet her lips and the blood pulsed through her veins. "All of it."

She could feel the heat of him, like the sun, like the reflection of her own burning flesh. She fought to think.

"I never intended Hunferth to see us. Mildred made a mistake. He found her and he questioned her until she had to tell him where I was." Poor Mildred. "A fine warrior like Hunferth thinks a woman has no power and should have none." She made a sound of bitterness, so much bitterness inside her. The fine warrior-merchant called Einhard moved. She saw the sharpness in his sun-gilded shadow, the size of him. She refused to step back. She thought he would press closer but he did not. She kept speaking.

"I will not let Hunferth dictate to me. Not any man. Never. I will not marry you. I will never marry. I will not be——" She stopped the heated words, the ones that pressed in her heart.

"Not be what?" The grey-green eyes held her, uncomfortable eyes, full of storms. "Not be what, princess?"

"Trapped," she said. The answer grated in the tension of the air, the tension between them. She had let out far more than she intended, different things, things that went deep, far too deep. She had only intended to turn his offer aside, firmly, but with the thanks that were, after all, his due.

"Trapped?" He did not move. They were not so very near each other. But she felt the potent spell of his closeness, the closeness that had been theirs along the narrow walkway of the harbour. In the firelit chamber that was his. She wanted to move backwards again, to break the spell, but she could not.

"Is that what you see?" he asked.

"Yes," she said and the bitterness caught at her throat. She could see his shadow, foreshortened by the high sunlight, dense. The golden light gilded his bright hair, the turn of his shoulders, the heavy lines and the smooth power. Warmth. His warmth like the sun. It was as though she could feel it, the way she had felt it in the intimacy of his bedchamber, warmth that enfolded her. Heat.

"No prospect of happiness?"

"I…" Her voice hesitated and he did take a step towards her then, a single step. It brought them back into closeness, into the closeness that was intensely familiar and now erotically charged. Because of what they had done. They could never be strangers again. Such a small movement, a step across the white shell path. It could have been accidental. But he knew the erotic charge was there. The shared heat. She could reach out and touch it.

"Have you seen no one who was happy in another? Are you so alone?" he said.

Having your happiness rest in someone else. That was worse. That was where the greatest trap lay. She had only one person left to love. She had seen all the rest die, or be parted from her. There was only her brother, her brother who had let his happiness rest in someone else, so much that he would have died for her.

"That kind of happiness is not what I crave."

"No?" He moved until he was all she could see, all she could feel. The bright sunlight rippled over him in waves. She could smell the tang of the sea in the summer air. She could see nothing but him; her sight dazzled and her breath caught. The sound of it was small and sharp, beyond disguising, not quite controlled. It was the same sound he had heard in the night silence of his room. "Then what do you crave, Lady Judith?"

He stirred, hot flesh under thin linen. She knew how he felt to the touch, how he burned. The way he said the word she had used, *crave*... How she had reacted to him, what she had wanted and desired of him.

What she had feared.

He was so close. The breeze blew his loose hair until it touched her. He knew what he did with his closeness and his taunting words. He knew what he did with the heavy fineness of his body and the masculine heat that radiated from him in waves.

"I do not desire the kind of *happiness* that you know." Carnal and earthly. Beguiling. Such a trap.

"So you keep your heart safe by giving it to nothing?" The

sharpness of his voice broke the heady spell, the beguilement of him that had lain over her like a drug.

"No," she said with vehemence, "not to nothing. I have given my heart to the king's cause. He has my loyalty, my duty, my—" She did not say it. Even his beguilement could not lead her so recklessly far beyond control. But he looked at her, in that way he had, as though he could see through all the woven web of her soul. He became utterly still, not a breath away from her.

"All the saints. Is that how it is? You think, you believe, that that is where you have bestowed your love."

She stopped, appalled. She had never betrayed what she felt, never once by word or deed had she stepped beyond the bounds of what was right. She had given her heart to the shocking brilliance of King Alfred from the first moment of his crowning in that desperate grief-filled ceremony at Wimborne, with the wounded body of his brother scarcely cold and an unwinnable battle waiting for him outside the walls.

She had seen him take an oath of loyalty from her brother, from her brother's friends, from the best men in the kingdom and she had wanted to give that oath herself. She had wanted to give the same dedication that surpassed all other claims on her heart, that would block out all the grief and the pain. She had wanted to give so much.

"No," she said coldly. "I gave my heart in loyalty, out of a desire to help someone else. It is a loyalty which is pure..." But her voice stumbled over the word and what she really wanted to say was *safe,* distant, nothing like the strange heated confusion she felt just from standing on the same path as the Frisian.

But that was lust, bespellment. He knew it and he taunted

her with it. By his closeness and his barbed words and his knowledge of her weakness.

"You would not understand," she said. "You would not know what a true feeling was."

She looked up. She caught one glimpse of something so strong, so violent, that the breath left her lungs. Then his gaze was gone from her, fixed on something else, something behind her and farther down the path.

She turned her head. Hunferth, and with him the stolid figure of the port reeve of Stathwic.

"Einhard—"

She glanced back. She saw nothing that she expected in his face, not the anger she must have called forth, not the carnal edge that so frightened her. There was only the ruthless control. And the dark shadows around his eyes, the starkness of his fine face and the way his skin hugged his strong bones.

"You made an offer that was forced on you," she said rapidly. "I forced it." She measured the distance of the approaching figures. "I will not hold you to that."

"No. Neither of us knows how to hold the other."

"No." He saw it. She felt a flood of unidentifiable feeling. It was relief. She fought down the bleakness. "So you withdraw—"

His voice cut her off. "No. I made the offer."

"But it is madness. There is no agreement. Nothing is settled. *I* have not even agreed." Hunferth was close, so close. "My brother would never consent," she said desperately, brandishing Berg's power like a shield.

"No," he agreed with infuriating calmness, immovable as a

rock in the middle of the narrow path. "If your brother has any feeling for you at all, he will not consent."

"Then—"

But he kept speaking. His voice low, the words so rapid she had to strain to hear them. "Your brother is a prince is he not? And I am a trader and therefore a hard negotiator. The negotiations for the settlement and the size of the morning gift will fail. In a little while, when all the interest in this dies down, the settlement will collapse. You will be free. No one will blame you. You will have your *pure* and respectable life back."

"My—"

"But there is one thing I cannot change."

"I do not—" She began and then broke off. She nearly lost his last words under the crunch of approaching feet on the path. She thought he said again, *I cannot*... Cannot what? Go with her to the king's shipyard at Derne? But then Hunferth was there and the port reeve, and Einhard had turned and was speaking to them.

She gathered her reeling wits and looked round in her turn, because she would not be pushed into anything—But they were not talking about getting her wedded. The port reeve was speaking, intent and obviously upset. Something about ships.

"What ships?"

But no one heard her. Einhard was already deep in a rapid exchange of questions, as though he had a right to demand information of the port reeve just as well as Hunferth, or any West Saxon.

"...how many..."

"Between two and a hundred. It was only a couple of village lads that saw them. It grew into a wonder-tale. But mayhap half a dozen?" hazarded the harassed reeve. "Hardly a doubt they were Viking."

"And no one knows the number of oars. But the look?"

She watched Einhard's eyes.

"The look? They could only be Earl Guthrum's ships—"

"The sails?" demanded Einhard.

The reeve shrugged. "Like a swarm of angry bees, they said. So—"

"Black and yellow." Einhard's face gave nothing, only the concern that was common to them all. But he had not moved and he was as close to her as a breath. The tension in his body, the harshness in each heavy muscle, was as clear to her as the sun's light. Hunferth seemed oblivious, the port reeve merely worried, deep in the demands of his job.

"Sailing east two hours ago and the wind in the bay north by northwest and the tide..." Einhard and the port reeve began calculating. Hunferth frowned importantly and then his jaw merely slackened. Of course to a land person it was...fascinating. She began to listen.

Finally Hunferth burst out, "Yes, but will they catch them?"

The port reeve had sent out his own ships. They had begun the chase but the raiders' advantages were too great. The reeve began to explain the chances. It could have been said in one word: *impossible*. The best they could hope for was to force the ships out to sea. With luck, they would give up and run back for East Anglia.

Einhard said nothing.

Hunferth muttered half audibly that if the fleet at Derne had been seaworthy and trained... He shot a venomous glance at Einhard's impassive face.

"Not that such a matter need concern you," he said aloud. "Your ships are safe enough here. Like your betrothed wife."

Judith could not allow that. Her pride would not let her. Not even on the level of the practical bargain Einhard had offered. It was not right. She would have known that from the start if she had not been mad, sotted and desperate. Filled with her own brilliant scheme and criminally reckless.

"I am not betr—" began Judith. Einhard moved. She lost the words under the sudden touch of his hot silk mouth. She lost her balance in the strong grip of his arms and she lost breath and her being and her sense of self under the deliberate assault of his lips. It was not a gentle kiss. She had the fleeting thought that it was harsher than he intended, like something hardly held back, something that had the power to slip the fierce control he held over himself. But she did not push him away.

For one terrible instant the same uncivilized response was in her, just as harsh-edged and driving. She responded like a man-starved jade, open so that she felt everything, the sensual shape of his mouth, the full lines of his body, the fierce tightness of the tension that had been hidden from Hunferth and the anxious reeve, hidden from all except her. She responded like a trusted lover. She felt the harsh beat of his heart. And then he pulled away. She heard the sharp hiss of Hunferth's breath, the indecently fast sound of her own. She turned, blinded, struggling for control. At that moment, Einhard spoke.

"But my wife and I are not staying here," he said. Hunferth's head snapped up. "Did you not know? My ships are sailing for the king's shipyard at Derne."

"WHAT KIND OF DEAL?" Skar's fingers tightened on the sword hilt.

"To your advantage. If you can meet the Jarl's terms."

"Terms...."

Jarl Guthrum's creature watched the movement of his hand. Skar spat. The man had no weapon. It was a condition of delivering his message. He would learn how to cringe before Skar's power. No weapon, but...the token that was King Guthrum's, the ravening bird shape in silver and gems, with its ripping beak and its bent claws, the wound-cleaver, the eagle that fed on the battle-slain.

Skar's hand unfurled. "You will have to forgive my impatience. I am not used to another man's terms." It was true. He did no man's bidding. He never had. Now he was driven to it. Because of thievery by the Frisian—

"They will be favorable terms, the share of plunder that is your due." The tone was well steadied. It was not wise to kill a messenger, particularly not one belonging to a powerful Jarl.

But there was nothing wrong with intimidation. It almost always produced results. He needed results. His fingers caressed the ridged indentations of the carved silver sword hilt.

"It is not enough," said Skar.

"Not enough?" The man's eyes shifted with the movement of his ringed fingers across the hilt. "Wessex still has wealth. The booty will be...considerable." The messenger raised his head in a fair display of arrogance. "How can your share in the riches of a whole kingdom not be enough?"

"Possible riches. The kingdom of Wessex is not yet Jarl Guthrum's." He fixed the man's gaze with his own, measuring the strength of will, the strength of the Viking earl behind the messenger. "It may never be his."

"It will." The reply was flat, absolute. It held a conviction and a strength far beyond the capacity of this man's—Jarl Guthrum's will to take what he wanted. Guthrum wanted a kingdom and was amassing the necessary number of ships and men. Guthrum wanted Skar's ships. The question was how badly.

As badly as Skar needed money to make good his ruined plans?

"What terms?" he repeated, as though he were a long way from being persuaded. Guthrum, holed up in East Anglia, had no reason to know how things stood in Dorestad.

"We regret your recent losses," said Guthrum's man.

Skar drew the sword. The movement was lightning-fast, beyond stopping, the thwarted rage outstripping mind and sense. Yet the uncontrolled viciousness of the movement proved not so very ill. The messenger's breath gasped, the primitive reaction of fear too quick to suppress, the sharp sound humiliatingly obvious in the silence. Perfect. Skar controlled the blade, forcing steadiness through each muscle. The man was brave enough but he was in a vipers' pit and he knew it. Every one of Skar's men had drawn a weapon when he had.

Skar turned the blade in the light. He could calculate any man's weakness and use it. He made sure this man knew. He smiled.

"It is only that your master is asking me to risk much. As he appears to know already, my ships are all I have." The tightness in his hands, in the visibly corded muscles of his arms was not feigned. His brother's losses had been huge. The cargo of furs, silk and amber had been wealth undreamed of and now it was gone. Stolen, along with his future. He knew by whom. He cut his mind off from that. The payment for that would keep. He would take it in blood.

He focused his gaze on Jarl Guthrum's man. "I will be risking all I own. I see the reward but, I told you. I do not take well to terms."

The man straightened. He held his ground. Skar's thwarted rage notched higher. This time he managed to control it.

"Perhaps you may persuade me." At a gesture from Skar, there was the hiss of sheathing weapons. He could see the sweat start on the other man's skin; he waved him forward.

The messenger watched him, watched the circle of armed men behind him.

"Jarl Guthrum does not take well to those who oppose his plans." The messenger did not move and the rich token glittered between them, the clawed eagle, the mythic old-one, sometimes called the deluder.

"It has reached the Jarl's attention that there may be opposition from a certain Frisian ship owner." The blade in Skar's slackened hand jerked. The messenger's eyes flickered. But the triumph was sour, the betrayal of weakness double-edged.

"I see you know who I mean," said Guthrum's man. "This Frisian has landed on the coast of Wessex. He appears to have stayed there. Frisians are good seafarers. The Jarl does not wish such a man to come to an arrangement with the Wessex king. He considers such an arrangement should be better made with him. You may be able to help."

"I—"

Guthrum's messenger stepped forward. There was sweat on the man's skin. But in his hand was the token of the ravening bird.

"We believe you have a dispute to settle with him." *We*. Guthrum, the ruthless conqueror, the devil who could gather information out of the air, information he should not have had the means to learn. Only Rorik in Dorestad knew— "You have your own reasons," said the messenger. "We would not stand in the way of that. All we ask is that you bring the Frisian to the Jarl's camp, preferably alive and with his ships intact. You may take any cargo they bear. The Jarl is not interested in that. He wants the man."

The blood pounded in his veins. "Alive?"

"You will find he is worth more so. But if not…" The messenger shrugged. "It is the ships and the crews that matter most to the Jarl. Just as your ships do." The messenger bowed his head, the warning clear, despite the sweating tang of fear. "The Jarl felt it would not be so hard to come to terms, particularly when they might be so…agreeable."

JUDITH CLUTCHED AT THE SIDE of Einhard's large merchant ship as the wooden deck turned under her feet like something living. The hiss of white water under the high raking prow with its dragon head, the wild freshness of the air, brought a deep exhilaration. Being at sea was the most exciting thing in the world. The open path to Derne stretched out ahead, the swan-road.

When her veil tugged in the wind she took it off and stuffed it into her belt.

There were fish diving and flashing silver in the sun. She leaned over the wooden side.

"Thinking of falling in?"

"I—" She was not in any danger, not really. But the big hand with the gold arm ring snaked out, catching her, pulling her back. She felt the hard familiar shape of the Frisian's body, warm against the wind. The ship heeled, sending her harder against him for a breathtaking moment without balance. But he steadied her effortlessly against the movement of the ship, a competent seafarer, a man looking after his betrothed.

It was a sham. Unsettlingly heady, dangerous. But she stayed in the circle of his arms. She was bringing back the prize, the man who would help to lift Alfred's half-built ships at Derne into a serviceable fleet. All she had to do was hold him.

The moving air tugged at her tunic and kirtle, but the heavy flesh behind her was warm, strong, and she could not move away. She could hardly believe he was truly here. It was a triumph. She had what she wanted. It was…beyond expectation.

Hunferth had seen no problem, once he had got over the shock of her betrothal. And Hunferth was the one who would be paying out the money. The ship bucked and the waves foamed with the sharp thrust of their passage. It seemed Einhard did not believe in wasting time once a decision had been made. The great single sail, blue as the sky above, strained, set to gain every ounce of force out of the wind. Their speed was relentless, the next thing to dangerous, almost…driven.

She shifted, the movement more abrupt than she had meant. His warmth held her steady.

"Judith?"

She felt the friction of her clothing moving against his, the touch of flesh underneath. The bright light danced and the boat surged. Her hair whipped back in fine strands, stinging them both.

"This must be the nearest thing to flying." The dancing golden air filled her lungs, its power rich as wine. The man held her and for a breathtaking moment, nothing else existed. "Have you seen how a hawk dives and rises and how rooks play at falling out of the air and nothing impedes them? This is what it must be like." She felt the quick, arrested movement of his body.

"Aye."

The word touched her, in the faint vibration of his chest, the sound of his voice. She tried to think that this was an arrangement for Hunferth's silver. But the boat glided, fast as a bird, smooth as a serpent, and the wind and the sunlight danced like madness. Above their heads the sky was fair as a jewel, endless.

"I wonder what it must be like to climb up to the top of the mast," she said, as though she were ten winters old again and running wild at the palace at Rendlesham, indulged, loved.

"Luckily you will not find out." His body shifted against her back, fine hard masculine strength.

"You think I would not do it."

He appeared to consider it. She turned her head and caught the masking sweep of his thick brown lashes. "I think you will not do it on my ship." He looked up, his gaze straight into hers. "I have no desire to swab the decks after you fall off." His eyes changed. In someone else it would have been the beginning of laughter. But he never laughed freely. Something tightened round the region of her heart. Something that held the latent power to cripple her.

Hunferth's silver. She moved away, tossing her head.

"If I were a sailor, I would never come back to land."

He stepped back, out of courtesy. As he should.

"Nay. You would not say that in an autumn storm, with the

freezing rain lashing you and the wind like ice. Then you would know the value of a home."

A home. Rendlesham as it was, a palace of golden light, a great hall with a high roof and decorated walls, all the other royal estates, her family's own lands… She clutched the side of the ship with her hands in the unsteady world. One could die longing for home. A seafarer, of all men, might know that.

"Like the man in the story?" she said. The ship surged under her feet. *"No one knows,"* she quoted, *"not he to whom it befalls in the fairest manner on land, how I, wretched and sorrowful, have spent winters on the ice cold sea, the wanderer's place, cut off from kin…."* As the last words, *winemægum bidroren,* took their place in the sunlight, she realised how cold the wind was. There was no shelter from it at sea.

The sailor she was betrothed to did not look at her. His gaze was fixed on the horizon. She watched the movement of his hair, the line of his shoulders.

Do you understand? She did not know how to say such a thing to the stark back in its fine, dark linen tunic. It was not a question she should ask, or even something that mattered between them. They had nothing.

"Einhard…" But he did not hear, his attention suddenly locked elsewhere. His head came up and at the same moment the lookout shouted something incomprehensible in Frisian. But then the words did not matter. She had seen what had caught his attention: dragon-ships, long, sleek vessels of war. Her heart fluttered despite all of her willpower. She had to fight not to step back. But then the movement of his body told her when he turned. It was not danger. Or at least, not of the expected kind.

"Einhard! What is it?"

He pushed away from the ship's side, the movement competent, deliberate as anything he did. He shouted some order and people started scurrying.

She could see for herself now that it was not a set of black-and-yellow sails, not the swarm of angry bees that had so frightened the port reeve.

"Einhard—"

He turned his head, courteous, but she could see the cold shutters close off the moment of unguarded brilliance in his eyes, locking whatever he thought inside his head.

"Princess? Best put your veil back on. Or perhaps you might prefer the red dress."

"What? Why—" But she could see the leading ship, skimming the green waves, fast and dangerous as a bird of prey. The bright pennant swirling from its masthead left a trail of golden fire in the sunlight. A winged dragon.

The Sea-wylf, the beautiful, predatory she-wolf of the ocean. The king's ship.

Einhard set his own ship to follow the white wake. He did not speak to her again. Just as well. He was a stranger. A paid stranger.

THEY ARRIVED AT DERNE IN good time. The small natural harbour was calm, sheltered and overgrown, named for those qualities and for one far more important. Derne meant hidden, secret. Einhard's ship dropped its stone-and-wooden anchor well back from the king's ships.

Her betrothed carried her ashore so that she would not get her feet wet.

No one spoke as they walked to the beached warship, except Mildred who kept muttering. Judith fancied that her maid might be reciting prayers. It was not encouraging.

They reached the sleek, lethal shape of Alfred's ship. There was a bustle of movement, the calls of sailors. And then the king leaped down from the oak-straked side. The sun glittered on the scabbard slung at one lean, powerful hip, on the torqued gold at arm and neck. Behind him, like an exotic foil, was the elegant, dark-haired shape of the Briton, Macsen, her brother's close friend.

They stopped on the landing stage, the men she had known for years, one bound to aid her out of friendship to her brother, the other a figure of complete power. If she wanted it, they would release her from the insane folly she had walked into. She could fall at the king's feet, explain it, ask forgiveness. She knew he would help her.

His men started pouring off the ship, house thanes, hearth companions, warriors, his chaplain. They all stared at the Frisian. The trader and mercenary. The attainted pirate.

All except the king. He looked at her. She took a step forward that was instinctive, unstoppable. The suspect merchant, who had been at her side, let her. She stood for a moment, isolated with her sovereign. True-born East Anglian princess and Wessex king.

There was a faint sound around them, the whispering of dozens of voices, hissing with unease, speculation. With rank curiosity. But that was not what she heard. The voice in her head was Frisian.

I have made the offer.

That was what he had said when they had stood on the shell

path and the consequences of her actions had stared them both in the face.

A princess was trained to know the value of gestures. She stepped backwards, taking it slowly so that everyone could see her, so that everyone knew her action was deliberate. She judged it exactly, so that when the movement stopped, she was standing at the side of her betrothed.

7

"WHAT, IN THE NAME OF ALL THAT is holy, have you done?"

It was not the king's question. The king had been patient, concerned as a proper sovereign should be for her welfare, the first instant of surprise glossed over by native kindness. Yet in the end she had seen a hint of shrewd speculation in the hawklike eyes that had sent nervousness crawling down her spine.

People said that there was no mind King Alfred could not see through, friend or enemy. She thought it was true.

And now she had to convince his henchman and her brother's friend that she had a proper intention to wed.

"Did you run mad?" inquired Macsen. The dark eyes measured her. "Is it Beltane or Midsummer Eve and I have not noticed?"

"What an ill-bred question that is." But it was impossible to outface Macsen, who was descended from long-dead emperors. He crossed one beautifully shod foot over the other. "I am betrothed to be married," she snapped.

"Just in time by what I hear."

"I—" *Hang* Hunferth and his flapping mouth. It was so unfair. No one in their right mind would pretend that any of her brother's friends had denied themselves pleasure all their lives. Or that Hunferth had for that matter.

She gritted her teeth. "He offered marriage," she said crushingly.

"He could hardly have done much else. What possessed you?"

She shut her mind on the vision of Einhard's skin, the erotic feel of his mouth. His touch…

"With a man like that. If he has got you with child—"

"Certainly not!" The trouble with her brother's friends was that sometimes they acted like her own brother.

"So what does Berg say?" asked Macsen.

"Nothing," she replied in a voice of ice. "Why? What should my brother say?"

"Then he does not know yet." It was not a question but a flat statement. Sometimes she had the urge to land a punch right in the middle of Macsen's flawless face.

"Berg is not here." But there was the next problem. She hesitated. She would not imply, even to Macsen, that there was something wrong, that she was in far over her head. Macsen would feel obliged to tell Berg out of that irritating sense of masculine solidarity, and Berg had enough worries. The friendship cut two ways.

"I have not sent to tell him yet." The only thing she could think of was what the Frisian had said. "Because there may be some problems with the settlement. I see no point in burdening my brother with the details of all that now. He has enough to deal with."

Berg's mysterious lover with the unexplained past had nearly died. So—she bit down on the thought—so had Berg. Macsen knew that. She saw the difficult calculation in the tightness of his face. The intelligent eyes narrowed.

"The man, this Frisian merchant, has you. And he has problems with the marriage settlement?"

Not off the hook yet. She tried not to clench her fist. "He has some difficulties of his own," she said dampeningly.

"Difficulties? With that last cargo?"

Why could her brother not have picked friends who could be dampened? "Well, how much do you get for blubber?" she snapped. "Or fish oil."

"*Fish oil?* It was wine, various spices and dyestuffs. Not to mention certain weapons. Do you have any idea how much that kind of cargo is worth?"

Wine and— She set her teeth. In any case, it could not be worth that much. Hunferth had bought the dangerous creature's loyalties with Wessex silver. "There are other difficulties," she offered. "With Rorik in Dorestad, with…" Best not to mention piracy… "And there is some sort of feud and—"

"Piracy," said Macsen.

"It…it was not exactly…" She had no idea what it was. Straight-out theft, as far as she knew. With violence.

"Do you have any idea what kind of a man this is? A virtual exile. He is at enmity with Rorik. Back in Dorestad he was embroiled in a blood feud with the Danish pirate, Skar. Although now it seems that Skar may have fallen out with Rorik because he has left Dorestad. Like your betrothed." The dark eyes fixed her. "In fact, there are so many similarities the two of them might as well bury the feud and join forces."

"No," she said, but coldness touched her veins. "Einhard agreed to come here, to help the king's cause. I was there when he said it. We had just heard about the Danish ships, Guthrum's ships. But Einhard chose Alfred."

"So you say." Macsen made a frustrated gesture. "We cannot contain Guthrum. We need more ships and more men."

"Which is why Einhard is here," she said. But the coldness seemed to spread. The terrifying ships with the black-and-yellow sails like a swarm of angry bees. The questions to the port reeve and the fierce tension in the body next to hers. "He said—"

"There was violence when he left Dorestad. People were killed. I do not know who or how many."

She made a strangled sound.

"Did he not mention that?"

"He told me there was a feud."

"Apparently the man will not let this blood feud go. If it involves you as his wife—"

"It will not."

"How can you know that?"

Because the betrothal will be over long before that. I am not going sailing across some dazzling sun-bright sea to Dorestad with him. There is nothing between us, nothing except this one purpose, here.

"Judith." Macsen leaned forward. The movement was sudden, designed to take her off guard. But it was the deadly earnestness in his eyes that did so. "You can still get out of this, I can help you. The king will."

The king. The king with Guthrum's fleet on the loose. The king who needed more ships, now, before it was too late....

"No," she said. Einhard was here at Alfred's ship base. That was the main thing. She had come so far with this and she could manage whatever was to come. She had to. The alternative did not exist.

"I have made a betrothal."

"And you will not give this man up?"

"No." She saw the moment when the intensity of Macsen's black gaze slipped beyond her. "I know what I am doing," she said desperately. "I will tell Berg in good time. When he and Elene are well. I am asking only that you say nothing until then. I shall be here among the king's men." He would never agree. He did not even listen....

"I shall be safe." She stopped speaking. The dark eyes focused. On the light first and then on her.

"Macsen?" she said in sudden urgency. "What did you see?" He hated that question. It touched on a separate world he never admitted to. A world comprised only of dreams. He would never tell her.

"I saw the burial mounds on the River Deben."

"Sutton Hoo?" Her spine tingled. "The barrow downs?" The tombs in the rich earth where her ancestors were buried... "What else did you see?" *Tell me.* He would not....

"A flame," he said with irritating obscurity. "Light." He stood up. "Invite me to the wedding feast." She watched his back fill the doorway.

"There won't—" She stopped herself just in time. He shut the door.

There would not be a wedding feast. She might be betrothed to a thieving murderer of dubious loyalties, but in the days to come she would find what secrets lived in his head and she would outwit him, bend him to her will, to what was right.

She had only to put her mind to it, and her courage.

JUDITH FOUND HER BETROTHED messing about with pitch.

"Caulking." She was getting good at this shipbuilding business. The day was hot, windless. She observed the sweating figure in the base of the half-finished ship. "Fascinating."

He looked at her. It was the kind of look that probably terrified innocent owners of boats into handing over all of their goods in return for the privilege of breathing.

Her heart skipped a beat.

"Messy," she observed critically as black goo dripped onto the planking. He swore somewhat violently. Her fingers dug into the ship's side.

"Needs care," she encouraged. He bent his naked back. The light gleamed off sun-bronzed muscle. He was missing half his clothes again because working this fast and this hard in the late-summer heat was no light task. Neither was it fit for someone with an injured arm. He seemed to take no account of that, as though it were irrelevant compared to what burned inside him. He looked... The word that had come into her mind on the ship journey resurfaced—*driven*.

No one else seemed to notice.

She glanced down from the side of the boat. Naturally, she would not gawk at the glistening sunburned skin. Or at anything else outlined by the tight coil of his body. *Mad...Midsummer Eve...* Macsen's words rang in her head. Macsen had not actually said carnally bespelled. He had not needed to.

Solid muscle bunched and slid. She watched the large, competent hands deal with the black goo. People said the pitch had bits of sheep's wool or some kind of animal hair mixed into it to make it stick. Revolting, really. She made a faint sound.

The gold hair spilled over his skin as he raised his head.

"Perhaps you would rather the seams of the ship leaked until it sank?"

"No, indeed."

He, of course, was the expert. No one could have faulted his dedication since the king and his men had left, whether it came to building ships or to practicing fighting tactics.

No one could have complained. Not even Macsen.

No one, in the whole of the shipyard at Derne saw anything amiss.

She watched him.

"Wifely duty," she said by way of explanation. She observed a struggle for patience. The sun-gilded muscle tautened. It was mildly terrifying.

He looked away with a studied completeness.

He was checking the work already done on the warship, adding finishing touches. He was alone.

She contemplated the distance.

She might, of course, make a disgusting mess of her braided tunic and her fine blue kirtle. She gathered the fullness of her pristine skirts and spared a brief and envious thought for the forbidden freedom of trousers.

There was no deck on the ship yet, but it was not so very far to the bottom.

She leaped.

She had the brief satisfaction of nearly making him jump out of his sinfully enticing skin.

"What on earth do you think you are doing?" he yelled like a captain about to hang one of the crew. "You could have broken your neck."

Perhaps he was going to offer assistance. She tried looking delicate. "Nothing broken at all." It had been a neat landing. Perfect. She was quite proud of it. "But are you all right?" she added solicitously. "I thought you were going to fall."

He would murder her. She took a breath. She pushed the thought of what he was capable of right to the back of her head.

"Mind the pitch," she said helpfully.

She had forgotten how hot his eyes could be. His gaze moved from her head to her feet. She thought she could actually feel it burn. Shivers touched her skin. They might have been back in the torchlit chamber with the masked anger and the feelings that had no control. His gaze stopped. She realised the edge of her skirt was caught on one side. He could see the curve of her leg. Her heart beat in a hot rush. She dragged at the bunched linen. It fell into place instantly, but it was too late. The terrible awareness that existed between them had come alive.

She stepped back. There were only the two of them in the enclosed wooden space of the boat. This was a stupid, stupid idea. But she could not stop. Macsen's words about piracy and feuding and death, her own suspicions, dug through her like a wolf's claws.

"It will be a fine ship," she said. The shape of the wooden vessel with its overlapping planks, sleek as a serpent, was clear, and he had made her know what it was like to skim the vastness of the sea.

"I am relieved to have your approval."

Her gaze flew back to the hot impenetrable green of his eyes. Was there meaning in his words beyond the surface, or not? She had played this bitter game for three days. The danger of it stared back at her.

Her heart beat so fast.

She made a regal inclination of the head, as though she had still been at her cousin's court at Rendlesham, now occupied by Vikings. There was no way back.

He leaned towards her.

"Princess?"

She was acutely, achingly aware of him. She took another step, masking the movement to put distance between them by the smiling turn of her head.

"But I did notice the oars stacked on the ground do not match," she said. "Do you suppose they have made them wrong?" She took a breath. He was so close behind her. He must have moved when she did. She could sense him without looking. "Perhaps I should tell them," she offered.

She turned round.

His hand was gripping the long line of the boat ell they used to measure the angle for each run of planking along the straked sides. She wondered whether the size of his hand would break it.

"The oars are supposed to be of different lengths to compensate for the curve of the ship. How long they are depends on their station, where they are positioned. I would not, if I were you, mention it to the king's shipmaster."

She could not quite look at his face, only at the graceful curve of his throat that was at eye level, only at the endless brutal width of his shoulders. Next step.

"Ah," she said. "You mean because your own man is not here to assist him today and doubtless he is feeling out of sorts from being overworked. Perhaps your man will be back soon, when he has finished whatever task you have set him?"

There was a silence. She watched the gleam of sweat on his heated skin, the shadowed movement of his chest, the way the sun caught the dark-gold hairs at the centre.

No one, in the organised chaos at Derne, appeared to have questioned the way Einhard's own men disappeared and reappeared without explanation. Likely no one had noticed. Her fingers, hidden in the folds of her skirts, fisted. No one save her.

"Even so." That was all he said. He might have been oblivious. He might— "Is there another question?" She saw his hand move away from the long pole of the boat ell like a golden blur and could have cursed herself for the small gasp of breath that left her dry throat. He would have heard it. But he gave no sign.

"Princess, you look tired in this heat."

He took her arm. That was all, the gesture formal, distant. They pretended to be distant with each other all the time. They both knew everything about pretence.

The touch of him burned through her skin.

"Perhaps you should leave me to get on."

Her cue to take her leave. He was not going to answer any more questions, however artfully put. He was too clever by half. How very much he wanted her gone. The tension between them was strong as fire, burning like his touch, the sense of his presence, the closeness of his sun-warmed skin, the wild, fiercely contained, erotic danger of him. He turned her, his size crowding her in the confined space.

"Come. I will help you back over the side. When I have finished here, the tide will be fair for sailing."

"Sailing?" The question this time was impulsive, part of a different need for knowledge and yet perhaps bound up in the other.

"Practicing battle tactics. Another thing you want to know about, princess?"

His fingers slid along her arm. Her skin tingled under his touch through the thin linen of her sleeve. The touch broke. It left her burning. She watched him swing himself over the side of the ship, clean as a spear's flight. The wound did not stop him. There might have been no damage at all. His strength of will was unnerving.

She stepped across to the wooden planking, bunching up her skirts. She watched his body straighten from the fast movement. She pulled herself up quickly, before he could turn. It was not dignified in a skirt. She dragged the material round her knees, precariously balanced. She could leap down by herself without difficulty. She should keep her distance from him. His double-edged words had warned her so clearly. But there was no way back from the path that her fate and her own will had set her on.

"Come." She watched heavy outstretched hands, a naked arm. Like a dangerous challenge. The light glanced over his skin as he moved and the tone of his voice was rough, yet touched with disturbing warmth. The wind caught her hair. The sunlight dazzled. So hot. She let go, stepping through the brilliant air.

He caught her, the helpless weight of her body slamming against his. He swung her round, the movement and the strength of him taking the impact of her fall. She stayed like that for an instant that was timeless, between one breath and the next, suspended in the moving air, caught in the strength of his arms. Her feet did not touch the ground. She saw his face, the light in his eyes. She felt the touch of his strong fingers at her back and at the intimate curve of her waist. She felt his heat.

The same heat burst inside her. It surged through her like a flood, uncontrollable, and with it came need. The same aching wild-edged hunger she had felt in his chamber when they had touched like this and she had wanted...so much. She had wanted him and the carnal knowledge that lay behind the hot brightness of his eyes, in the way he touched, in every blatant sensual movement. In the mysterious exotic shape of his body. She had wanted something indefinable, the dangerous closeness of another living person.

She clung to him, her fingers digging into his flesh. She felt the tightened muscle, the nearness of him, the fine skin faintly dampened with a thin film of sweat.

Her heart swooped. The sudden gasp of her breath was sharp as pain, a sound that could be heard. Perhaps he could feel her heart beat. He lowered her down, still holding her with the same strength, so that she need lose nothing of his hot earthy nearness, not unless she wished it.

She could not move away.

She stayed, touching him. The madness of the challenge, the secrets, were still there, dangerous as ever, but subsumed under the power between them like entrapment.

He held her close.

The slow, gliding movement when he set her on her feet had

brought the vulnerable lines of her body into his heat, enfolded her in its stark power, her thinly covered flesh tight against his naked skin, moving, the closeness like the most private of caresses, intimate beyond her dreaming. Sinful.

There was nothing of his body she could not feel, the solid living wall of his chest, the heavy swelling muscle of his thigh against hers, the tight hips—the hard ripened fullness of him against her flesh. His closeness and the slow, controlled, infinitely blatant movement dazzled her senses. The consciousness of him pierced her, burning through her mind, through every aroused inch of her skin, the sight of him and the touch of him and the fierce male promise of his body overwhelming. But even more intimate seemed the catch of breath in his rib cage, the knowledge of the way his heart beat, fast as hers.

Her feet had touched the pebbled shore, but she could not stand. She leaned into him. Nothing existed in the world but him and the heat in his eyes and his skin. Nothing but the wanting, the feel of him under her hands, the firm touch of his own hands on her. So near her. His face was inches from hers, their mouths on the edge of warm, shared breath.

"What is it you want, princess?"

This. I want closeness. The sharp truth hovered at the edge of her mind. Dangerous, fated for pain and disaster like any other closeness in her life, more so because *he* was dangerous. A pirate. A deceiver. Her body leaned closer.

"I—"

The movement of his limbs, the touch of him, dizzied sense. Power and strength and the undisguised force of desire, his body hot, open. Nothing hidden. She felt the breath he took to speak.

"Why did you follow me here?"

Nothing hidden.

Nothing of her would be hidden from him.

Deceit.

She tried to make herself think. "It should be known that we are sometimes together." Her lips, heated from the surge of her blood, swollen as though he had touched her, formed the words with care. Her mouth was so close to his she nearly touched it. "We are betrothed."

The smooth fall of his hair brushed the thin skin of her neck. "Wifely duty?" He was so big. So close. No one else near them.

"Aye." Her heart beat faster. "What else could there be?" The awareness of him swamped her, the tightness of the dense muscle under the hot skin. She took a shallow breath. "I am like the Frisian wife in the fireside tale," she said lightly. "She has a welcome for her provider when his ship is at anchor. She takes him in and washes his clothes and gives him all that love could ask." She produced a smile. "I am sure she would have been interested in ships, too." Her lower lip brushed his, the faintest touch. Enough to make her heart skip and the breath catch in her chest hard against him. But this time there was no reaction in the hot muscled strength of him, not by sound or deed or even by breath.

Nothing, where before there had been all. Or so she had thought. She felt cold, straight through.

"Einhard—"

Mildred's words, half heard in the hazy disaster of that first night, stirred in her head. There had been a wife. Once. What did he feel? She knew so little of him, only that dismissive mention from Mildred of something long confined to the past. But she sensed sharp feelings, harshly guarded.

"A woman interested in ship building and battle tactics, is that it?" His mouth slanted over hers, but not touching. She suddenly knew he would not give shape either to what he thought or to the kiss that almost existed, even though the heat of his mouth and the closeness of his body would have told otherwise. The familiar sense of isolation locked round her, took its accustomed place. Closeness was beyond her grasp, beyond either of them. She straightened her spine.

She could not wish it. It led to destruction.

She looked up into the shadowed lines of his face. The strength was so clear, the strength and the ruthless purpose. The bright heat of passion flickered, but it was mastered, so mercilessly. She was glad of that mercilessness. It meant she could tell part of the truth, a part that was so strong.

"I would know all that you can say of battle tactics." She met the ruthless gaze, felt the cold warrior's strength, not the warm man's. "Tell me what that is like."

The hard-edged muscle shifted. "A battle at sea? That is something you want to know?"

"Aye."

It was as though the harshness in the solid muscle she touched moved to his eyes. She made her gaze hold his, so close she could see nothing beyond that dense brightness against the skin bronzed by seafaring.

"Are you surprised?" *That this is what I want to know because it drives me? Yet it is something I will do, must do. Because I have to avenge those who have died or I will never rest.*

Because I have to stop the loss.

"What is it you wish to know?" The danger, the secrets in his eyes, matched the terrible depths hidden inside her.

"What it is like, fighting in a battle."

"Forming the fleet into line before the start? Lashing the biggest of the ships together to form a fighting platform while the others are free to skirmish? You want to know how to direct that?"

She watched the harshness in his gaze. She met it head-on. "In part. I want you to tell me…"

"The next step?"

"Yes."

"Why?"

"Because I want to know." *Because I need to know. All the things that perhaps there are no words for.* Her voice could not frame it. She sounded merely obstinate, willful. Stupid.

"Tell me." The need made her voice hard, the bitter need to know all the things that her brother had been through. All that this man knew. She watched his eyes freeze over. His body still touched her so intimately, and yet not intimately at all, cut off from her by the knowledge and the bitterness.

Perhaps by something else, by the power of the secrets in him that she could not fathom. She watched the fine mouth move so close to hers.

"Shall I describe boarding? Or perhaps the iron rain that precedes it? The hail of arrows and then the spears and the iron-shod stakes. And the stones."

"How do people survive it?"

"By luck. By the use of a shield. Or not at all."

She thought of how desperate it was. How it must feel. She

leaned against the living warmth of his flesh and felt the movement of his breathing and the beat of his heart. She felt his strength and she thought of the iron rain.

"The end comes like a land battle, once the ship is grappled the fighting is hand-to-hand, each man against the other."

"Yes."

The flesh warmed by the sun and the heat of passion moved restlessly under her hands.

"You would be a fool to wish to know more of that."

"Would I?" she said passionately. "Why am I such a fool when a man of my station would not be? Do I not suffer the destruction of all that I hold dear? Can I not do what I must to defend it? I will fight to defend what I love. That is the end I see."

The abrupt movement of his body broke, the hot uneasy spell that had held them. Broke her hold.

"The end is that people die." His eyes were dark, black-shadowed as they had been in that appalling moment in his chamber.

He moved away from her. She tried to hold on to the hot, sun-warmed flesh; but she might as well have tried to hold back the power of a flood.

"People die," he said. "Or they are—" He stopped speaking. His head turned, the fierce movement of his body arrested. She saw what he saw, the solid shape of another man in the boat's shadow. Tatwin, the monk in training. His friend.

Tatwin took an uncomfortable step back, glancing from her own face flushed with passion to the bitter wildness of Einhard stopped in midstride, moving away from her.

"I did not mean to intrude. I came only to say that the men are ready."

Einhard stilled, his body poised between the shadow and the light, like a creature returning from another world.

"For the battle training," said Tatwin.

"Aye." That was all he said, that single word, and then he turned away.

"I will come." Judith had taken a step forward before the power of thought or reason could form in her head.

"Why? So that you can see how all that I have described will be carried out?"

Her feet stopped, slipping in the loose shingle. The monk caught her arm. She did not know how much he had heard of what they had said. What he had seen...

Einhard's long stride never paused. "No, princess. Find some other source for your amusement." His words dismissed her, the way every man did.

Bastard.

"Wait, lady. Leave him."

She stopped because it was pointless following. Her eyes narrowed to slits. "He believed I spoke for my own amusement." She thought of the deaths that had touched her, of the losses that went on every single day. "He thinks there is nothing in me but that."

"Lady—"

She watched the breadth of the Frisian's back, the bright swing of his hair. He had almost reached the men gathered at the edge of the waterline beside the ship waiting for him.

"Fool." She became aware of the monk soothing, drawing her aside. "How can he not see?"

"I am sorry. There is little he can see now beyond this quest of his. Where it will bring him..."

"*Fæhth.*" The fell word struck the air. Blood feud. *The end is that people die.*

She watched the competence with which he moved, the controlled power and the unshakable strength. "And is there nothing beyond that?"

"No," said Tatwin.

"Then—" They saw someone running, flat out across the treacherous shingle, the way a man might run from disaster. She saw Einhard turn. The flying figure reached him, spoke.

Tatwin swore. The messenger gestured, back towards the hazy shadow of the woods. At the same moment, she heard the pure, clear sound of a horn. It had only one meaning. She was already moving towards the two figures silhouetted on the shore, isolated in the presage of disaster. She began to run.

8

SHE REACHED EINHARD before Tatwin did, her light weight and supple strength an advantage over his bulkier power. Judith skidded to a halt in the treacherous stones.

"What is it?"

Tatwin crashed to a stop beside her.

The messenger raced off at some sign of Einhard's. Einhard's gaze caught hers for one instant and then transferred to Tatwin. His eyes were distant, intent. A look she had seen before.

"Well?" said Tatwin.

"Vikings," said Einhard, then, "no," at Tatwin's instinctive glance at the ships. "By land. Riding. A war band. Perhaps as many as fifty."

"Fifty?"

"Aye."

She could see the men from Einhard's ship with their weapons. So few. The rest were out to sea. There must be some of Hunferth's men ready. The shipbuilders…

Einhard shouted to the milling disorder.

"Vikings from where?" said Tatwin. Stupid, stupid question. What did it matter? They had to be Earl Guthrum's. The men crashed through the surf and past her. She was counting, her thoughts racing ahead to what had to be done. To the time and the distance to the wooded slopes. To the numbers. Always the numbers. Tatwin alone had not moved. Einhard stopped. The bright head turned.

"From where?" repeated Tatwin.

"I am going," said Einhard. The blank gaze fixed for one instant on his friend's face. "Will you come?"

The dark head shook in negation. "No, not on this path."

She watched the set of Einhard's naked shoulders as he ran, his men streaming before him across the shipyard. The others already had the horses saddled beside the gates. She could hear Hunferth yelling. They were Alfred's trained men, fast and efficient. But there were not many horses to saddle. There was no time to wait for the rest of the men to return from the sea.

She could see the bristle of spears, the steel tips catching the lowering sun. Tatwin watched.

Even bishops led troops when it was needed and he was not in orders yet. He could fight.

"You will not go?" She watched the men mount and wheel round, the earth flying from hoofs. "Tatwin? It is only five miles to the forest. Five miles before the Vikings are within sight of here."

If but one of Earl Guthrum's men saw what they did here, even if this first attack were beaten off, they were finished. They could not defend this place. Their work would be lost. No burgeoning fleet to match an invasion. Everything would be forfeit. All the effort. All the lives.

She watched Einhard's back, the spears ranged behind him.

The end is that people die.

"He is your friend. There are fifty Vikings. How likely do you think it is that he will come back?"

Five miles.

She turned, running in the direction of her chamber. Tatwin stayed standing.

"TROUSERS?" MILDRED PUT DOWN a kirtle embellished with tablet woven braid and boggled.

"In the oak chest." Judith dragged ells of fine-woven linen over her head. "There. With the *byrnie*." The seam of the underdress ripped. Hang it.

"You have a *byrnie*? In the... Is it the lord your brother's?"

"Berg's? If it was Berg's it would drown me." She grabbed the chain mail shirt. Links of fire-hardened, close-riveted metal flowed through her fingers, supple as water, steel-hard and chanted-over with rune magic.

Battle-hard.

She let go of the *byrnie* and grabbed the trousers, hopping on one foot to get them on. Mildred caught her elbow.

"You will be excommunicated for wearing such things."

"Really?" She seized the padded undershirt. *By whom? A false friend like Tatwin?* "Hand me the *byrnie*."

"But—"

"Quick. Help me get it over my head." She hoped warriors had handier persons to help them get dressed. "Ouch."

She knelt down, shoving the cosmetic case out of the way and lifting the sword belt out of the chest. The sword was clean, oiled, stored in its scabbard lined with sheepskin.

It would not be clean for long. Her throat closed.

"All the saints, Mildred."

Her companion helped her up, clutching at her arms. "Why must you do such a thing?"

The sword banged against her leg when Mildred tried to fasten the belt buckle. What if her courage did fail, after all? Despite everything she had concentrated her life on since the devastating battle at Hoxne, since she had come to Wessex. She shut her eyes. But it was not the lost green slopes of East Anglia she saw, not Wessex. Not even the king's face. It was Einhard's back.

"There is a Viking war band five miles away."

Mildred finished the buckle.

"Pass me the helmet." It was old, made of iron decorated with engraved copper. It had a face mask and a single rune. *Cen.* No one knew why that particular symbol had been chosen. Mildred held it out. Judith seized it and stuffed her hair inside the leather lining.

Mildred carefully adjusted the short skirts of the chain mail *byrnie* as though it were a court dress. Stupid thing to do. It made her eyes burn.

"Thank you." Judith's voice sounded oddly controlled.

She hesitated. "If I do not come back can you tell Berg…" What? "Tell him… Well, just give him this." She stripped the boar-shaped ring off her finger and put it into Mildred's outstretched palm.

"You can have my things. There is some money, enough to live on." She wrenched the door open. "You must go and see Ber—" She could not say the name. "He will look after you."

She started running across the grass towards the stables. She thought Mildred waved.

SHE HAD NOT BROUGHT A SPEAR with her to Derne. Such things were impossible to pack in a lady's luggage. If only there had been time to pilfer the armoury. So, it would have to be close quarters. Unless, of course, the lighter throwing-spears were discarded on the ground by now, spent.

Almost there. She heard the screaming. A sound like no other, it belonged only to a battlefield or a massacre. It pierced the soul.

It was familiar.

The noise blocked out the hot Wessex sun, the present. Her skin was shivering as though it felt the cold east wind of November at Hoxne. Her mouth filled with the acrid taste of despair, loss. She set spurs to the horse.

They were not hard to find, Guthrum's men. She pulled rein. The sweating horse stopped short, hooves dancing, the tension in its heaving muscles matching hers.

She was aware of the feeling she had had in the high-roofed hall when she had seen the assassin prepare to strike, the sense of being balanced on a cliff edge, one step, the slightest movement forward, and the world changed. Except that things had happened so fast then that the decision had almost made itself.

She could, of course, turn back.

But the thoughts in her head would not let her. They were the same.

One had the courage or one did not. One's life had a purpose or it was empty for all eternity. Useless.

She suddenly wished she had kept the ring, to show who she was, where she came from, so that Guthrum's men should know her. The Vikings had taken all that she had. Her life. The reins bit into her unadorned hands. She had forgotten gloves.

She threw herself down from the saddle. It was so much easier in trousers. She landed light as a cat.

She could see someone in the middle of the battle, shouting, using a sword. She caught the glimpse of dark-gold hair, the subtle turn of brutal shoulders. Einhard. There were so many round him. Screaming like hounds round a stag. She heard the Danish words.

There was no choice.

Judith unsheathed and ran.

A TRUE BATTLE WAS NOTHING like training. Training had a clear set of rules. What she found was chaos. She got nowhere near Einhard. She was trapped between a treacherous fall of loose shingle down to a stream and an impenetrable thicket of blackthorn. The mail and the thick trousers saved her from most of it. She had not yet drawn blood. Only hacked away at shields and once barely stopped herself from being decapitated. The helmet had saved her. The man beside her went down. He was not dead. He moved.

This was the worst place to be. She could no longer see Einhard. She had no time to look. Sometimes, she thought she heard his voice.

They kept coming. She felt exhaustion more than fear. She was strong, but the effort of survival, of attacking, was beyond bearing. It could have been minutes since she had got here, or hours. Time had no meaning beyond the effort in her breath and the burning ache in her limbs. There was nothing but the immediate circle around her, the primitive need to stay alive. And Einhard's voice. She had the sudden thought it was yelling at her. She could not focus.

Someone hacked for the man on the ground. She saw the glitter of a steel blade. She saw what the weapon was. The man on the ground was helpless, utterly vulnerable for all that he was so powerful, so much more skilled with experience than her. He was brave. It could have been Berg on the ground. It could have been the martyred king her cousin, dying in blood.

It was as though a dam burst inside her head. The fear and the exhaustion vanished. There was nothing, nothing but six years of rage and unhealed fury and the bitter inexcusable sting of helplessness. Like a curse. She would break it.

Her arm swung, her whole body, all of her light weight honed on balance. Years of training. She struck.

The blade fell true.

After that, things happened so fast she had no recollection of them. Only of the movement of the battle changing, swirling against her, not like a collection of separate men but like one great monstrous beast. The ranks of the warriors round her were driven backwards. They shouted to her. She knew she should fall back, too, but that would mean leaving the helpless man, abandoning the small square of ground she had fought over, letting a Viking win. She fought, with all the skill she had and the mad rage drove her, beyond fear or sense or sanity.

Someone cut her out of the press. He fought like one possessed, with the same rage she did. The injured man on the ground moved, as though he would try to help her. She saw the bloodied hand reach out towards the fallen axe. He would have no chance. He must have realised because the instant his gaze fastened on the man who had cut her off, his hand dropped away.

The rage burst again. Her body swung round, trying to block the fallen warrior from harm, even though some sane part of her brain knew she had no time because the other man was on top of her. But he did not strike. He caught her, dragging her fully armoured weight towards the stand of oak trees where before there had been the solid wall of Guthrum's men and now there was nothing. Just this man.

She struggled, maddened, insane with anger. He was shouting, but the rage still flamed its way inside her, too strong after six years of pain to stop. He was so strong. She could scarcely move the sword because of the way he held her. She could not control its direction. It did not matter. His superior strength did not matter. She did not care if the blade caught her and it was she who died. She swung anyway. The blow was badly aimed but still dangerous. He would have to let her go. He did not. The blade sheered off a net of steel, jerked out of her hand. She made a sound. She realised it was Einhard just before he hit her.

She stopped, her mind spinning in the grip of madness. The only reality was the sting of his open hand on her flesh just below the edge of the helm, which was already half off her head. He held her sword. His own lay on the ground where he must have thrown it. Unarmed and she had—

"God's wounds. I could have killed you."

"Me? It is you who could have been killed, you witless fool. What in heaven's name are you doing here?"

"The battle. The—Guthrum's men…"

"Fled. Where you were standing blocked their escape. It is over now and they are gone. But you—" She could see the anger in him, incandescent, the kind of anger would kill its target. Her. "How could you have done this? What, by all that is holy, are you doing here?"

He shouted. The ferocity that had cut her out of the deadly battle clung to him like a black wave. She could sense his shock, deep and tearing.

"The same as you," she said.

He spat something execrable in Frisian. Her hand went to her face. His eyes changed, though the anger was still there, like something unhealable. His gaze locked on her hand where she touched her face. "I have hurt you." She could hear the deep shock, now. It tore him as much as the anger. She suddenly realised he looked stricken.

"You are trying to say that *you* hurt me?" It was such a stupid thing to worry about after the viciousness of the fighting, after the Vikings, the weapon that— A strange sound rose up in her throat. Laughter. Hysteria.

Perhaps it was screaming.

He caught her hand before she was ready for it. His fingers imprisoned hers in human warmth, vital touch. She choked off the appalling sound. He was so close she could see the living heat in his eyes and the way his chest moved under the glittering metal skin.

"How could you do this?" He was no longer shouting. She could scarcely hear his voice and yet the power of it shivered across her skin. "Why?"

"I...I had to." Her own voice swooped. She started again. "There wasn't another way."

She swallowed. It hurt her throat. "It was because of who I am." She had never said that to anyone.

She felt the warmth of his fingers. The grip of his hand was hard, too hard. It had scratches like hers. No time for gloves. She did not even know how he had managed the chain mail *byrnie*. He must have carried it with him. He had come for her in the battle. His closeness stunned, overwhelmed.

"It is because I..." *What?*

I saw how your face looked when Tatwin turned aside. I watched your back when you rode out. Then I saw all Guthrum's men around you like a pack of dogs. The thoughts formed so clearly in her head but she could not find the voice for them. "I thought..."

"What?"

She sought for the words to say. She felt cold inside now that the madness of her rage had gone. Frozen. "I thought it was the end. I thought about what you said. That people die, and I had to do something. I could not leave it. Not this time."

She could feel the heat of him against the wind.

"You could have died."

"It did not matter, not compared to all the other things. I did not care so much." She swallowed. The deeply hidden horrors burned. "It was almost as though I wanted—"

"No!" he shouted in his Frisian seafarer's voice that yelled orders across ships, across battles like this one. "That is not what you wanted." His hands had moved to grip her arms below the edge of the chain mail, holding her. So close.

"Not you," said the foreigner who had fought the same Wessex battle she had. "You were made for living." His chain mail was tainted with dirt, horrors, like hers, the brightness dulled. What she could feel was the touch of his flesh through the linen sleeves of her shirt, the strength, the heat of his skin and the power with which he held her.

"You are alive," he said.

Life. It radiated from him like light. His hands moved across her flesh. The instinctive response leaped deep inside her, primitive, strong. The response to another human being. She did not want that. That kind of connection was doomed. It was not stronger than the carnage of a battle field.

But as his hands moved, the response inside her flared.

He sensed it. He felt it through her skin.

He pulled her closer. There was no gentleness. He could not manage it yet. But she did not want it. She wanted what he offered now, clear strength and the bitter overmastering power of life. Heat.

She needed his warmth. She needed the heat that burned.

His lips touched hers and she caught his mouth, taking from it, the heat and the fierce touch of him, the raw power. Life. Enough to blot out the blood and the merciless horror and the unfit wish for death. For this moment with him. Only him. He was the only one who could see the blackness. His heat burned through it, shattered the ice inside her. She clung to him, her hands uncivilized, savage with need, desperate with wanting. Witched.

She felt him loosen the war helm and free it from her head. Her hair fell down, cascading over the gray metal covering her shoulders, drowning it in light. She felt him touch it, burying his hands in the silken thickness, urgent as the touch of his mouth. His fingers plunged deeper in the disordered mass, finding the hidden curve of her neck, the shape of her skull, turning her head, drawing her closer to the insistent hard-driven demand of his mouth, to the burning, urging, sense-blinding caress of lips and tongue, the heat of sex. Its primitive shared needs.

She pulled at him, drawing him closer, dragging at his balance, and the tough, heavy weight of him bore her back against the oak tree. She pushed into him, tasting passion and wildness and through it, a golden thread of care. The kiss turned molten, the press of his body intimate. The solid mass of his thigh nudged between hers, pushing up the short, thigh-length chain mail. The daring freedom of trousers let her own legs wrap round his, take the intoxicating shape of his thigh against her. He moved restlessly. The heat coursed through her veins, cutting deep inside. She was aware of tightness, of the ache between her legs, sharpened and intensified by the friction of his movement. She gasped.

He pressed closer and her hands clawed at him, at his back, the tight line of his hips, the taut muscular swell of his buttocks. She already half knew the shape of his body. The heightened, maddened sense of need in her mind told the rest. Yet the hard mesh of metal under her fingers defeated her, hiding what she sought, a barrier to touch, closeness. The steel links nipped at her flesh. The battle-net had been impenetrable even to the fire-hardened edge of her sword. *The sword.* If she had harmed him in her frenzied battle rage, because of her madness…

A sound like a sob escaped her throat, hot and desperate and full of animal fear. He heard. The kiss broke. The sudden with-drawal of his body was abrupt, shocking. The savage, careful touching, the madness, stopped. She stood, free and alone, a being apart, the way she always was.

But it was no longer true.

She was not the same person. The imprint of his body, the warmth, was still there, as though it would be there for ever.

She heard the harsh sound of his breath like something taken with pain. Still close— She watched the line of his body where he leaned against the oak, the bent head.

She touched his shoulder, then the stark line of his face. Hot skin, sheened with sweat, his gold hair damp with it. Like her skin, her own hair at her temples and the nape of her neck. So much shared.

"Einhard—"

His eyes were black. "What I did just now was mad. I would have taken—" He bit it off.

"No—there was nothing that I did not want, or—" He did not hear her. His head turned. His attention shifted, locked else-where. She heard it—the faint rustling brush of leaves, fast, stealthy, the sound of another person moving through the oak-wood. Not closing in on them, but moving away, surely, with an unknown purpose.…

He took her arm, turned her, the pressure of his hand different, urgent in an altered way. But she could still feel the heat. Her breath caught.

"We must go." He picked up her sword from the ground where he had flung it, and handed it to her. She stared at it, dazed. It was a moment before she could bring herself to touch the hilt.

"Hurry."

She grasped the hilt. Their fingers touched. Her senses lurched and then there was nothing but the cool hardness of embossed silver under her hand. She saw the rent in the sleeve of his *byrnie*. Gaping links of hammered steel.

"My blade struck you. It struck you when I—" Her voice gave out.

He glanced down, saw the damage as though for the first time. "The blade did not touch me. Only the chain mail."

I could have killed you, left you crippled. And yet you still held me. You did not let me go.

"Sheathe the sword," he said. "I have wiped the blade. Hurry before someone sees you."

Fright snaked through her. "You do not think anyone guessed in the battle that…"

"No. But in another five minutes they would have." He reached for her fallen helm.

"Then how did you know?" She watched his averted head. How had she picked him out in that first moment, even in the midst a battle? How did she know half of what he was thinking just by the turn of his shoulders and the tilt of his head? He ignored her question, because it was pointless between them. He gathered up the helmet.

"Put this on before one of my men sees you."

"One of *your* men?"

He turned. No more than half of his thoughts were known to her. No more than half.

"Hunferth has gone back to the shipyard to see that all is well there. It was my men who undertook the pursuit. To make sure none of the Vikings fled in the direction of the harbour." His eyes were blank.

A small shiver crawled over her heated skin. She took hold of her hair to twist and coil it up behind her head. He held out the helmet, face unreadable, so controlled. The visored helm dangled from his hand.

"Where did you get such a thing?" He sounded mildly interested, as though that was where his attention was.

Her hair fell down. Her hands would not obey her. She tried again. Oh, for Mildred's skilled fingers. She glanced at the helm with unseeing eyes, just as he did. "I suppose you might call it an heirloom. I do not know how long it has been in our house. They say it should have been placed in the burial mounds at Sutton Hoo with its owner. But for some reason it was not. It was always around the hall. No one would use it because it was supposed to be enchanted. So I did." She struggled with the cascade of waist-length hair. "It was rather difficult for me to find anything else."

"Enchanted?"

"You know. People used to chant rune-knowledge over weapons and armour when they made them so that the magic would sit inside them. I think some smiths still do it, whatever the church says. This one would definitely have been chanted over. Look at the rune, almost hidden underneath the crest."

His hand went tight. His attention suddenly and utterly focused. The frightening thing was that his face did not change.

"Kenaz," he said, giving the old name, in the old language. There was no expression in his voice at all. "The torch."

The deliberate control, the act of will, was utterly and ruthlessly back in place. Unbreakable. She did not say a word. He helped her with her hair.

"THE SAXONS ARE THERE."

Skar shifted his weight. The anticipation of action surged through him. Beneath his feet, the timbers of the ship hummed, riding the punch of the waves like some powerful beast.

"How many?"

"No one knows. No one has ever got near the harbour." Mord, his errant brother, shrugged. "Enough to make difficulties for us."

"Difficulties?" He spat it, the impatience a living force. "What do the Saxons matter?" He pushed himself away from the ship's side but Mord's gaze slid past him, out across the foaming water and towards the faintly discernible line of the shore.

"They say there was some sort of battle, that a raiding party was beaten off, defeated. There were deaths." His gaze stayed fixed on the distant shoreline. Mord, loser of cargoes, had been lucky to escape with his life from his own particular defeat. Skar's hands gripped the high side of the merchant vessel. He did not take well to defeat. Neither, at one time, had Mord.

But Mord had taken injury and humiliation from an attack that had been vicious. Something in him had changed. It was one more step on the road to vengeance.

The hunched shoulders shrugged again. "Guthrum's men. They do not realise what they nearly found. They fell back to East Anglia. They never got near the harbour."

Skar's mouth twitched. "That will please the Jarl." But the defeat of a raiding party was only that. Guthrum merely bided his time and built his strength. Anyone with eyes knew it. Skar was driven by need and Guthrum was the only possibility.

He made a mirthless sound, his mind already moving forward to that other problem, the one that involved unredeemed loss that was personal. The problem that demanded blood. He shrugged in dismissal.

"Then there was some skill on the part of the Saxons."

"They had Hunferth. He is one of Alfred's men." Mord looked up. "They say that they also had foreigners, men who shouted out in an alien tongue."

The oakwood bit into his palms. Foreign. If that was so then the hunt might be drawing close.

"What kind of foreigners?" he said.

"No one knew." Mord shifted. "But they thought they were shipmen."

"Turn the sail." He shouted orders at the man with the steering oar. The boat came round, nose in to the shore. The black-and-yellow sail was adjusted instantly to his command. The other ships followed. His blood surged. He still had this much. They were good ships. His own fleet, built from nothing, and now he had a mix of merchantmen and warships.

Just like the foreigner, the Frisian who had been born into the arrogance of long-established wealth, who yet had the greater arrogance to want more, to take it. Thief.

"Skar! They will sight us. The king has watchmen now."

"They will do more than sight us." It was past time for cowering in the shadow of defeat. He yelled and the ship heeled to the wind.

"You cannot mean to land, not at Derne with the king's men there. You will—"

"It is Einhard who is there with the Saxons, do you hear me? Einhard. It must be. What I will do is take vengeance for your wrongs. For mine. Now." Mord was a fool, always so cautious. The familiar impatience was riding him, the will to act. He caught Mord's shoulders. "We take our payment in blood, regain what was lost and the future that goes with it. Can you not see?"

"I can see disaster if you challenge the Saxons now. More loss."

The weakheartedness, the taint of cowardice, maddened him.

"I will act for what is right," he yelled. Mord might have suffered. He might suffer still, but he was a younger brother. Skar took the decisions. He always had.

"You will act," said Mord. "But you will not think."

"What?"

"You will not think. If you sail into Derne like this, unprepared, not knowing what strength you will meet or how many, Hunferth's Saxons will have you. And if Einhard is there, you will not be able to take him. You will not meet Guthrum's terms either by the Frisian's death or his capture."

"Guthrum—"

"You will risk all the ships we have left for no gain."

"You think I am afraid of risk?" he bellowed.

"No, I do not think you fear to take risks. I think you cannot afford to."

The words hit him like a spear thrust, deadly, cold. He wanted to yell, rage, but nothing came. He wanted to strike out.

Mord leaped back. But he was still speaking, the words like deadly bale. "You will take risks when you do not need to and that is the action not of a brave man, but of a fool. You would lose everything we have, every chance to get away from here. Think of that."

Skar stopped.

"Think of what you want," said Mord. "Do not let the Frisian take that from you because he pushed you into a trap. Just the way he pushed me."

Mord's hand shook his arm, speaking until the anger lifted, just fractionally. But the driving urge was still there. It would never die. He knew what he wanted. He would get it. There would be another way. He stopped listening.

There were always more ways of taking vengeance. He would do it. It was he who was strong, others who were weak.

He watched the wind.

"Turn the ship back." He gave the orders. He could not pull closer to the shore. Not yet.

If the thief was not accessible, then the thief would have to come to him. If there was to be a trap, it would be Skar's.

He thought. He was quite capable of it. It was he, Skar, who had the power. Always. Einhard was—

The only thing he could admit about Einhard in the depths of his heart was that the devil would stop at nothing. It was one of the greatest strengths a man could have.

Something caught his eye, something small, a nuisance scarcely regarded.

He shook off his brother's restraining hand. The answer was obvious. He could force Einhard to do anything he wanted, submit to his basest demand, grovel, lick the soles of his boots clean, take death crawling like a worm on its belly. The man would do it. He would beg to.

How satisfying to turn your enemy's greatest strength into his greatest weakness. All he had to do was wait, allow himself to be found. Einhard would come to him. The man would not be able to stop himself.

He extended his hand.

"Come here."

The unregarded nuisance, the prisoner, the little Frisian whelp, came. Just like his father.

9

LIGHT AND NOISE SPILLED from the rough communal building that served the shipmen as a hall. Judith sat outside. The sound of singing wreathed past her head, blindly triumphant. She covered her ears.

Hunferth was feasting Einhard, the hero of the hour. Einhard who had fought steadfastly until the sweat had darkened his hair and blood had mired the fairness of his armour, and every breath burned like fire and every movement caused hurt.

There was a cost to high deeds like his. She had seen it. She had known it and understood that price through the desperate touch of his flesh against hers, the suppressed pain. She had felt the same feelings through her own body, through fighting. Einhard had saved her life.

She did not go into the lighted hall.

Vikings from where, Tatwin had asked, and then he had looked at the man who was supposed to be his friend and had said, *no, not on this path.*

Einhard, loyal to the end, had helped Hunferth win and then,
It was my men who undertook the pursuit.

She remembered the deliberate blankness of his grey-green
eyes.

The night scents breathed round her, summer grass and un-
identified flowers lightened by the indefinable tang of the sea.
It was cold, but she could not go inside, even though the battle
was won and she knew she had played her own part, however
small. She had stood her ground and she had not fled screaming. She had proved her faith after so many bitter years. Perhaps
there was a man in this encampment who would not be alive
but for her.

And now she was sitting here shaking like an autumn leaf with
a half-empty mead bottle for a companion, even though it was
over and no one knew the reckless thing she had done. No one
except Einhard.

It was the first time she had killed someone.

She looked at the mead bottle.

Inside the warm, crowded, firelit hall they were all together,
all the men, English and Frisian. Celebrating the fact that it was
not they who were dead. Drowning whatever it was that they
felt, not just in the mead bottle but in companionship. She could
hear their unsteady cheering. It sounded like a name. *Einhard.*

Einhard. He had held her afterwards as though he had needed
her as much as she had needed—what? Him? A dangerous
stranger? A man's touch?

Einhard.

She saw him. He simply appeared out of the darkness as
though her thoughts had summoned him, as though she had

called to the other half of herself. He stopped, a darker patch of shadow like a black wraith. She could distinguish none of his features in the starlight, but the black silhouette of his body was unmistakable.

She had touched that body, touched him and held him and—

"Will you drink all of that?"

"No." She thought her voice sounded as unstable as the rest of her. But she could not do anything about it. Not now. She held on to the flask.

He sat down. As though it was perfectly ordinary to find his betrothed hiding out in the shadow of one of his stupid boats. There was silence. The sea lapped on the shingle below where they sat on the edge of the grass.

"Going to share it then?"

She handed him the hardened leather flask and watched with envy as he drank with a perfectly steady hand. Shadows moved on the moon-blanched curve of his throat.

She knew nothing about him. And everything. Just as he knew all about her.

He put the bottle down.

"That's better."

"Is it?" Her voice cracked. She tried again. "Does it…" What was the use of pretending? He could hear her voice. There was light enough to see her shaking. She ought to be ashamed. She thought that she was.

He just sat there.

She forced the words out. "Does that make it better?"

"Sometimes." He shot an assessing look at the bottle. "Not really."

"Then what does?"

"Nothing. Perhaps time." He turned his head. "Perhaps telling someone what the hell you were doing." There was no rancour in his voice. Just inquiry. But there was something in his dark shape that was implacable. She thought that if she moved, she would not get beyond two steps.

"I told you," she said stubbornly. "It is something I had to do."

"So you mentioned. You did not say why."

She got up. At least she tried to. Her muscles would not work, so she could not get farther than to her knees. He moved round so that he was sitting in front of her, trapping her in the small space beside the half-finished boat, blocking off escape. She could see the fine line of his side, the dark curve of his bent leg. She could see solidness and perfection.

Implacability.

"I cannot say why," she choked.

He seemed to consider whether this was a reasonable answer from a mad woman crawling around on the faintly muddy ground at midnight. "Perhaps not yet."

"Not ever," she said, incensed. She tried moving again. It did not work. She felt desperate. "What I want to know is how to get over it." He stayed where he was. She swatted one irritatingly perfect knee out of the way. "What do you do?"

Stupid question. He stayed like a black rock, drank with a steady hand. She had seen him through the open door of the hall celebrating with Hunferth and the rest, eating, walking round, roaring with his strong voice. Just as he had when she had first seen him at Stathwic, Holofernes surrounded by the hearth-troops, shouting and impervious. But on that night, she had seen him after the feasting, in the quiet light of his chamber, borne down.

He was not impervious.

Her hand rested on his shadowed knee where it had fallen. She could feel his warmth, the rich deep-boned heat of his flesh. He did not do anything obvious and deeply mortifying like take her hopelessly shaking fingers.

But he let her touch him.

"So what did you do?" she asked. "I mean the first time you ever struck someone in battle and—" *killed them.*

"Me? I did try the mead. Well, actually it was some imported wine from Byzantium, on account of my not being a prince, but a successful merchant."

She hit his knee again. She was past caring about such things as rank, or even whether he planned some double game of his own. All she knew was that in this moment, he was the only person living who could help her.

"I thought you said drink was not the answer?"

"So what did I know at that age? I had not quite sixteen winters." He paused. "Besides, it was really expensive wine."

A year older than she had been when…

"Trust a merchant to think of the price," she said out of habit. Her voice shook.

"Not a good bargain though. It was wasted on me."

"Then what else?"

"Now that," he said in his dark-edged voice, "is not a tale fit for a maiden's ears."

"You—?" The heat of his solid flesh burned through her hand.

"Not another question." She heard the faint thread of silver.

Lightness. "We will draw a veil over the fumblings of a drunken sixteen-year-old with the local light skirt. I refuse to answer however hard you may beg me for details."

"Beg for— I am not going to—"

"No? Well, that is disappointing." His gaze traveled to where her hand rested on his leg. "I could show you how it should be. I improve with age."

It was outrageous. It was meant to be. The lightness leaped. She felt the sudden choke of laughter in her throat. And yet the consciousness of where she was, of how she touched the warm, tough, heavy lines of his body scored through her. Sudden heat blossomed inside her where there had been none before, only the cold shaking through her bones. She suddenly felt insanely jealous of a nameless woman who had obliged a muddled sixteen-year-old boy ten winters ago. Shameless harlot.

She was still shaking.

"Come. It is too cold here. I will take you back."

"No." The word came out like a breathless screech, with the blind and desperate force of a defensive blow. She tried to moderate her voice. "I do not feel like sleeping. I will not go back to my chamber."

She swallowed.

"You will not stay here, alone in the dark." She heard the sudden implacability in his voice. More than that, she sensed it in the almost imperceptible tightening of the muscle under her hand. Her breath skipped.

"No. Later. I cannot… I will not go yet. I would wake Mildred. I do not want to upset her." How could she say that she could not face going back to what was normal, ordinary? To someone as blamelessly straightforward as Mildred? Not with the blackness still clinging to her and her head full of such thoughts.

"Thank you for staying," she said formally, as though this were some court function. "But I am quite all right now." She had managed to stand up. She was not quite sure how. She would walk away from him. In the other direction along the shingle beach. No reason for him to follow.

She had a brief impression of his shadow, of the fast cold whisper of air past her skin. Then she collapsed.

It was so unexpected, even though the normally functioning part of her brain told her immediately what he had done. She recognised the trick. She had tried it herself a dozen times. She knew the counter for it, but she had been so convinced he would not follow her that she could not think fast enough, let alone move. She tried to turn but she thudded into his chest. She landed hard, the fast grunt of his exhaled breath felt as much as heard. The sharp contact made no difference. He was too strong and she was far too late to keep her feet. She felt the rock-solid band of his arm behind her knees and he had her. Helpless.

"Let me go." The words were low, intense. She did not dare shout because the sound might bring Hunferth's guards and she could not bear that.

She contemplated breaking his nose, but the sound of a full-on fight would bring the guards as fast as screaming. He saw her make the calculation.

"Put me down," she snapped against the smooth fall of his hair.

"No. Later."

Bastard. "I knew that trick. I could have snapped your knee."

"You think so?" But he had felt the well-trained way she had turned. He made a disgusted sound. "I suppose you practice wrestling holds, along with swordplay. Why could you not take up your time with embroidery like any other decent female?"

"I can embroider," she said indignantly. "You should see the wall hanging I made with Queen Elswith. It shows Cerdic the first Saxon King arriving from the sea to found Wessex—" He began walking. "Don't..." She clutched at his shoulder. It was like solid rock. Not rock, but smooth and lithe and resilient under her palm and her fingers. Her fingertips abruptly found skin, the warmth of him above the neckline of his tunic, hidden warmth and the curve of his neck under the dark shadowed curtain of his hair.

Her fingers were unsteady against his skin.

"Don't what?"

Don't let me go. The words beat in her head. She was leaning against him, her arm round his shoulders, her hand buried in his hair, the nape of his neck. Her body rested against his, against the solid, muscular, intimately familiar shape of him. Familiar because she had almost lain with him. Because of the kiss they had shared after the battle. She remembered the power of that, as though that searing shared heat could penetrate the coldness of her bones.

She could not speak.

He was warm.

Alive.

She came to herself when he kicked the door shut and it

slammed home into a solid wood-planked wall. It was his room. He put her down on the bed.

"What are you doing?"

He glanced round the silent, lamplit chamber as though assessing it. Then he looked at her lying in his bed.

"You did not want to go back to your bower." He was leaning over her, one hand on either side of her torso, close, almost touching. The lamp glow made gold out of his hair, fire and shadow across the stark planes of his face, darkness across the full, heavy line of his body.

I could show you how it should be. I improve with age.

Her mind dizzied with the prospect of how it could be. With him. And her body, already half attuned to his, tightened without her will, flicked by the edge of desire the way the smoky red light flickered across his skin. She felt taut with wanting, frightened to the depths of her soul by the intensity of it. It was crazed, out of control, an abyss with depths she could not imagine. He moved. His hand grazed her arm. She bit back the gasp of breath. It could have been a scream. His gaze locked with hers. The uncontrolled heat, the wild, primitive drive they had both felt among the trees after the battle, scored through her. He looked at her as though he could see that, the desire burning through her skin, through her wide-open eyes. As though he could also see the fear.

He moved back. She thought that that was what he had been going to do anyway, that the touch of his hand had been inadvertent. But then he had seen what was inside her, things that should not be there.

"It is all right," he said. "This afternoon's madness is over."

But that was a lie. For both of them. She did not know whether he knew it. He lay back in the bed, beside her. Not touching. But he had carefully positioned himself between her and the door. He looked like a predator.

"You can tell me now how this all came about."

"No. I cannot."

But strangely enough, the very danger of him, the wild, hot, unacceptable emotions locked inside him, only half-understood, made it possible. The hardness with which he handled his own feelings, the hardness of the feelings themselves, made her trust him. In this one aspect of their dealings together, if in naught else.

"You can tell me how it was," he said. "How you first wore that appalling monstrosity of a helmet and your ridiculous war-gear."

"It is not ridiculous." Her voice sounded cautiously better, like the first step on the path.

"Ridiculous," he repeated without the slightest mercy. "I can see you in it now. So how did you begin your career? East Anglian princess beheads six of her subjects and then has her wicked way with a helpless and grateful stable lad?"

She shivered uncontrollably and was aware of his heat, of the solid masculine body beside her. Of the way he could touch.

"There was no stable lad." Stupid to start by defending that particular gibe when it was the least thing that mattered. But perhaps that was the start.

"What, no stable lad? What kind of a princess were you? Was it some fine jewelled *nithing* of a prince spouting sweet words, then?"

"No. Even though, believe it or not, I wanted a prince, one of those precious *nithings* who would spout sweet words to me.

But there was no arrangement, not even a political one. When I was of an age to be betrothed, I was at Hoxne."

That was how it began.

She felt the shock that went through him. Even a Frisian pirate would have heard of the great battle at Hoxne, the battle which had wiped out the kingdom that her ancestors had held for three hundred years, that had existed for countless years before that. Of course, he would think she was speaking in general terms. She did not have to tell him things that—

He moved round in the bed until he was facing her. She could see what was in his eyes.

"You followed the East Anglian troops there, to the battle at Hoxne, just the way you followed Hunferth's men and mine today."

Her heart lurched. He had been so angry at what she had done this day, when he had seen her and known who she was. The anger had blazed. The anger had still been there when he had kissed her.

It had begun when she had asked him about sea battles. He had despised her, just as any man would.

"It is all right," she said, her words bitter with mockery. "I might have been at Hoxne all those years ago, but I did not even get to strike a blow that counted." Her scorn cut the lamplit air, yet it was the worst admission she could make. That had been the thing she could not get over. The uselessness, the bitter sense of having failed, of watching defeat, a defeat which was final and yet ended nothing because the nightmare went on and had to be lived through, even now.

He pulled away, the movement so abrupt it had to be instinctive. It told her all she needed to know. She slid across in the bed. There was room. They no longer touched by one tiny fraction of skin. She could see the door.

"I will go."

His hand snaked out and caught her.

"No," she said. "Do not. There is no point."

He said something vicious.

She watched his hand on her arm, the way their flesh touched. Like something melded, living warmth. As though the fire was still there underneath, as though it meant something. Impossible. "I failed then because the odds were too great, because of my own lack. I had to put that right. How could a man like you possibly understand what I felt?"

His hand flattened out. The heavy fingers moved slowly, as though a gesture as simple as that masked something savage.

She could not read his face because, like her, he was watching the small improbable point of joining between them.

"We all fail—" Something was cut off. She was right about the savagery. He was ruthless.

"You went to Hoxne for what you believe in. Because you have faith. That is what you feel so deeply."

The restraint inside her nearly shattered. She stared at his hand on her arm, the painful scratches on his skin, the edge of a bruise.

"Perhaps you also went for the sake of this brother you have. Perhaps for a father?"

"No father. He was long dead, and my mother. There was only myself and Berg. That is how it always was, almost ever since I can remember." And now even that closeness was impossible to hold on to. She swallowed. Einhard the Frisian did not move his hand. She did not want him to.

If he moved his great stupid ham fist she would die.

She finished it off. "They killed my cousin."

"Your cousin?"

"The king. The king of East Anglia that was. Edmund."

"The king—the new saint."

"So they say." She stopped. His hand tightened again on the exposed flesh of her arm, just a little. She could feel him. "He was martyred, made a sacrifice to Odin. I was there. I saw him die."

His hand cupped her skin. But the familiar coldness, six empty winters, drowned the feel of him.

"It was the end, the end of everything I had known, the end of who I was. I do not think there is a way to get over that."

He pulled her back, down into the shelter of his arms.

"You have to tell me everything."

There was not a man who drew breath who did not know the fate of East Anglia, the first kingdom to be attacked by the Viking army of King Ivar, the second to be destroyed. Having bought its way out of trouble once, East Anglia had turned and fought, had risked everything on a single battle and had gone down fighting an invasion army that had never been defeated.

He did not mean that. He meant, what had happened to her.

She was lying at his side, her head on his shoulder. Her long hair spilled across his body. He still had hold of her arm. She could feel the utter stillness of him and beneath that, fire.

"It was a disaster. I did not know what to do." She tried to find the words that would fit into the silence, into the strong remorseless curve of his body round hers.

"Berg, my brother, would not take me with him to the battleground. Of course. So I went by myself. But I had to come late,

hiding." Her fingers clenched. "Trailing afterwards with the servants and the baggage train. The battle was long begun and I—"
He was close. The slightest movement made the light catch his hair.

"My plan was to find Berg. I wanted to surprise him, to show him that I had courage equal to his, that I would sacrifice anything, just as he did." She took a harsh breath. "I wanted to stand alongside my kin, the royal house. I wanted to be with my brother. But I never got near him."

Her hand was fisted in the neck of Einhard's linen tunic, her fingers twisting the material. The coldness of her hand touched his skin.

"I could see Berg in the center, in front of the king and his standard, fighting with the king's bodyguard and his own. I could see him so clearly. But such a press of people separated us, so many men, all screaming and dying and—" She swallowed it back. But there was no mercy in her memories.

The end is that people die.

"You see, I thought that I knew. I had been brought up with a warrior for a brother, with his friends and his male kin. No sisters. I did not want them. I would do anything Berg and his companions did, even fight. I had a lot of licence. I was a princess, and an orphaned one at that. People indulged me in all the things I wanted before I was of marriageable age. I learned to fight and so I thought I understood. But I did not."

She paused.

"Hoxne was like madness." Underneath the loosened laces at the neck of his tunic, was the warmth of his skin. "It was like the battle today, only a thousand times greater." She watched her hand on his flesh. "I know you understand that," she whispered. "You understand what warfare is like."

"Yes."

She thought of the way he had found her out of the chaos. He had forced his way through to her across a battlefield. She knew what effort that took, what determination. The determination had been the first thing she had seen in him, the depthlessness of it. He had showed her that life mattered. The knowledge had not just been in his words, but in his touch. Her body still ached with that touch, as though the imprint of it would be on her for the rest of her life. And yet they were strangers, bitter strangers at that, forced together.

Her hand twisted against his flesh. "I did not achieve what I wished. The tide of the battle broke over me and I was swept away with it." Her sight dimmed until she could not see the bright light of the Frisian's room, the glow of his hair. There was only the battle and the men in it moving like grey ghosts, the cutting wind of November on her skin and the sound of screaming, and then nothing. Blackness.

"There was only confusion," she said. "I cannot even tell you what I did. It was useless. I remember finally falling and then nothing."

Somewhere far away, in the late summer at Derne, in the brightness of the closed chamber, Einhard moved. The stillness, his hidden tenseness, broke on the harsh intake of his breath.

"I was not hurt," she said rapidly because it was what a person as strong as him would worry about. "Not much. I wish I had been. But it was nothing and no one touched me after I fell, no one even thought to take the richness of my sword or my armour. That is the truth. There I was, a fifteen-year-old fool with dreams of saving a kingdom, dedicated to training in arms and with no experience of how to use them. I had never ridden out against raiders like my brother, never struck a blow except in practice. I was in a battle the size of the world's ending and I might as well not have been there."

She thought he spoke. She heard the deep rough sound of his voice, but she could not hear the words. She was too far away, locked in the past.

"When I came to myself, it was over. Finished. The standard lay in the mud and the king—well, you know what they did. There are no words for it. I saw it. I saw every muscle break and I heard every sound, and then he was dead. Ivar had him made a sacrifice. He wanted to give Odin, the chief of the gods, a king's blood, my own kinsman's. There was no defence." Her voice shook. "At least Berg did something. He tried to stop them. They must have been afraid the other men who were still alive would follow him. They struck him down. It was an axe blow."

She could see the blade moving and the past battle began to merge with today, with now. She was suddenly and completely aware of the lamplit room, the soft Wessex air, of the Frisian, the way his arms held her and the tight hot contours of his body. Heated closeness.

She said the next words, the ones that set her apart as some-one driven and unacceptable. They came so clearly.

He held her tightly. But she knew he would let her go.

"I failed at Hoxne. But I swore to myself then that I would not stop until I had done what I set out to. I wanted vengeance for my cousin's death, for the way they had made him suffer, and I wanted a blood-payment for what they had done to my brother. But more than that. I wanted to stop what the Vikings did. I wanted to stop the loss and the destruction and all the harm. I wanted to do what in a man would be natural, but in me was not. I wanted to strike the blow myself."

He did not let her go. Not yet. She could still feel the bright power of his body and his heat. He held her as though he would never release her. There was not much softness in his touch, but the bitter completeness of his strength was a relief. Something she could take in her madness, however briefly it might be given.

"Everyone thought Berg would die of his wounds, most of all me. I cannot tell you how it was, watching day and night and seeing——" She shut her mind on the horrors of the sickroom.

"We had to hide in the marshlands in case any of Ivar's Vikings realised that someone with a claim to an empty throne was still alive. But Berg did not die."

Yet she had lost her tie to him, to the only person she had left to love. She had lost him in a way she did not understand, something beyond the horror of watching maiming and near death.

She stirred restlessly in the narrow bed. The man moved with her. She felt the slide of his limbs against her, the solid heat of him. His hold adjusted, the warm cradle of his arms looser, as though he thought she would want to be free of him now that she had said what she must.

It was what a decent woman would want. She was not decent.

She lay against him. She could feel his warmth and his deliberate stillness; more subtly, her mind told her the power of his attention, the focus of his thoughts, centered on her, on what she said, on the words she had never told to another living being.

Mind and body shivered in response, pierced through and desperate with longing. She did not know how to express that. No true way existed. They were nothing to each other. There was no future. They were just two people swept together for one moment in a tide of violence.

"Tell me the next step," he said. The lamplight caught the heavy gold on his arm, the foreign carving of the dragons' heads. Her hand was still fisted in his tunic.

"When Berg was well enough we came here to Wessex, to the last stand, the only place where it was still possible to fight. The king took us in."

"Alfred."

The dark-mouthed abyss opened between them, black, shocking. All of it said in that one word. A gulf without bridging.

"The king of Wessex still fights," she said. "I would stand by that. By him——"

"Aye. So you said. Because that is where you have given your heart." He moved round. The heated glide of his body across hers, the tangling of their limbs was hotly intimate, invasive. The lamplight spilled across his face, like sunlight pouring down across the shell path at the harbour. She had felt the closeness of him then, the earthy carnality, and he had taunted her when she said she had given her heart in the bounds of duty, as though that were only half an answer, half a life, as though there were so much more. Another world that could be stepped into, a world that did not admit restraint, a world of feelings that were raw, dangerous, intensely real.

She would never take that path, the path that led to dependence on another's feelings. It would destroy her.

"I gave Alfred my loyalty. His kingship, this war, was not something he chose." Four brothers dead, leaving Alfred to take the throne; Alfred, who saw good in people, who would grapple with any problem and take any burden. Alfred the fierce warrior who loved books and sought what was right.

"My brother swore his loyalty at the king's crowning. So did his friends, like a circle that held magic, warriors of the dragon banner. Berg said the oath he had made was to two kings, to Alfred who held Wessex and to our cousin who was dead. But I...I could not swear. Even though I felt just as Berg did, just as strongly as any warrior there." She took the breath that framed the truth, her truth. "I made the oath on the inside."

She felt the intimate warmth of Einhard's body, human and intensely real. She kept speaking, all the words that had to be said, so that he knew her madness.

"But only Berg fought. There was nothing for me. I was placed with Queen Elswith and I tried to say that was enough, that even so I gave my duty. But the bitter force inside me would not stop. I had to do something, achieve something. The memories were still there."

"And so you found your chance." His eyes were hot, so hot.

"Yes." She moved, such a slight movement, but they were so close her hand brushed the curve of his thigh.

"A...A chance. I talked my way into accompanying Hunferth. It was not so unsuitable. Hunferth is a vague relation by marriage. He could look after me and it must have seemed the perfect way to appease my restlessness at last, letting me go on a mission without danger, a simple matter of persuasion."

"Such a simple matter." His hand moved over her arm, tracing its length from her wrist to her shoulder. His touch burned. Even though they lay together in the frank intimacy of his bed, even though the primitive man-edged closeness of him had enfolded her, it was the first overtly sexual move he had made. The sharp erotic tension between them had been there all the time, felt by both, as a deep undercurrent of danger. Now it was open.

"Easy." The edge of his thumb brushed the curve of her breast where the tight line of her arm pressed against it. His hand came to rest at the vulnerable column of her neck, locking on the smoothness of her skin, finding its place. Staying. Imprinting the touch of him on her flesh. He would feel the tightness of her breath in her throat.

She could not look away from the bright dangerous heat of his eyes.

"All for the sake of your duty," he said.

She thought of what she had done that night, to another human being, to the one who touched her now. The recklessness of it.

Yet there had seemed no other way. The recklessness had been part of the force that drove her without mercy. The same force that had driven her into battle. She watched his strength, the bright force in his own eyes. Like a mirror. Like something driven.

"Yes."

The dangerous light flared. Something sharp leaped inside her. Then the brightness was extinguished, damped down.

She had not pulled away, but she was shaking. She wondered if he felt it. Her mouth was dry.

"The same duty that sent you rushing into battle this day."

Not a question. Because the dangerous eyes could see straight through her. She thought about what had made her ride out, take her place in the screaming chaos amongst the trees. The same force that had been in her for six winters.

"Yes."

But there had also been him.

10

THERE WAS ALSO YOU, not just duty, but you.

Judith could not face a truth like that. She wanted to pull back from the infinitely unsafe man in the bed with her, but his hand moved across her skin. The familiar heady sensation of his flesh on hers flooded through her, more intimate than breathing.

She could sense the tension in him and all the things held back. She could see the hidden fire in his eyes but she could also see other things. Shared memories. The bitter graceless edge of facing violence together. The frightening thoughts formed in her head, the image of his back, the turn of his shoulders as he had ridden out with the earth flying from the horse's hooves and not one backward glance.

I rode out and took battle for you.

The idea was too new, unacceptable.

"Aye," she said wildly. "It was duty that made me do what I had to. And this time I made a difference."

His hand tightened on the bare flesh of her neck. She caught the glitter in his eyes.

"You nearly took death."

This time he could not dampen down the light in his eyes. The same light that had burned in the moment before his mouth had taken hers, filled with the brilliant flame of desire and life. Such life. She had been lost in it.

Or found.

Her body trembled.

His gaze held hers. "It was like madness in you."

"I... It was because of the man the one who was injured. He was on the ground." She swallowed. "Helpless." Her eyes watched his, sought not just the cleansing fire, but the depths in them that would make him understand. "I could not stand that they struck him down and he could do nothing. It was like Hoxne. First the king and then my brother. All the horror of it. All the things that were wrong, that I wanted to avenge. That I wanted to stop. They would have killed that man today, even though he was helpless."

She did not know whether she could get the last words out.

"It was the weapon." She was shaking so much now that she could not speak. Even her lips trembled and she would never get sound past them, not something intelligible.

But she did not need to. She saw his gaze narrow in the fierce concentration that had never left her, not even when they had both recognised the black abyss of division between them. She could see the thoughts move behind his eyes, the shifting of memory as the images of the battle played across his mind. He sorted them. The connection with what she had said was made.

The weapon the Viking had wielded on the injured man had been an axe blade. The same weapon that had maimed her brother.

He understood. Both the meaning of the things she had said and perhaps the shadows of the feelings she had no words for, the feelings for which things as clumsy and limited as words did not exist. He saw and he was not shocked by the demons that drove her.

She closed her eyes but the tears still spilled out of them. She was so cold.

She felt the warmth of his mouth settle over hers. It was the gentlest touch she had ever felt in her life. Her senses swam, dizzied, as though she were falling, drawn in to the spell of his touch, the dark insistent warmth. The tenderness. It was so unexpected. He should not be capable of such feelings.

Yet his mouth moved over hers.

Her body twisted, following his lips, but the light touching went on. She could feel the heat, the deep sensuality held back. She could feel so much. Care.

Fear touched her. She was frightened even of the idea of the care that smooth caress implied. She had shunned it. Ever since she had lost the fabric of her world. The tears leaked out from her under her closed eyelids.

He touched her tears, with his pirate's battle-scratched fingers, as though he was that mythic prince she had dreamed about, as though she mattered. He should not have done that. Stupid Frisian bastard. Why did he have to do such a thing? Why did he have to act as though he knew what sorrow was and what it meant? As though he understood how much it hurt? The pain inside gathered round where her heart should be. She felt the warm, steady, careful touch of his hand and the control clamped down inside her for the last six years broke.

She thought the storm of weeping would never stop. The pictures ran through her mind, Hoxne, the dead bodies on the frozen earth and the sound of Danish voices shouting. The battle today, the injured man on the ground, the axe blade. The fear, the merciless fear of what happened to people. Berg moving towards the captive king. Einhard rushing towards the battle. The summer sun catching the spear tips at his back. The hard remorseless power of his body as he had cut her out of the fight. His face, savage with anger, bright with passion in the moment before he had kissed her, his eyes dark, black with need, with some feeling he could not express.

Pain.

Her arm moved round the warmth of his body, questing, until she found the solid weight of his shoulder. The crazed thought formed in the aching mass of her head that he needed the human connection with the same bitterness that she did. Stupid. Her fingers curved round his neck. She could hear the sound of her own voice sobbing. Like someone broken. She came to herself eventually.

The appalling heart-bitter sound of the crying stopped. Her breathing slowed to match the rhythm of his. She was lying on top of him in a tangled heap and her fingers dug into his neck. He had not stopped holding her even though she had wept like a madwoman.

She tried to pull herself away but her limbs were so heavy it seemed impossible. He tightened his arms and she collapsed, dishevelled and helpless, sprawled out across his body like some untidy *hor-cwen* who belonged in the darkest stews of the water-front.

She could not move. Even the slightest pressure from his arms round her body was enough to lock her in place so that they seemed to touch at every point.

He had seen her cry. He had seen her lose control of herself the way she had not since the day her mother died when she was five winters old.

She turned her head and her hair rippled across his chest.

"I am sorry." Her lips touched the heated skin at the slitted neck of his tunic, the firm rise of his collarbone.

"I never weep."

She could hear the rustle of the pillow as he moved his head.

"As well you told me. I could have got myself confused."

"I mean I do not usually weep."

"No. I do not think you do. Or confide what you think."

She went still.

"Not even to that painstakingly loyal maid of yours."

"Mildred?" Mildred was West Saxon. Judith had been more or less foisted on her from the moment she arrived at the Wessex court because Mildred, the widow, needed employment. No one had known quite what to do with either of them. "I am the bane of her life."

"That is not what the daft wench thinks. Mildred would stand your friend."

Mildred… Judith thought of the small unsteady hands adjusting chain mail like a court dress.

"You should let her give her friendship, but you don't. I do not think you even confide in that brother of yours."

Her breath caught. "My brother and I are… Berg is… You do not know how much he has borne. How everything changed for him. He—"

"Changed only for him?" His fingers traced the path of dried tears, touched skin still flushed and faintly damp with weeping.

"Changed for me. Changed…in me."

He made her see the truth, Einhard the Frisian, about the way she behaved with people, cutting them off if they got too near, in case they mattered so deeply that their loss or their pain could kill her. She must have become that way with everyone. Distant. Cold.

Even with Berg.

"It was me who changed."

"Life changed you." His hand lightly stroked her face. "That is what it does."

She could feel the faint movement in his breathing as he spoke, feel the vibration of his voice against her body where it covered his.

"You understand that," she said. "You did from the start."

The slight movement of his body, almost imperceptible, jarred the warm cocoon.

"Einhard?"

His fingers resumed the light, rhythmic movement across her face.

"It was there in your words when you spoke of your home, when you said Dorestad had been sold off to the Vikings. Your voice changed when you said those words, your eyes." She moved round. "It was in every muscle and bone of your body. I saw it then." Her hands moved over the thick, harshly muscled wall of his chest. "I feel it now. You cannot deny it." The tightness beneath her fingertips intensified frighteningly.

"You understand," she said with all the desperation in her soul. "When you fought today, you fought for the king's cause."

The tightness slipped the rein.

"I fought because I had to. Because there was no other way forward—" He stopped. There was a small deadly silence.

I do as I will. I will take what I want.

The hidden feeling bound inside him, that she had so blithely assumed she understood, now filled the close-locked air of the room. It burned the open vulnerable length of her body where it lay against his.

"You did what was right," she said, the desperation in her voice horribly exposed. "You chose that."

The statement hung in the air like a question, the kind of fatal question in quest stories that plunged the asker into the wilderness without any hope of regaining what had been lost. She watched the darkness of his eyes and the fear licked through her veins. His eyes were so blank she was afraid that the secret would remain for ever locked in his head.

She was afraid that he would speak it.

"You chose to do what was right." She kept her eyes on the blackened gaze. "You risked your life for it." The powerful body that had fought so bitterly held still. She took a breath, the next step along the dangerous quest.

"You could have stayed here with the ships. You could have left the battle to Hunferth's men. You did not." Her voice took on a fraction more confidence because he had neither moved nor spoken. Not yet. "You did what was ri—" Something flared in the black gaze.

"You cannot believe that."

Her mind, all of her heightened senses, sought to take in the lightning change in his eyes.

"I told you when you asked me once before. I take my own path. In the end, I will not deviate from my course by one hair's breadth."

She struggled to assess the meaning of the fast, fleeting expression she had seen. Bitterness, anger. Something more savage. Pain—

Now there was only the blankness like a shield wall. The heavy body moved, its strength effortless.

"I will take what I want."

"You fought when you did not have to," she said stubbornly. "Just as I did. You did more than that. You saved my life at the risk of your own." Her hand rested on his sword arm, on the flesh and blood that had moved to defend her. "When you saw I was there, in the battle, nothing would have stopped you from reaching me."

He had touched her afterwards with such power. She could sense the same deep reaction now, their physical closeness, the tension in him, dangerous as a weapon. She used it.

"I could have died," she said. "You knew it."

They were the words he had used. *You could have died.* She had felt his anger, the force of his formidable will to deny that grim danger. *You were meant for life,* he had said.

"The tide of the battle had moved against me. It was hard to defend myself against so many. If but one blow had struck true, I would have been helpless." She kept her gaze on the dark power of his. "You could not stand that thought. Neither of us can. That is our own private nightmare. We cannot bear the thought of someone helpless when we should aid them—" The weapon struck. Not as she expected. The unreadable expression flared in his eyes, like black fire.

"You do not know what you speak of."

"Yes, I do," she said, her own volatile feelings catching the flame from him. Like anger and yet not so. "I see more clearly than you."

"No." The denial was harsh. He turned, the movement sudden and unexpected, filled with the kind of strength she had always envied. But she did not envy it now. It seemed rather something to be fought down, something with its own life that could lead down the path of hell. It must be a burden to have such strength.

She looked up at his face. "You risked your life to save mine. When I was so bitter I did not care about death. You said that life was important."

The sharp line of his body cut the lamplight, the fireglow clinging to every harsh muscle under the thin linen tunic. It left his face in shadow, his eyes like pools of darkness. She understood the measure of bitter pain in that darkness. The reason for it did not matter to her, not in this breathless moment between them. What was underneath did.

"That is what you believe in, life's power. You told me that not just with words…" Her hand lighted on his shoulder, touched the same body that had forced life into hers, infused her with its heat. "But with flesh and bone."

She could feel the same force of life now, burning, brighter even than the shadows that still held death.

"That was what mattered between us. It is still what matters." She touched his face and felt the instant reaction in him, hot and primitive beyond the reach of her words. The consciousness of it flooded her veins, intense and unstoppable, faintly frightening. But she had glimpsed the pain locked inside him.

She closed her mind to everything else as the heat enfolded her. The heat of the life she needed. The heat of him. Her mouth caught his.

THE BURST OF DESIRE was instant at the first contact of his lips. It overwhelmed, like the power of the banked force locked within him. Her mouth was lost under the utter blinding intensity of the kiss. She could feel nothing but the caress of his lips, the smooth invasion of his tongue. Then the tightness of his body over hers. She gasped, her own body tensing. For an endless moment, the kiss deepened and then it eased. He drew back.

She clutched at him. "Don't—"

"You are afraid."

"No." But… His gaze caught hers, held it. His face was darkened. His eyes jewel deep. The rise of breath in his heavy chest was fast, shallow.

"You are still a virgin."

She caught her breath. "Does that matter?"

"Yes."

He had said as much before, when she had hidden in his room. She had half accepted that as a reason not to continue.

"It can have no meaning. I am not a girl anymore. Not after today."

"It does matter."

"Why?"

"Because I am not the man for you." His chest rose sharply. "I cannot see a future. There is naught I can give."

She watched his face, the strong brilliant lines of it and the shadows cast by the flame of the lamp, the other shadows that were not material, the ones that lived in his eyes.

"I cannot think about the future." *I am not strong enough.* She held his arms. "All I know is that you are what I need now. Let me stay with you." Her hand moved across tight muscle. "Show me what life should be." Her fingers touched his skin. "I cannot live without your warmth. Show me."

She expected some force, the release of all the harshly bound strength that was there in every line of his body.

She was prepared this time. But it was not so. The supple heat of his mouth drew her in, bringing her closer. At first there was only the touch of his lips, the movement of his mouth filling her with the knowledge of him, with the awareness of his heated flesh on hers. She sank into it, falling. Into the darkness.

His arms closed round her, bringing her close again, into the hard familiar shape of his body and she was kissing him, as she had in the forest glade.

Her hands closed over his shoulders, her lips parted under the warm dark urging of his. She felt the brilliant intensity, the hunger inside him like a flame in the dark. Such hunger.

The power of life.

His tongue entered her mouth.

She closed her eyes, and the endless hunger built. The dizzying dark surrounded her, with him like a flame at its center, catching the fire inside her, igniting it. She pressed closer, hardly knowing what she did.

His embrace tightened, holding her body under the stark heated planes of his and then his hands moved, tracing her shape, exploring the soft contours, moulding her flesh. This time there was no body armour to block sense, nothing but the light material of her summer dress, nothing but the slide of the thin linen across her skin, the heat of his hands.

He shifted, turning his weight so that the lighter, more vulnerable length of her body followed and they were lying facing. She felt the moment of pure stillness, the slight hitch in the smooth movement of his hands.

Her eyes opened. He was watching her. Just that. For one instant outside time. The depths of his eyes were wide, darkened with the moving shadows, filled with such things. They flitted across the burning depths, shadows beyond her grasp. If he would tell her, she would see through them. She would understand. Know who he was.

Tell me.

The words formed in her head. But he broke the meshing of their gazes, the severing deliberate. He was already moving. His mouth claimed hers and his hands slid over her waist, pushing higher, higher until the edge of his thumb touched the curve of her breast. It made the desire tighten, as he knew it would, sharp, intense, swamping everything, mind and body and feeling. The sensation he evoked dragged her under. She was drowning in it, but her hands stayed, touching him, smoothing over the heavy muscles of his shoulders so that he would know that she wanted him.

He moved, angling the strong length of his body against hers. She sought to hold him. His hand cupped her breast. She gasped, the sensation so intense that she almost wanted to draw back. But they shared this blinded closeness and the lure of feeling his hand on her was too great, too filled with magic. She moved. Her spine arched, pressing her aching flesh closer against his touch. She felt the reaction in him, bright and fiercely danger-ous, filled with an inner anticipation, mysterious.

His hand tightened. She moaned. The soft pressure increased and then relaxed, increased again, the rhythm of his touch overwhelming her with a need she could not control. Her hands slid from his shoulders, the touching lost. But he did not stop. His fingers brushed across the hard tightened bud of her nipple and the maddening sensation shot through her, too in-tense, and yet not nearly enough, the thin barrier of her cloth-ing unbearable.

She had had one glimpse of what his touch could be like on her naked skin. He had taught her that on the first night, taught her the wanting, even though she had been afraid of it then.

Her hand moved, covered his where he touched her. There was a moment that was breathless, filled with the force of de-sires held back, at least in him, clamped down by a control that was wire-thin.

Desire that was incendiary.

She wondered whether she was still afraid. Not just of the act itself, but of the intimacy.

She could draw back, even now. He would let her. The con-trol was that harsh, ruthless.

Her hand stayed. Her slender fingers threaded themselves with the thickness of his and this touching was something more, the next step on the path. His hand moved in hers.

It was he who paused.

"Will you touch me?" Her voice broke the silence, the shared sound of their breathing and the heat intensified, burned deep inside her, danced across her skin. "Touch me as you did before…" She watched the sleek, taut lines of his body, the shadows in his face. "I want—" *you*. She could not say it. The word had no place.

"I want your touch."

His eyes darkened. The desire between them snapped tight. He slipped the ties of her tunic and the thin shift underneath to bare her flesh. She felt his hand on her skin, felt the caress of his hard palm and his skillful fingers. Her body tightened, alive with anticipation. He bent his head. Her body shifted, meeting the movement, pressing closer. She felt the hot, wet touch of his mouth. She cried out. But her voice was formless, a raw sound of need. His hands on her body tightened. She felt the caress of lips and tongue on the aching, swollen peak of her breast, moving, building the pleasure and inciting the desire until she was nearly mindless with it.

When he loosened the rest of her clothing she did not draw back. Her body trembled, but his hands were so sure, so smooth as they bunched her skirts, slid the tunic and long kirtle over her head. She turned her body, moved to his hot urging, felt the heat of his gaze on the shape of her body through the thin covering of her shift. The linen sheath hid nothing, the curve of her waist, the line of her legs. She could see the curbed desire in his eyes.

His fingers found the hem of her shift. Her breath caught as he pulled the last garment away, freeing her tight, heated flesh.

The desire in his eyes flamed, the brilliant intensity of it suddenly and shockingly visible. Her breath tightened. For a moment he did not touch her and the heat burned between them. The leashed power was frightening and yet it was what she wanted, the only fire that had power over the dark.

She reached out over the minute distance that separated them and touched his hand.

"I do not know what to do."

"Then let me show you." His hand closed over hers. The gesture was like a bond that reached beyond the flame of desire, deeper. The simplicity of it, a token of comfort. She realised that her need for solace was as great as her need for the cleansing fire of desire. That that was what he offered. That each step he had used to draw her on into the flames had been made with care.

Her heart swelled with feelings she could not afford to see closely. She moved now on instinct alone, on a power that now seemed double-edged, hers as much as his. Her gaze fastened on the harsh lines of his face, the intentness, the wholly unanticipated beauty of it. Her arm moved, drawing his hand with hers, lower, to the gilded buckle at his waist.

"Will you—"

The heat flared.

He undid the buckle, the movement of his hand filled with an incredible sexual charge. The leather parted. He freed the belt from his hips, in one smooth motion drew off the linen tunic. Dark shadow sheeted over the brightness of his naked skin, the firelit play of living muscle, the taut line of his flesh.

Judith's own desire tightened, matching his. When he moved towards her, she came into his arms. The heat surrounded her.

Their flesh melded, skin to skin. His mouth sought hers. His touch incited, inflamed flesh already aroused, ignited desire that was bone-deep, tinged with the madness locked inside her.

Their bodies moved, twining. It was no longer play, but something deeper. She felt his thigh slide between hers, the way it had when they had embraced in the forest glade, the movement urgent. His hands moved over her naked skin, the touch a torment, impossibly intimate. The touch moved lower, across the dip of her back, finding the curve of her hip, sliding round across the fullness of her buttock. The aching low in her belly, the deep moist heat between her legs intensified.

She gasped against his mouth. Her body writhed. His hand moved lower, across her thigh, drawing her leg upwards and bending her knee so that her thigh draped over his, holding her body opened to him. Her heart beat wildly, out of time, her breath tightened. The fierce ache in her flesh grew, hot and urgent, seeking a release she did not understand.

His lips brushed hers, softly, like the reassurance he had offered before. His hand moved round, the touch slow, his fingertips tracing the open vulnerable skin of her inner thigh. The sensations inside her screamed in anticipation. His fingers found the tight curls that covered her sex, the soft delicate folds of her flesh. She cried out, the sound ragged, desperate, choked off. She became utterly still, afraid he would stop, afraid he would go on. His fingers settled, gentle, not drawing back, yet not forcing her where she would not go.

She had shared so much with him, danger, the risk of life or death. She had trusted him with a part of who she was.

She pressed closer against his hand and felt the answering fire in the powerful mass of his body. Yet the touch of his fingers on her swollen vulnerable skin was soft. The way he touched her, the combination of strength and care was darkly exciting, intensely arousing.

She moved against his hand, against the deftly skilful exploration of the intimate secrets of her body that no man had touched. He brought her to the brink. He must sense her readiness, her openness to him. The need. The soft glide of his fingers quickened, touched some part of her that sent dizzying waves of sensation spiraling through her body. She gasped, moving against his touch without will, in some knowledge that was primeval.

Her breath tightened, loud in the stillness, loud in her own ears. The bright sensation inside her built, intensified. She pressed closer to him, opening in a way beyond understanding, primitive. The heat consumed her, burning out the protective urge to withdraw. The crippling, long-held horrors that haunted her, the fresher horrors of today retreated, just for this night, this moment.

"Einhard."

There was no consciousness left in her but the need, the sense of his touch. Of his closeness.

Her body flowered for him. She did not draw away, not while her lover's fingers traced the delicate aching flesh of her sex, caressed its folds, slid inside the tight damp hotness of her body, heightening the already overmastering pleasure. So that the slick glide of his fingers brought on the fire that burned everything in one dizzying burst of white light.

11

IN THAT BRILLIANT fire-struck moment, Judith's world changed. Because of another person. Because of a gift.

She held him, her arms round his back, her head buried against his neck. Her senses filled with the clean scent of his skin. She could feel the strong tough wall of his body, the soft fall of his hair, the rough line of his jaw and the warmth of his neck. His heart beat fast.

Her body trembled, filled with pleasure, heavy with an exhaustion that was blindingly complete. The deep exhaustion dragged at her, yet she moved in the protective circle of Einhard's arms and the smooth heated lines of his body turned without effort to accommodate her.

She was looking down into the dark fathomless pools of his eyes. His face was tight. His hand reached up to catch the wild, tumbled mass of her hair, touch her still heated skin, flushed with the mad flood of desire.

"Did you weep? Judith?"

She realized the skin under his hand was wet, streaked with fresh tears, as though once she had cried, the bitter barrier was broken and she might weep again. She had struggled so hard against tears, afraid of their power. The truth shimmered on the edge of this new world. If she had to weep, it did not matter. She shook her head.

"I am happy." She watched the stormy eyes. "It is because of what you have given." She reached out, the display of feeling unlike her, part of the changed world. "You said you had naught to give." She touched his hot, moving flesh. "It is not so—"

"No." The reaction was violent, deep as the measure of the untamed strength if he had not controlled it. She made some small sound. It was shock, not fear. She would have called it back.

But he heard it.

His gaze raked over her widened eyes, her clenched hands. "You see. There is nothing. Nothing that I could give you. It is as I told you from the start."

The cold-bloodedness in his gaze cut off every emotion he had ever felt, that he still felt. Or perhaps that cold-blooded ruthlessness was the true core of him, the savage will that was tough enough to exert its mastery over every feeling.

Her body glowed with the warmth of his lovemaking, the power that had released the demons. That power was strong. Stronger than isolation.

She unclenched her hands.

Einhard's blank gaze did not change, emotion held down by a strength that was inexhaustible.

No one had strength that was inexhaustible.

The flame of the lamp flared. The light flickered across their combined skin. Two separate people, touching. Connection and isolation. Her hand flattened out against his flesh. She felt the reaction, sharp, physical. She felt the harshly held tension, exhaustion, the tightly wound strain of battle, pain. He was wounded, alone. But she still felt the strength.

"Can you not tell me what lives in your mind?"

The shadowed eyes flickered and she was reminded of that moment in the chamber at Stathwic when she had seen what she should not, the wild despair like madness. In the changing of a single breath it was gone, swept aside by the bitter unmerciful strength that had carried him beyond that moment of defeat, that would carry him now, far beyond her reach. Alone.

The rush of fear was dizzying. Like taking the step that led to battle. Her head bent. Her lips touched the strong heated brilliance, the fine graceful line of his neck.

She was strong, stronger than she had ever been in her life. She realised the strength was on the inside, something unbreakable, something that endured as though it had always been there and it was only she who had not known its measure. Something that had needed his gift to take life.

She could not fight his physical strength. But the power locked inside her, shimmered.

She moved on instinct, her body sliding round, taking its accustomed place, touching him as he had taught her.

"I want to stay." Her breath touched his skin. "Let me stay." Her fingers touched the broad plane of his chest. She could feel the fast beat of his heart. "Let me——" What? He would not have her maidenhead. He meant his words. *No future.* She closed her mind against why. She closed her mind against everything she did not know about the act of love. Against all the things she did not know about him.

Her hand moved lower, across the warm flesh at the center of his chest, down, between the heavy-boned ribs, lower, across the lean flexible line of his belly. The heat of him burned her skin.

Power.

Her fingers brushed the line of his dark linen trousers, hesitated. She could see the hard-edged shape of him. Feel his strength. The slow movement of her hand stopped. She forced her head up and made herself look into the depths of his eyes. Blackness and flame. The moment hung, breathless, charged with power, beyond her limited knowledge. She had touched him this way before, on the edge of that hot carnal knowledge and he had stopped her. She knew he had the strength to do that again. If he chose.

Do not choose that.

The words burned in her mind. The dangerous unknown connection between them hung in the balance. Her fingertips moved over tight linen, over the firm flesh underneath, the heat of him. Her hand stilled, all of her caught on the edge of the unknown depths. She understood the force of need now. It was no longer foreign. The rush of feeling was dizzying, powerful with a deep and heady anticipation he had taught her. *Shown* her. If she could give that back…

"Show me." She had to force the words past the dryness of her throat. "Show me how. There must be a way to…" *She did not even know the words to use. She could no longer look at his face.*

She had closed her mind to female whisperings about love because such things were not for her. Now she rued it. Her fingers moved. The only guide was instinct, instinct and the sure strength. She touched him and the hot wave of anticipation flooded through her, tightening her newly heightened senses with the hot, intense memory of pleasuring.

Pleasure.

"There must be the same pleasuring for you. The same…" *Gift.* Her mouth touched the warmth of his skin where her head lay against the solid strength of his shoulder. Her lips closed again over the taut skin of his neck. She touched him, waiting, filled with wanting. Then the magic happened. She felt the heat of his body all round her, the closeness of his arms, then his mouth on hers, matching the kiss, driving it higher, further, evoking pleasure. She felt the warmth of his lips in her hair, on her skin. His fierce bone-deep reaction to her touch.

His mouth captured hers again, possessed it. The kiss was demanding, heated. For one split instant, the savage control broke and she saw what was underneath. She did not draw back. It was what she wanted, release of all that hidden feeling. She felt the hunger he could no longer hide, sharp as the edge of pain. She met it.

The heat inside her flared without control, her response to the need in him overwhelming, fierce and possessive. The desire intensified until she was crazed, reckless, her touch on him carnal, unbridled, pierced through with passion that was uniquely hers. Her own arousal heightened with the sight and the awareness of his. Her naked body moved over his, open to the touch of his hand, his heated mouth. Her hands helped his to remove the dark linen that covered his lower body, sliding the material over the tautness of his hips, the powerful thigh, the long graceful line of his leg.

Her breath caught, her gaze trapped on him. She leaned over him, her hands on the hot heavy muscles of his thighs, aware of their shared nakedness. The blood raced in her veins. She felt hot, aching, filled with the same desire she had experienced before, restless and taut, unbearably excited.

His hand reached up to touch the tumbled weight of her hair. The tangled mass of pale gold trailed across his skin. She watched the slow movement of his hand. He drew her head downwards and his lips brushed hers, the caress light, tantalising. The touch inflamed. Her breathing tightened, became shallow. She felt his hands frame her face and then move, down the delicate column of her throat, over her collarbone. One hand touched the globe of her breast. She sensed the tension in him notch higher. The knowledge was like some mystic power, deeply arousing.

"Einhard…"

The light touch of his fingers trailed down her body, across the quivering sensitivity of her belly. She made some sound. No word this time, just a sound of need, hunger. His hand captured hers, covered it, drew it slowly across the taut heat of his flesh. She gasped. His skin was so smooth, hot, burning. She felt his powerful body clench, the harsh muscles beneath her tighten.

The fingers of his free hand traced the delicate rise of her cheekbone, soothing. She watched his face, fascinated both by its harshness and its intensity.

Her fingers moved on the heated skin under her hand. She saw the reaction in the hard masculine lines of his face, the dark pools of his eyes. It was fierce, stark, dark with need.

His gaze held hers. His hand where it covered her fingers moved, guiding her touch along the length of his shaft, the blunt rounded tip, smooth skin sliding over rigid hardness. His touch showed her the rhythm, achingly slow, light. So at variance with the urgent tightness of his body. She sensed that, sensed the bitter need. When her touch quickened, he slowed it. She made some sound, but he caught her closer, his hands on her flesh as though the need in him could never be satisfied without the knowledge of her own pleasure.

Without giving.

The thought pierced through her, lodged in her mind but she could not hold on to it, to anything. Her body responded to the play of his hand, to the remembered pleasure, to the pact of sensual touching, of physical release. She was so aroused by her touching of him, by the flagrant hunger she had seen in his face, that the first sensation of his fingers on her slickened skin, parting the intimate folds of her woman's flesh made her shudder. It was fast as lightning. The erotic glide of his fingers, the sense of his hunger, his desire for her, sent her spiraling over the edge. The sensation was so deep, deep as though the first time had never been, as though her hunger for him would never abate but would always be renewed.

The intensity swept her over, into the madness, the only conscious thought that she wanted him. Her body cleaved to his, boneless. The heat, the strength of him, the sense of his presence engulfed her. He was all she wanted. His hard hot flesh filled her hand, the closeness of his body. Her hand moved possessively, the touch wild in her madness.

She felt the harsh movement in the powerful muscles, the catch in his breath, the rough thrust of his body against her hand. There was no control, only the passion and the driving madness, long held back. She understood it, recognised it for her own. The release was bitter, like pain. She would not let him go afterwards. When the black mist of exhaustion claimed her, it was with her head on his skin.

She thought closeness must be like that, pleasure and pain, joy and sorrow, all she had turned her back on.

The flames in the hearth flickered without focus before her eyes. Her thoughts flickered with them, impossible to pin down—death, the battle, loving. Her eyes stung. She shut them. The sickening weariness hit her and the flames were behind her closed eyelids, firelight and torchlight and Macsen's voice when it spoke of dreams.

Einhard slept beside her. The last awareness in her mind was of touching him. In the warmth of his arms it seemed impossible there could be no future.

EINHARD WOKE TO DARKNESS AND the sound that spelled warning, the eerie drawn-out note of the wood owl. The awareness was instant, complete, something as practiced in him as a conjurer's trick. The fire in the hearth was almost gone. Embers gave but grudging light.

It was enough.

He moved. The girl close beside him in the bed never stirred. She slept, deeply and completely. The spent fire gave enough light to see the bruising weariness round her eyes. She still touched him, her skin warm against his body. She smelled of freshness and exhaustion and sex. The fine strands of her hair clung to him. She touched him like a lover, like one who had shared complete intimacy. She was turned towards him as though she would share even this.

Her hand rested on his arm, white and small. It had the bruises of one who had dealt death, and risked it. She had achieved what she had wanted, the East Anglian princess. She had laid her demons and struck a blow for her much-loved lord, Alfred of Wessex. That king had not been what he had expected. He had been...more; a man and a ruler who would not give up, a king who might even have given a Frisian mercenary his faith.

He could not take that.

He stirred, gritting his teeth as the movement flowed back through the injured arm.

Alfred of Wessex would never win. No one could.

The long wavering note outside the walls was repeated, cutting through the night air like a presage of death. The woman sighed in her sleep as though she heard it. The faint exhalation of her breath touched him, clean and warm as her mouth, soft as her skin touching him.

He disengaged himself. Her bruised hand was too small to stop him. He crossed the room. She did not wake. The woman—Judith.

He dragged on his clothes, using his cloak over all to hide the last betraying gleam of skin. The dying fire flared as he opened the door.

The tidings the messenger brought were what he waited for. He could not take it in. He had to force himself to the stillness required to listen, to assess the value of each word through the harsh beat of his heart. When he did not immediately speak, his man tried to tell him what the news meant. Einhard cut him off with a finality that was savage. The flow of well-intentioned words stopped. The messenger stepped back into shadow, the way a man does when confronted by a hell-spawn. It was what he had become.

The man bowed his head.

There was no need of further words. His orders were already set. They had been so since the moment he had made the decision to come to Derne.

The Serpent waited for him off the coast, out of sight, not a high-sided merchant vessel but a slipway wolf, a longship, iron-beaked, low to the water and fast. An instrument of death.

There was little enough to take with him from the firelit chamber. Everything he owned was already on board the Serpent. It was better that way.

He turned.

"WHAT DO I MEAN BY GONE?" howled Hunferth, his face suffused with an alarming shade of dark red. His mouth worked on various possibilities. "I mean gone," he bellowed with crushing logic. "Decamped. Fled like a wolf after carrion."

"That is foolish," snapped Judith. Her head ached with tiredness, with— "I cannot believe..." She lengthened her stride to keep up with Hunferth. Her long skirts snagged infuriatingly on fruiting brambles. Mildred trailed behind.

"Yesterday after the battle you were thanking the Frisian for your life," she said. Yesterday she had bedded him.

She had woken up alone.

"Yesterday," snarled Hunferth. They rounded the screen of blackberry and sand-spurrey. "Look."

The beauty of the inlet spread out before her. Early sunlight glanced off the rippling sheet of water, pure and unsullied. Empty where a compact fleet of graceful ships had ridden at anchor.

"It is a mistake," said Judith. "It does not mean..."

"Mean what? What are you trying to say? That it is a mistake that not one treacherous Frisian remains in this camp? That four ships slipped out of this harbour before dawn? That the coast guard saw them at the change of light heading out for the open sea? Or—all the saints, I am not going to deal with swooning."

"No, indeed you are not." There was no need for it. Judith began the urgent task of removing a blackberry twig from an expanse of her pale-blue linen kirtle. It was difficult because her sight had blurred. She took a lot of care with her skirts, as though it mattered. "Open sea, did you say?"

"Making for Dorestad, apparently," muttered Hunferth with less heat.

The bramble began to work free in her fingers. If she concentrated on that, she would be all right. The fine air and the brilliant world would not crash around her dizzied head like four walls collapsing inwards.

"Dorestad?" she said. "You are jesting."

There was the small matter of Rorik and piracy and...whatever else her beguiling lover had done. Of all things, of all the terrifying possibilities, surely he would not have gone back to Dorestad.

"It does not make sense."

There was a wholly uncharacteristic hesitation in the heavy figure beside her. Her heart tightened. Hunferth's dusty boots shifted. She thought for a moment he would not speak. She hoped he would not, because her exhausted mind, beginning to function again, had already made the leap.

"If it was not Dorestad," said Hunferth, "there is only one other place, one other master your precious Frisian could run to. That being so, if I were him, once I had let my ships be seen heading out for the open sea, I would double back later, towards the coast of East Anglia." The bramble stabbed through her thumb. She swore. It was the kind of oath that belonged in an uncleaned privy.

"Precisely," said Hunferth. "Earl Guthrum would turn away no man who could barter several sets of oars. As I would not."

"No." The reaction was violent, not based on any reasoning at all. "Einhard would not do that."

"Saint Beren's bones," yelled Hunferth. "Can you not think past *for-licgan?* Just because the man can get up your skirts for the mere asking, woman, does not mean he does not understand his own worth. I am quite sure Earl Guthrum can afford to pay him more for the use of his ships than I can, or yo—"

Mildred smacked him over the back of the head. It was difficult to say who was more surprised, the incensed battle veteran or the outraged maidservant.

"I regret the need to be outspoken," said Hunferth with terrifying clarity. "Princess." She saw him resist the temptation to rub the back of his skull. Mildred gazed at him, the whites of her eyes showing. "But that is how matters stand."

Judith thought all the blood had drained from her body, that she would turn round and be sick. "So what will you do? Go after him?"

"With what, lady? A half-built fleet? I cannot risk what we have or jeopardise the progress we have already made. He will have calculated that. The spies I have in East Anglia have even now got the message through to me that some of Guthrum's ships are close. The only thing I can hope for is that Einhard does not bring them down on us too soon." Hunferth attempted a calming breath. "There is so much good work done already. So much the Frisian had—" One meaty fist slammed against a palm.

"The job was as near as done. It still could be if we have only a little more time. I can tell you one thing, princess. If I found your lover, I would kill him. Bear it in mind."

"I am aware of duty."

"Good. If you will excuse me, I have a messenger to send to the king." He paused, as though he would say something else, as though there were a thread through the bitter frightened anger that might be regret, even pity. But there was nothing to say, so he turned and walked away.

She understood it, just as she understood what the potential consequences were. Failure. She imagined the king's face, the battered restless energy turning to meet the new challenge.

"What will you do?" Mildred's voice echoed her own question.

Swoon despite Hunferth's scorn. Slit my throat. Walk out into the beautiful brilliant water until I drown.

"I do not know." She sat down on the ground because it was much easier than standing.

"But…what happened last night?" said the woman who had disposed of two husbands.

"Precisely what Hunferth said." It was so clear. She had asked for it. No, not asked, begged, and Einhard had obliged. While all the time he had known, planned, this.

"Oh, Judith. It was such a dangerous thing to do. He is not the kind of man who…"

Who what? Knew how to keep to his word? Even wanted to give it? Who recognised the terrifying value of any kind of connection to another human being?

"I thought there was…" Something. The something she had seen in his eyes, guessed at, convinced herself existed. "I thought there was magic. There was not." It sounded stupid. Pathetic. Sniveling girls' talk. She felt Mildred's hand touch her shoulder.

Mildred would stand your friend, and the look in his eyes, the sound of his voice, as though he understood.

She stood up.

Bastard. Why had he said such things?

What he had said was that he would walk his own path, never deviate. But why such underlying deceit? He had fought alongside Hunferth. It had been the extra numbers of his men that had swung the fate of the battle. She shut her eyes. It was his men who had so conveniently undertaken the pursuit afterwards. They must have brought him news of…something. What? An inducement from Guthrum to divide a useful Frisian ally from Hunferth? Or something else?

Tatwin had said Einhard had fought alongside Hunferth for his own ends. He had been planning—

"Why Guthrum?"

"What? Lady…"

"Why join with a Viking when one of them has outlawed him, when he is engaged in a blood feud with another, when he has lost his home…" *Fæhth. A blood feud* and the sound of his voice when he had said it.

Plans.

"What colour are Earl Guthrum's ships?"

"What colour are— I do not know."

She would get nothing out of Hunferth. Besides, his responsibility lay here. And her responsibility, her duty? She tried to thrust the thought aside. But it came back. It was, had been, the mainspring of her life. She had been brought up to follow duty in the court of East Anglia. She had given her word, in her heart, at the court of Wessex, oath-sworn. Yet if her heart was divided now? If duty opposed— What? Love?

Judith could not think on it. It would kill her. She began to walk back up the well-worn path, following the print of Hunferth's great boots in the soft ground. But the only thing she could see was Einhard's face. The sun beat on her back but all she could feel was the still air of a torchlit room, the pure heated glide of Einhard's skin.

She could see his eyes.

"Where are you going?" said Mildred.

"Home."

"Home?"

"Yes." The unknown Viking Skar, who had pursued the blood feud, had to be in Danish-held East Anglia. Earl Guthrum's ships were there, at sea, and somewhere along the coast was a Frisian mercenary with a private fleet, someone who had discovered the secrets of Wessex and kept his own. Someone who was infinitely dangerous.

She had to get there.

Home. Her skin shivered.

Somewhere.

There was one other person who knew where. She would bet her life on it.

She would have to.

She crested the rise.

"BLACK AND YELLOW," said Judith.

Tatwin stared at the hazy blue horizon. The wind whipped his decently short brown hair. She imagined him shaving it in a tonsure. He was an honest man. He was not going to lie to her. He was finding it hard enough to evade.

"That was the colour of the sails seen off the coast at Stathwic," she persisted. "Einhard questioned the port reeve. I was there when he did it. I am asking you whether those were truly likely to have been Guthrum's ships as the reeve believed."

"I cannot say." A proper priestly answer, a confidence respected.

There were lives at stake.

"You cannot say. As you could not help your friend in battle yesterday when he needed it."

The charge struck home, with the force of an arrow. It must have been a less-easy decision than she had thought to stay standing while Einhard rode out to face a threat that had seemed overwhelming.

"You cannot tell me that you do not know all." Much more than I can guess or even know to ask. *Vikings from where?* The question that Tatwin had known to ask yesterday burned through her mind. "You know who owns those ships with the black-and-yellow sails as well as Einhard did. Is it Guthrum he is chasing, or that other man?" *Skar.* "Someone, perhaps, who is engaged in a blood feud?"

It was true. She could see it. Tatwin did not have the iron will required for dissembling. Not like Einhard.

What have you done?

"If you will not say it, I will. Einhard has not set out to meet Guthrum. He follows the man who owns the black-and-yellow sails, in pursuit of this feud. He has set out after someone who commands at least as many ships as he does. Hunferth has just told me that some of Earl Guthrum's boats have put to sea. Close. I doubt that Einhard knows that. Earl Guthrum has a line of communication to Rorik who has still to punish piracy. That makes for interesting odds."

She took a breath. It all depended on her next words, on how deep Tatwin's loyalty ran.

"There is one more chance to change things. You are the only person who can help me with this. I have to go after Einhard. I have to find him. Otherwise he will not live through this and everything he has done, everything I have tried to do, will be lost. Your friend is sailing into a danger that is greater than he has the slightest awareness of. The numbers are against him, just like yesterday. Worse than yesterday."

"If you think that that would make any difference, that Einhard would deviate one step from the course he has set himself, you have let friendship blind you."

Athelbert's bones. That was it. The comradeship with Tatwin, however strong it had once been, had not been able to stand against the unswerving will that had set Einhard in pursuit of his goal. Just as her friendship, her love, had not. That was what Tatwin was telling her.

There was no future. Nothing that could be done except what, in the end, Tatwin had chosen. To let him go.

Einhard would not turn back. Not for her. Yesterday he had survived despite the odds. This time it was far less likely.

Even if he did live, the mad hope of him coming back here to aid Hunferth's desperation, of his believing in all that she believed in, was impossible.

It was a defeat that was complete.

She watched the hazy horizon, blue and impenetrable. Empty. "I had thought things were…" Changed. That the new world glimpsed in the hearthlight, in the shared warmth of someone else's arms, had truly existed. "That things were different."

She caught Tatwin's gaze. For a second the friend's eyes, God's thane's eyes, held hers.

"Things are different," said Tatwin. "You have seen it." He glanced away. Then he said, "I have a ship that is seaworthy. That is what you wanted, is it not?"

12

THE SAIL CAME OUT OF NOWHERE, out of the haze on the horizon and the shadow of the curving promontory, not black barred with yellow, but a single colour, bloodred.

Judith clutched the side of the borrowed boat that was seaworthy. They were less than a day into their insane attempt at pursuit. Tatwin began swearing. The approaching sail, the taut swelling sides of the oncoming ship moved fast. There were others behind, but the vessel far in front drew the eye. It was fine, low-sided with a high gracefully curving prow, not a merchantman like Tatwin's boat, but a dragon, long, low and infinitely menacing, a warship.

"Outrun it…" Tatwin's shouts became incomprehensibly nautical. Judith's hands gripped the oak-planked side of Tatwin's laboring ship.

"Is it gaining on us?" asked Mildred.

Judith reached out and linked her arm solidly with her maid's. The other woman was quivering. It was not fair to bring her on this crazed mission. But Mildred would not be gainsaid.

"I am not sure." She kept her words carefully neutral. But the sleek grey craft was gaining. Somehow, by the very position its captain had chosen, the other vessel was shadowing the wind from the huge green-and-white sail above her head. Even a land-person could calculate the effect.

Suddenly there was no more dissembling. The ship was so close she could see the banner snapping from the mast, a great eagle, the clawed carrion-bird on its field of red, and the stream-ing trails of red linen falling from the bronze weather vane like blood. The menacing banner of Earl Guthrum's ship. Her stom-ach lurched. Mildred moaned.

Behind them, Tatwin yelled the most appalling curse. But the sound of his voice was different.

"What?" she shouted. "What is it?" She whirled round to face Tatwin. "What have you seen?"

Mildred stifled a shriek.

Their own men had the arrows out, bows strung ready for Tatwin's signal.

But he did not give it.

"He will turn," said Tatwin, the relief in his voice obvious. He turned away, shouted orders. Then he said, "Saviour's blood," which was desperate for a would-be monk.

She looked back over the ship's side.

"Athelbert's bones." She could feel how her face had gone white and the blood seemed to have drained from her veins. The other ship was bearded. The prow had been plated with iron, fixed with a series of metal spikes. It was barbaric, the most chilling threat she had ever seen.

The ship was not going to turn.

Tatwin was yelling. The green-and-white sail came down in a kind of fast organised chaos and they put out the oars, which seemed mad to Judith but the sturdy merchantman seemed to rise out of the water with the stroke of the oars, skimming the surface like a great bird, its maneuvering suddenly controlled. She knew how a sea-fight worked. She had made Einhard explain it to her. She dragged Mildred behind a linden wood shield.

Nothing happened, no deadly hail of missiles, no yelling.

The land was close, closer to the red-sailed longship. If Tatwin could force through the gap—

There would not be time. She could see it. Her heart raced, the fear, the bitter madness of yesterday's battle rose in her mind. Mildred clutched the shield. Judith unsheathed her sword. There was a rending sound of wood cleaved by iron.

"The ship has hit us," screamed Mildred. "We will drown."

If they were lucky.

"Stay behind the shield." She stepped out. There was no deadly flooding wave of seawater. Little damage. Then she realised. The iron-plated hull had sheared off the oars. Tatwin's ship was helpless. The other, sailless, was lashed alongside. Its crew boarded. Someone huge, shadowed in the sunlight, lithe as a hunting wolf, leaped over the side. She thought the fast beating of her heart would kill her. She tightened her grip on the hilt.

"Drop that."

She stared at the huge shadowed figure. It was a moment before her dizzied mind could take in the evidence of her eyes. Her gaze fastened on the brilliant face, the light-green eyes in the bronzed skin.

She grounded the blade.

"Einhard."

He yanked the sword out of her hand. The gesture was violent, far beyond compromise. She swallowed and gave up the hilt. There did not seem to be much of a choice.

She stared at the familiar planes of his face. On the edge of awareness, she sensed that Tatwin had come to stand beside her.

"Einhard..."

He turned his head at Tatwin's arrival. Sunlight slid over the heated skin and strong-boned features she had touched in love.

"Why are you here?" The question was directed at Tatwin, as brutally uncompromising as his touch on the sword.

Not a familiar face at all.

"I might ask the same. What you are doing here, sailing under that banner." The great bird, the storm-cleaver, coiled and uncoiled above their heads and the bloodred streamers fanned out in the wind.

"Skar is seeking Guthrum's ships."

"And he will find you, in Guthrum's fleet?"

"I will do whatever it takes."

"You would not bind yourself to Guthrum."

"I will bind myself to no one, only take what I seek."

"And you seek—"

"You know what it is."

The sharp exchange stopped. *Guthrum.* The name chilled her. *I will bind myself to no one, only take what I seek.* She did not understand. Tatwin did.

Skar. The Viking name was as blank and loaded with danger as Einhard's voice.

She had thought that if she found him again she would understand, that the fierce, gentle, unrestrained intimacy they had shared would have given her the key she needed. It had not. The stranger stood, weighing her sword in his hand.

She had to try. It was why she had followed him.

"Einhard, you—" His voice drowned hers.

"Why have you come here?" The same question directed at Tatwin, as though she had not spoken, as though she had no existence. Her heart beat out of time. She tried to find the right words, any words, something that would break the spell of harshness. She saw his chest swell with the breath to speak. "How could you have brought the woman?"

The woman. He might as well have said the sack of grain, the pet bitch, the *hor-cwen. Just because the man can get up your skirts for the mere asking, woman.*

"It was my choice." Her words cut across the sunlit air. Both men turned to look at her, but it was only Einhard she saw.

"Then it was foolish."

"Foolish?" Her gaze caught his and for an instant there was everything they had shared in the long night, in the first passionate moment of aliveness after the battle, like a flame, true and hot enough to burn through steel.

"No." She actually moved; the belief in what she saw was so strong. But then it vanished, like flame behind smoke, hidden. He turned away, before her gesture, whatever it might have been, could be completed.

Not a flame hidden. Extinguished.

"Foolish," he said. "Beyond permission." He tossed her sword to one of his men, as though it were nothing, as though she were nothing, not only herself, but all that was in her head, all that she had experienced yesterday, all that she had shared of her inmost thoughts.

Permission.

The shock held her silent for one frozen instant, bitter as the hurt and humiliation, and then the rage swamped her.

"You have to go back to Derne," he was saying to Tatwin. "You could never follow me into East Anglia now. You cannot maneuver the ship without oars. There is damage to the hull. The ship is too vulnerable."

"The ship is too vulnerable to take back to Derne."

"Have you no skill? I would not have thought it beyond the meanest seaman's capabilities. Hunferth is desperate enough to pay you. Perhaps a quarter of the pathetically inadequate amount he offered me. Of course, you would have to get your money in advance and then get out before the Saxons lose."

"I am not going," said Tatwin. "Please, will you…"

She was so angry that if the blade had still been in her hand she would have used it. She wanted to yell at Tatwin not to crawl. That she would happily take the ship back to Derne herself. If she could not use it to sink Einhard's entire fleet first.

The rage-maddened words stormed through her head but some other part of her brain kept focused, caught by some invisible layer of meaning.

Things are different. That was what Tatwin had said.

She watched the priest-in-training try appealing to reason. After that, he blustered. Einhard simply attacked, forcing Tatwin into a state approaching incoherence. It was deliberate, as ruthless and calculated as crippling the ship without destroying it.

But friendship could not bear the same treatment without

being destroyed. Only one thing in this appalling disaster was certain. Einhard was not stupid, not even in the more ephemeral realm of the spirit. He knew what he did.

Chills ran over her skin.

Things are different.

She did not know whether she believed it anymore.

"You have to go." Einhard turned away, back to his men, to his better, faster, more dangerous ship, the other ships that had now closed in behind him. The end of the discussion, of the battle. Defeat.

Defeat.

"Mildred." She whispered it. She swallowed. She never asked help from anyone. It was like trusting yourself to them. "Help me."

She stepped forward. There was no time to explain, but she felt Mildred follow. She slid a protective arm round her maid's shoulders.

"You cannot send two women back in a broken ship."

There was silence. She did not think it would stop him. She did not think it had even registered. He took two more steps. His hand rested lightly on the side of Tatwin's ship where it rode against the oak planking of his own.

"There is less danger in that than in sailing to East Anglia."

"The ship is damaged. You said yourself that it is vulnerable. Einhard——" He did not look round. Some sixth sense gave her the words to say. "*You* damaged it."

He turned.

Her grip on Mildred's shoulder tightened. She was not sure who was supporting whom.

"You cannot send me out to sea in that." She pointed an accusing finger at the small hole in the bow. Mildred moaned. Einhard cast the damage a glance that held fury.

"Tatwin is capable of getting this ship back to Derne."

"Then Tatwin can take the ship back. Tatwin might be capable but…" She let the sentence hang and tried to look helpless. She wished she had not elected to wear trousers and a sword belt. She wished he had not seen her in a battle rage. Mildred sniffed into the trailing ends of her veil. They stood, clinging. The boat rocked in the swell.

"I will not take you to East Anglia."

The leash on her temper broke. So did her clever attempt at subterfuge. "Who are you to say I cannot go to East Anglia? I live there. It is my home, was. It does not belong to Earl Guthrum. I tell you if you do not take me, I will go alone." The words streamed out, vicious, inappropriate, probably fatal. But the terrible pressure of feeling inside her would not let her call them back.

"My kindred are still there——" *Living and dead.* The words choked off. Her mind filled with the vision of the mist over the burial grounds at Sutton. The burial grounds and Macsen's forgotten words. *Light.*

"I can do it. I can find my own way back to Wessex afterwards by land if I have to. I have come this far and I will not be turned away." She raised her head. She kept speaking.

"You want to find out the movement of Earl Guthrum's ships for your own purpose." Her eyes locked with his. There was no denial of her words, only an act of will that was set, a purpose that was unswerving. It was frightening, alien because she did not know its foundation. Yet she recognized that depth of will, even the cost of it, to the very edges of her soul.

"I have my own purpose just as you do," she said "Even if I do not go with you, I will find my own way into my own country." She took a breath. "A set course." The recognition leaped like a flame in his brilliant green eyes, match and counterpart, soul deep. It was like a victory. But there was no triumph to be had. Neither did she think there would be a changed future.

He took her aboard.

She gave Mildred the choice of remaining with her or with Tatwin. She did not believe Einhard would have prevented whatever her maid chose. But Mildred would not be parted from her. Tatwin received no choice. Nothing he could advance would sway Einhard's mind. He had enough men to hold Tatwin's crew at bay and Tatwin knew it.

She managed only a few words as they parted.

"Tatwin are you sure you can sail that ship?"

"Well enough."

"Please, tell me," she said, as her small store of traveling goods was dragged past her and Mildred made her way towards the warship that was the image of one of Earl Guthrum's. "Tell me if there is any hope. Tell me what he is seeking." She did not truly expect God's thane to answer.

"Princess, I would once have said that what he sought was redemption. Now I think it may only be destruction. But I can no longer read him. Only you can do that."

She did not know whether she believed that. Einhard handed her across the ship's side himself. His touch burned. *Flame.*

EINHARD PACED THE DARK GROUND of East Anglia. The moon broke the clouds, almost full, a hunter's moon. The restless beat of anticipation stirred in his blood. They were deep in Viking-held territory. Impossible even to wait out the night. There was no sleep. He hardly needed it now. The hunting urge consumed him. Behind it was rage. It was so strong he could have howled at the waxing moon.

The princess slept, wrapped in furs next to her faithful maid-servant, silent as a prisoner. Which was what she was. Neither of them, after the first few moments on board his ship, had taken the slightest pains to disguise it.

Yet she had walked into this. For the sake of her beloved homeland, even though her kingdom was irrevocably lost.

The East Anglian night shades lightened. His ships rocked on the black water, moored for the night, silent, only the slight creak of the anchor rope, the faint restless slap of water against the hull.

He strode off, turning towards the faint glitter of light along the water, too restless to stay in the night camp even though the woman's presence dragged at him. He followed the line of the water's edge, as though the black shadows could lead him to his goal.

Some small creature erupted from the dark, disturbed by his footsteps, a black shadow. A water vole. It vanished into the hollow reeds at the water's edge. He stopped. The narrow wake disappeared without trace.

No trace.

He was so close to his goal, closer than he had ever been. The knowledge filled him at a level that was not rational. The reeds shivered. The creature was still there, hidden. It was only he who could not see it.

Thieto, his small son, would have followed it out of curiosity. Thieto would have stopped to make a useless whistle out of something as interesting as a hollow reed stem.

For a skillful child he was remarkably bad at it.

Einhard squatted down. It was simple, really. He had never quite grasped why Thieto was so very bad at it. He unsheathed the knife at his belt. He could accomplish such a matter in seconds. Thieto always pulled a face and then—

The blade nearly took his hand off because he could not see. The only thing before his eyes was Thieto, the small captive, the other soul who lived in Skar's hands and waited, helpless. The rage slipped bounds.

He tried to force it back because Thieto needed more than that from him. He could not fail his son, fail the memory of the fragile mother who had borne him nearly eight years ago and died of it. He owed Geva's memory that much, the safety of her child. His.

He could see his son's face in the black rushes, in the moonlit water, in every moving shadow. He did not see with material eyes. He thought he was mad. He reached out as though he could touch the elusive figure. But it vanished with the physical movement.

Stay. He spoke the word in his mind, as though the apparition had been real, as though that other soul that was indissolubly part of him could hear. *Wherever you are, wherever Skar is, you have only to stay still and wait for me. If you do that I will be able to find you. Thieto . . .*

"I will come for you and no force in the three worlds will be able to stop that."

He had spoken aloud. The shadows of the reeds shifted, light and blackness slid across his vision. But it was only the wind in the hollow stems. His hand dropped to his side. The wound in his arm throbbed. The night air closed round him, empty. The night that somewhere held Skar, farther down the coast, hidden. There had been many false trails. But this time he would find him. There was nothing to hold him back. His fingers rested on the knife hilt.

He was suddenly aware that Judith was there. He heard her move, even though her steps were light as those of the spirits that lived in the trees behind her. He watched her pick her way slowly across the cold ground. He stood up. The knife was still in his hand, white in the moonlight. She would have seen it, yet she came on.

She looked at him as though he was quite sane. It was a great mistake. He let the half-finished reed-pipe he could not give his son fall from his hand. He sheathed the knife, but it could make little difference. The blackness must pour off him in waves.

Judith kept walking towards him, just as though she had a place in the madness, in the barbarous ruthlessness of what he was engaged in. She stopped when she faced him. The moonlight caught the pale brightness of her hair and her face, elf-fair. She waited. His hand rested on the sheathed knife. He did not know whether she had heard him speak. But Judith said nothing. Perhaps that was what made it possible. She touched him.

She did not ask why he was here, what he did. He could not have answered. What he did was a thing apart, outside the civilized realm she lived in. It admitted no turning, and success or failure stretched out to death. She must sense its shadow on his skin. It was in his heart. But she did not seem to have fear, or even the horror that afflicted Tatwin. She was herself. She almost had the power to make him believe things that were impossible. That power had drawn him from the first moment he had seen her in Hunferth's train, outshining the king's man with her courage. Such courage....

It was a liability.

She moved closer, silent, as though nothing else were necessary, as though the barbarism of the blood feud, the uncivilized anger, the way he would betray all she believed in, had no relevance.

Her body leaned into his. The smooth lines of her were delicately full. The long cloak muffled her light warmth, covered her decently, but the barrier no longer existed for him. The awareness of her was already burned into him because of the bond they had shared, the complete intimacy that belonged to night.

He could feel the faint tremor in her finely drawn muscles, the slight unevenness in her breathing. It could have been fear, but she leaned into him, as though she knew he would accept her. As though there was trust.

Her breath sighed against his skin. "Sometimes I think I am crazed," she said. His own breath caught in his lungs, a black sound she would hear. But she kept speaking. "It is because I am here, in East Anglia. I did not know it would be like this, or that I would feel such things, terrible things without names. Things there is no way to describe."

It was impossible to get speech past the tight sinews of his throat, the locked tension of his jaw. She had her arms round him.

"There are no words." Her voice, low, intensely intimate, vibrated against his body, as though she could see inside his head, as though there was a bond where none could exist, even in pain.

Then she said, "You understand that."

He had learned to suppress any visible reaction to such words. But she touched him. She would feel the bitterness, the depth, the appalling unacceptable power of it. Yet her hands sought the harshened contours of his body, seeking his touch as though he could help her.

She had lost this land whose rich earth they stood on. It had once been hers.

He pulled her against him and she came to him, despite everything that cut them apart from each other. She turned in his arms. Her body touched his. Its fierce familiar beauty stole sense, burning him.

"I lost everything," she said, like a continuation of his thoughts. But her finely curved lips formed the one word he could not. "Family," she said. The word blinded him, but she moved in the darkness where he could not. Her lips touched his and the last fraction of separation broke, the last thread of control that kept him from her. The smooth heat of her mouth gave to him, opened under the desperate ill-controlled pressure of his, drew him in. She must have sensed the wildness inside, the old rage and the locked-down blackness. She must have known that he fought it. Yet the soft fragile curve of her lips followed his in the same mad need.

He tempered the strength.

She moved with him and her heat filled his hands.

She wore nothing under the heavy cloak except her thin shift. The fine supple curves he had seen, touched, known the warmth of, were open to the urging of his hands, his mouth.

He knew how she responded, the smoothness of the flesh beneath the linen, the sounds she made when he touched her, the scent of her skin, the measure of her desire and the slick scorching heat.

Her neck arched and he sought her skin, mouth and tongue taking the unique taste of her, heat and desire, the shuddering flame of arousal. The need. The reaction of his own body was instant, full, driven with a hunger that was complete. Need he could not contemplate. Or give in to.

The slender lines of her pressed against him, against the barbaric hunger of his mouth, the weight of his body, the blood-hardened outthrust of his flesh, the unslaked need.

He softened his touch, but she followed, pressing closer. The heat of her thighs opened, moulding round his. The thinness of her shift was no barrier to his hand. When he touched her skin, it scorched him, burned hotter and hotter under the fast path of his fingers until he touched her intimately. It was relentlessly swift, unsparing as his own feelings. Yet she was already moist, her flesh softened, the dampened folds heated and sleek against his fingers.

He touched her and she gasped, tightened in his hold. For a moment she held still, a fraction of time without breath or sound or form and then she pressed down on his hand.

Heat surged through him, the knowledge of her desire like a fire-flood, his own need complete, a force beyond bearing. The heat and the closeness and the life of her were what he craved more than breathing.

She writhed under his touch, the movement uncontrolled, frantic and desperate against the smooth glide of his fingers.

Unskilled.

She could not defend herself against him. He could take his fulfilment now on the open ground beside the water, in the black night shadows, not only in last night's way, but completely. She would not draw back from it and he did not know whether he would stop. He did not know.

He heard the check in her breath. Need. Desire.

Or the bitter desperateness that branded his own soul.

She made a helpless sound. She had no defence, no experience and no concept of what he was.

He drew back.

She tried to hold him, as though she could not surface out of the net of desire, as though the need were something beyond the moment and the physical desire and the vulnerability of her mood, that vulnerability mixed with the headstrong courage that was her doom.

But he knew what the truth was. He had nothing that could requite what a woman like her wanted or deserved.

He broke her hold.

Her gaze caught his, wide, dazed. It was the vulnerability that set his decision.

He stepped back.

She stared at him, shocked.

"Why…" Her voice choked. He watched her finely held strength conquer it. She raised her head, much as she did when she had some brutally dangerous sword in her hand. She spoke clearly, "Why did you let me go?"

Why. He cut down on the madness. "Because I—" He stopped. His madness was not her burden. "There is nothing I can give you."

"Nothing? Nothing but—" she kept her head straight "—lust?"

Her hand pushed the fine mass of her hair out of her face. The moonlight caught the ring on her finger, the twisted shape of the golden boar, the possession of an East Anglian princess. It was part of the true barrier, the gulf that was real.

Her fingers were not steady.

He fought the urge to catch her hand, to touch her again. The damage was done. The mistake was deep, bitter. He would not compound it.

"There is nothing that has a future."

She stared at him.

"Yet you did want me, even though you believe there is no future. You still wanted me enough to…"

The answer was in his eyes, in every ferally tightened line of his body. She must read it. She must have felt it through her skin. The wide gaze held him, the question still there and with it the look she had tried to suppress that first night before Hunferth, her high pride caught on the edge of humiliation.

It was not her fault. None of this was.

He said the truth.

"I have told you there is no future that I can see. If what you are asking is whether I still wanted you enough in this moment to take your maidenhead from you out here on the cold ground, under the sky, the answer is yes."

Something flickered in her gaze, a dark expression too fast to read. He finished it.

"That is all that I am."

The dark expression surfaced again. He realized what it was. Acknowledgement.

She walked away.

13

"WHAT IS GOING TO HAPPEN?" Mildred's hands clutched the side of the boat.

"I do not know," said Judith. They had been placed back on board the iron-bearded warship like any other part of the ship's stores.

The sea beneath them was pure, ruffled by a fair wind, and the sleek low-sided ship was fast, smoothly and expertly handled. But there was something in the air this day that had changed, a suppressed force that trickled over the skin and made the spine tingle. The kind of force that Judith had recognised in Einhard yesterday.

Anticipation.

Mildred's knuckles were white.

"Nothing bad will happen," lied Judith. She glanced at Einhard, the lethal shape of his body, the force that crackled round him like fire. She looked away. The sea hissed under the moving deck. The wind caught her hair, light, full of summer's brightness. The boat flew. But there was no joy this time.

"It will be all right. You will see. It is only—"

"Do you know where we are?" Mildred's question cut across the meaningless flow of her words. She caught her breath.

"No. At least, more or less, but not exactly. I never sailed this part of the coast. Why?"

"They do not know, either. At least, maybe they know, but they cannot make up their minds."

"What?"

"They are talking about it."

Judith glanced at the small knot of men gathered round the tall figure of their captain. She listened to their voices, low, rising as someone made a particular point, interrupting each other, jumbled, except when Einhard spoke. The words were incomprehensible.

"How," inquired Judith with great care, "do you know?"

"I can, well, I can…"

"What?" Judith looked at her maid as though she might dissolve and reveal some uncanny spirit like a wood-wose.

"I can more or less speak Frisian," said Mildred in a rush. "At least, not so much. I mean it is years since I heard— But it is quite similar to English. What is the matter? Are you not well?"

"Perfectly well."

"Oh. You see, my nursemaid was Frisian. Some woman abandoned by a husband who never came back from the sea for her and left her desperate. She never got over it, poor thing, but what I mean is…"

Left her desperate. The sunlight glinted over the moving fall of Einhard's hair, the heavy turn of his shoulder.

"What are they saying?"

"If we go too far north we could miss him...something or other...slip out to sea while we are stuck down the river and lose him entirely or be trapped," gabbled Mildred.

"I—"

"They do not like the south, either."

"I—"

"There are three rivers, you see."

"Saint Athelbert's bones."

"Einhard is going to choose."

The burial mounds on the River Deben. Flame. Light.

They must be near there. Three rivers leading inland from the sea, lying in close proximity, the Orwell, the Alde—and the Deben. Macsen's face, the unfocused gaze, the eyes that saw something else, into another world.

"It is quite difficult for Einhard," said Mildred. "You see, he has nothing to guide the choice he has to take. Are they by any chance looking for someone?"

"Yes."

"Do you know who?"

Earl Guthrum and the rest of his red-sailed fleet, the sea-force that will gather and tear Wessex to pieces if it can. Skar, the unknown Viking.

Her lungs tightened. It was not Macsen's otherwordly certainty she saw, but Tatwin, asking questions, bitter.

You would not bind yourself to Guthrum....

"Judith?"

"I do not know who. Not for sure."

I will do whatever it takes.

She watched Einhard make a particularly forceful point. She

stepped closer to the group of men. She could not distinguish their faces. She could only see one. He raised his head. She could not look at his eyes. Only at his hand lying on the sail rope, his fingers curved round the twisted fibers. So strong. Ruthless.

At some point they all stopped talking.

"Lady?" It was the captain's voice that broke the silence.

Einhard.

She stared at the solid, well-shaped flesh that had called magic out of her body, touched her with what some desperate, bewildered part of her had called love, but had been something else entirely. Nothing except lust. He had told her so and that had not stopped her from wanting him. She must be the *hor-cwen* he thought her, that Hunferth had thought her.

Can you not think past for-licgan?

The perilous decision pressed on her, fatal, worthy of impartial judgement, not the drives of need, of wanting.

She still wanted him. Even now.

"Judith?" She flinched at the use of her name. He moved in the sunlight, at the edge of her vision, smoothly, perfectly balanced on the pitching ship.

"What is it?" The deep voice was sharp, the intent in it relentless.

He was such a dangerous man.

She looked up.

"I know this part of the coast well." It took a strong spirit to lie, especially to someone like him. "I recognised where we are." She did not glance at Mildred, who spoke Frisian. "Farther along are the rivers. Will you follow one? I might be of assistance."

"How?" There was a fractional pause. "Why?"

She was aware that Mildred had come up behind her, as though she thought Einhard might strike. But he had never harmed her. He had not even taken all that the madness in her blood had made her offer.

"Judith?"

He had never harmed her. She tried not to shift under the full, remorseless focus of his attention. She tried to set her mind solely on the decision.

"The correct choice might depend on what you seek."

She held his gaze, attempted to read it, to see past the barrier of his will to all the things she had once believed lived in his eyes, in his mind. She tried to choose her words well.

"The southernmost river will take you to the trading town of Ipswich, the northern as far as Snape." She watched the changes in his eyes. "The middle course leads past the royal palace at Rendlesham." *Light,* Macsen had said. *Light.* "And the *hlæw,* the burial mounds at Sutton Hoo."

She could feel the anticipation in the air turn molten. Like the heat in his eyes. Flame.

A flame burned true, pure.

It could also destroy.

Her hands clenched into fists. If he sought Guthrum and not the yellow-and-black sails, it would be difficult to stop him whatever she said. If that was his will, to change from the service he had already given Wessex to aid her enemy, then the damage would be great. What she did now might only hasten it. The consequences would be murderous. Earl Guthrum would welcome him, pay him as Hunferth had said. Einhard would gain, and perhaps that was what he needed to further his own purpose, the purpose she did not know.

Things are different. The words of God's thane echoed in her head. The group of men shifted uneasily. Mildred caught at her sleeve. What she was most aware of, was Einhard's eyes.

"If I were looking for a place to anchor my ships, to wait." She tried out the words. "If I were seeking to find someone else." His gaze locked with hers. She took a breath.

"I would choose the middle river, the Deben."

THE NARROW MOUTH OF THE waterway lay ahead, the middle river. It was too dangerous to follow its course now, in the gathering dusk, before it was known what, or who, was there.

They anchored in a sheltered inlet and made camp. The weight of the decision Judith had made, the appalling possibilities, wracked her. In the blinding light of the sun reflected off the sea, with the impetus of the speeding boat beneath her feet and the sense of something unknown, waiting, it had seemed right.

It had seemed right under the greater and more dazzling influence of Einhard.

Now it seemed merely insane, criminally and recklessly foolish.

She made sure everyone was sitting, absorbed in either eating or talking, before she got up and walked away. They permitted her a few minutes on her own.

She could not sit still.

Athelbert's bones. How could she possibly explain this to Alfred and his *witan?* If there was a king and a council left after Guthrum unleashed his fleet.

If she ever got back alive from this.

She was not sure she wanted to.

"Athelbert's bones." Then she added something that would have curdled Mildred's blood.

The composition of the shadows changed. There was no sound, only the awareness tingling over her skin. She did not turn round.

"Why are you here?" The question that encompassed everything burst out of her. Her voice cracked like a whiplash.

"I came to find you." It was blank as a wall, the answer kept ruthlessly in the present moment, as though that were all that could exist. It was certainly all that the two of them could have. Their only connection was a series of moments shimmering beyond reach. She had made deliberate use of that sense of time suspended last night, in an attempt to deepen a connection that was ephemeral. She had tried to turn it into something else, something it could never be.

The bitterness broke, snapping a temper already lashed by guilt and fear over the unforgivable risk she had taken.

"Why would you come to find me? Will you drag me back to the camp like the troublesome prisoner I am? What did you think I would do, run off on my own into the night?"

The black bulk of his shape blocked her path.

"You said you still have kin here. It is not so far to Woodbridge, or even to Rendlesham. The king's hall was at Rendlesham."

She looked away. *Was.* She stared out at the dim shapes of the land, the black water. She was on familiar ground now. It unrolled all around her, the contours of the land, the tidal river hidden from sight to the north, the winding paths of the water and the lofty, richly decorated walls of King Edmund's palace on the eastern shore.

All forever changed. And she might have helped to hasten the same wind of destruction on Wessex.

"I will not leave," she said, "until this…this *quest* is over, one way or another." She turned her head. "Victory or defeat. Success or failure." The night breeze caught her head-veil. "Which is it, Frisian?"

"Success." The same breath of wind rippled the edge of the dark cloak that hid the solid mass of his figure. "There is no other possibility."

But she had seen too much to accept that. She could see what might happen. Her fault.

"There are always other possibilities. Right down to death."

"Then it will be death." He never moved. The single-mindedness was complete. Chills flicked over her skin.

"You mean that you would give your life, all that you are, to this quest? This blood feud?"

"Yes."

She knew it happened. She knew the power of feuding could feed on itself for generations if it was not checked. But she could not accept the rightness of this, of what he did. It seemed a negation of all the life that was in him, the person he was, the way, sometimes, he gave.

It was so bitter, so utterly desolate.

"Can you be so determined on the course you follow now? Is that really your will?"

He did not so much as attempt to answer. The whole of this

course of action was by his will. It was always possible, in some way or another, to compound a feud, to end it if you wished.

"You will not change." It was as though the scales of self-deceit, of fond imaginings, dropped from her eyes. The black figure did not move, did not change. It was only she who had been so blinded by her own conceit, her own wish to shape the world as she wished it to be, that she had created an illusion. What she saw now was the truth, a man who would pursue his own will to the exclusion of all else and was therefore unreachable. There was no connection, no common ground. Nothing.

"I have been such a fool."

"Judith——" He made some move towards her, but she pulled back. She would not touch him. She could never touch him as she had last night, not with the weight of her own guilt and her own blind arrogance round her neck. Round his.

"What is it that you are going to do? Who do you expect to find along the river? Guthrum? Is the Viking earl part of your plan of vengeance? You need not fear to tell me. There is so very little I could do about it. I have been stupid, have I not? You must have laughed at what I said, at what I... What I wanted to do. I have achieved nothing. I have merely led you here, straight to your goal." Her voice cracked on laughter, wild, slightly insane laughter. "I had such pathetic belief. I thought I could make a difference to what happened. I thought I would do something wonderful to save Wessex from the fate that has overtaken this land. And now I have hastened the same destruction." She stopped because her voice was hysterical.

She turned away. The darkness took her; the familiar shapes and sounds and scents of her home closed round her, fresh leaves

and the breath of the east wind and the tang of the water. All
the beauty that had surrounded her since childhood.

"Judith!"

It was him, in his single-mindedness and his ruthlessness.

She plunged down the slope, into the heart of East Anglia.
But she could not see its familiar shapes, its beauty. Her eyes
saw the Danish army spreading out for what seemed like miles,
shouting out its victory, endless, not to be defeated. Not by
someone like her.

It will be death. She had brought it here herself.

She began to run.

She knew he came after her. He no longer shouted but she could
hear the fast tireless beat of his feet, sure, skillful over the black
uneven ground. Her heart tightened. The madness gripped her.
She hardly knew why she ran, what or where she hoped to gain.

She ran from him.

From the unbearable pressure of her own thoughts.

She could hear him closer, ever closer. Gaining. She could
not allow it.

She ran on until her breath stung and her body ached and her
mind became blank because she could not bear what was in it.
She ran until the running itself became the purpose, as though
by it she could outstrip her thoughts, everything.

Such things were not possible.

He caught her.

She felt the sudden hard grip of his arms, the blank harshness
of his body. She twisted, training working with instinct. But he
knew the same tricks she did. She went down, hard, cushioned
by the solid rolling mass of his body beneath her. There was no

room for mercy, no time. He had made the move, forced it. Their combined weight slammed into the ground. The fast impact hurt him. It made no difference. He held her, the grip of hand and arm and solid leg hard, as though he thought she would fight.

She felt his breathing, as quick and forced as hers, sensed the harsh readjustment to pain, the determination that covered it. As it covered everything.

She should still struggle. But the madness, the urge to flee what could not be escaped, were gone.

She was not harmed. She tried get enough air into her lungs to speak.

"I will not—" Her voice failed. He still held her. She tried to breathe. The ache in her lungs burned. Eventually, it got better. "Let me go."

She became aware of the way their bodies were entwined. Her back lay against the solid wall of his chest, pulled against him by the unbreakable band of his arm. She could feel the push of his rib cage beneath her as he fought for breath, the denseness of his flesh under the tunic. Her hips were pressed into him, her legs caught under the sleek powerful weight of his thigh, trapping her against him, against his heat and his strength and his fineness.

"Let me go." Every word, every breath, resonated through the closeness of his body.

There was a tense space of nothing. Just the awareness of him, of the intimate way he held her.

"You must release me." She swallowed. "I—" What was the point of pretence? She would not run, not now that she had come to her senses. To flee from the bitterness of what she had done would be cowardly. It would mean abandoning Mildred. "I will not run."

Nothing. Just the harsh sound of his breath and the feel of the tension in each thickened muscle.

"Do you believe me?"

"Yes."

"Then——" Then what? He just held her against the solid warmth of his body, while her breathing returned to normal and the burning ache drained out of her limbs, leaving them heavy and exhausted. Cushioned on warmth. On such closeness. She could have cried with it.

"It was my fault." The truth was there, unavoidable. She faced it. "I thought, I believed things which were wrong."

She looked at the darkened arch of the horizon, the brightening stars, the familiar shape of the land. Lost.

"You are going to go to Earl Guthrum." It was a relief, finally, to say the words, even though they damned her with the guilt of her own folly. "I should have known from the beginning. You did not hide it. It was only that I thought— Oh, that things were possible." *Stupid things.*

Her hand rested on a patch of skin, only lightly touched by the sweat of exertion, hot, so powerful.

She forced the words out.

"It is you who were right, not me. You told me that I was fighting for a lost cause, that it would ultimately fail. You never...never deceived yourself with visions like I did. You said you would follow your own course, take what you wanted. You will go to Earl Guthrum, and that, perhaps, will lead you to the next step in the feud, the blood feud with this other Viking, the one called Skar. That is the truth, is it not?"

THERE WAS THE CHOICE. Einhard could tell her or not.

The resistance to speaking of what had happened, at first instinctive, had been toughened over bitter time until it was stone hard. He sought words.

"I have no intention of aiding Earl Guthrum in what he is planning." His voice cut the night black. He did not say he would not seek the Viking Guthrum if he had to. That assurance did not exist.

He felt the shudder that ran through her, unsuppressible, like an acceptance of what he said, though he had never given her any reason to trust his word. Her smooth weight moved against his body, against the breath that still came too fast. He was achingly aware of her rich curves, the closeness of the way he held her, of his own reaction.

He loosened his grip. Her slight body turned in his grasp, the small strong muscles tense as a wild cat who wanted to spring. He expected her to move. She had the assurance she needed. She was free of him as she wanted. She—

"Then what do you intend?" Her voice was careful, almost even. "To find this other Viking, the one called Skar? To further the blood feud?"

"Yes."

Her hand was fisted in the neck of his tunic. She did not seem to know that he had let her go.

She stayed, in the sham of closeness.

But he had let her go, even in the moment when she had saved his life. Before he had even met her.

He moved, gaining his feet, taking her with him. The jolt of pain through the infuriating weakness in his arm made him stumble. She caught at him.

"What is it?"

"Naught."

The unguarded movement he had not been able to avoid, the undeserved pity in her voice stung at the volatile mass of feeling tapped inside him.

"But——" she began. He cut off her words.

"It is nothing. Let it go." When she did not release him, he pulled free of her touch, suppressed the pain. There was no time for the lingering weakness caused by the assassin's knife, exacerbated by the battle. Later. After tomorrow.

"We must get back to the camp."

He thought everything was controlled, hidden. He had so much practice. But she stayed still, staring at him.

"We must get back. Come." It was beyond the disaster in his head to make it appear a request rather than an order. She glared at him, standing straight, her pride like fire. But he had already turned.

"Why?" Her voice followed him. "So you can make your plans for tomorrow's move, for the next step in the feud? Is it so important to you, planning your way to this death you have spoken of?"

"It was not I who chose the stakes."

The rustle of her footsteps sounded behind him.

"But it is your choice to accept them."

Choice. The dark foreign landscape vanished and he was back under the wide cloudy skies of Dorestad, stepping ashore at the river port, at the head of four ships and the cargo that replaced the wealth that had been lost. Enough to secure the future, not just his, but for everyone who depended on him.

The future.

And then they had taken him and shown him, the bloodied corpse, one among six, with so many wounds, past counting. Because there had not been a fight, only a massacre. Not something it was possible to stand against.

"What choice?"

"It is always possible to compound a feud, to arrange compensation, an honour payment, not murder." Her footsteps quickened to the same angry speed as his. Her voice held the same blank, frustrated edge as Tatwin's. "How can you pursue that kind of death?"

She caught up with him.

"You are not cold-blooded. You do not choose destruction for the sake of it. I have seen. You saved my life in battle. You have done so much work at Derne. You see things. You understand how much loss hurts. You gave me understanding that no one else has, so much that—"

"No."

He could not stand that. She did not know. Either the reality of what had happened or the reality of what was inside him. He stopped walking and turned round.

"The one thing I will never do is ask for peace."

"But you could—"

"What? Offer terms? Make the sacrifice?" The words, held back for so long, beat at his lips. "Such a sacrifice has already been made. Do you know how it is done? You send out messengers first. Through them you arrange and receive a promise of safe conduct, someone's oath. You agree on a meeting place. You go there with the number of men you have agreed. Because you have the promise of safe conduct and witnesses, you leave your weapons and your armour aside. You step from the bright daylight into the hall, half dark, blinding you. Then you…"

In his mind, he saw the corpse, the others surrounding it, the dead bodies of all who had gone to make peace, how they had been cut down without the means of defence. Cold, mutilated flesh. He stopped the spate of words, all the unfitting details she did not need to know.

"Such a sacrifice brings no guarantee of peace," he said. He thought of Skar and his men and the blood that must have mired them. "It will end only in betrayal and death. I will not walk openhanded into another man's power, to be slaughtered like—"

She stared at him. "Like what? Like *who?* Like…like someone who was close to you?" The anger in her voice faded; behind it was a growing horror.

He was past the point of dissembling. He said it. "It was my father and six of his men and then my—" But his voice gave out. That other was not a death. He would not accept it. If it was so, he did not know how he would survive it, even if his pursuit of Skar left him untouched.

Her eyes fixed on his face. "You will kill the man responsible, this Viking called Skar."

It was not a question. Her horror was clear. He turned away.

THAT WAS HER ANSWER, complete. Judith's heart thudded out of time. It was the truth, only bloodier in detail, more transfused with horror than she had expected. That was the explanation she had sought.

She struggled to take in the implications. That Guthrum was not his goal had left her weak with relief. But for the rest—

Einhard swung away from her, no sign of the physical cost of the chase, the crushing fall. No sign of the emotional cost of what he had said.

She watched the solid back. Earl Guthrum was not his *first* goal. What he wanted was the other Viking, Skar. He had every reason to seek a death payment and he was going to take it. She had seen the preparations for the morrow. They had been thorough, as ruthlessly complete as anything he did. She had not fully understood either the planning involved or its import. Now she did.

She watched the harshly controlled force of his movement, a man with a need to take vengeance, a man with the physical strength and the implacable will to do it, an age-old truism. There was her answer.

The cloak swirled. She saw his shoulders flex.

He had spoken of his father and she had seen the grief and the anger, but there was something else.

She stepped forward, far too fast for thought. Family failing: leap in first and think later.

"What happened to your wife?"

He stopped.

She waited. The deadly, catastrophic question was gone from her lips and the selfish, insecure, life-damaged part of her already wanted to bury the words. His head moved. She did not even want him to turn round. She was so cowardly she did not want to see what might be in his eyes.

But there was something, some other terrible hurt as yet uncovered.

"Was she killed, as your father was? Was she part of this feud? Did she—"

"She was not part of this."

He turned round. His eyes held the pain her question must have called forth. But it was different from the bitter fire that drove him now. It was something older, tempered because he had to accept it.

Whatever drove him now, he would not accept.

"She was not involved in this feuding. She died nearly eight winters ago, soon after—" He stopped speaking.

The darkness of full night was nothing to the blackness in his eyes and through that blank dark smouldered the restless glitter of flame. She felt the touch of fear, the way she had the first night she had hidden in his chamber and inadvertently trodden on demons.

This was not inadvertent.

She tried to think out the next step, to let her mind catch up with the recklessness of what she had started. If what he was engaged in now had not encompassed the breaking of a bond as strong as that of man and wife, then what?

If she had a clue…any information about him. But she knew so little and there was nothing he would say. What did he seek?

Death.

It was obvious in the strength and the single-mindedness of him.

If only Tatwin could have broken his duty of silence and told her. Tatwin said he had believed it was redemption.

Redemption or destruction.

Redemption meant life. Surely it might encompass something

or someone still living, redeemable, recoverable, lost. *If I were seeking to find someone else* and the way his eyes had looked when she had made her insane decision to lead him here to the edge of the Deben…

What else was as strong as the bond to a wife?

"It is a child."

14

JUDITH HAD BLURTED OUT the words before the thought was half formed. Einhard's eyes blanked off. He did not move.

"You are looking for a child," she said.

His stillness was appalling. The terrifying blankness in his eyes could have been complete. He might have been dead inside.

But she had seen too much, intimate and unguarded things, things he wanted to keep hidden. The black wall was there because what was underneath was too bitter, too intense to be let out. The fear inside her changed. She had the sense of saying something to him that was so infinitely cruel, so filled with pain that it could not be contained within this world.

"Your child."

She did not dare to touch him, not even to take one step nearer to him the way she had done when she had waited in his chamber the first night, when she had seen the despair that should never have had a witness.

She did not know what to do, how an impulsive self-absorbed

idiot like her could possibly help. She was miles out of her depth. She watched the strong figure with its terrible, limitless determination and thought her heart split.

She had understood less than nothing. She had not even had the ability to guess what had driven him. She had been so obsessed with her purpose that she had thought only of that. She had believed a foreign trader would sell his sword and his ships to Earl Guthrum because he would pick what seemed the stronger side in the forthcoming struggle. For his own ends, for a blood feud that had seemed—

"Einhard." She moved, and then wished she had not. The tension stung the air. She kept very still, terrified that he would turn from her and she would not be able to follow or to say what was right.

"Will you not tell me?"

"There is nothing to say."

The blankness seemed impenetrable, a welling of strength intended to repel. He would not speak of it. If there was one thing her fractured life had taught her to understand, it was that. She had never spoken to anyone of the effect the disaster at Hoxne had had on her. She had not even been able to talk to Berg. The shell she had created around her feelings had only thickened with time until it had become so strong she had not even been able to find words for a message to her own brother when she faced death.

The only person she had talked to was Einhard. The return she had received had been understanding.

She did not make the obvious mistake of moving again. She was blocking the only path through the tangled growth of the wood. Not that that would stop him, but it was something, a small boost to her courage. It was like facing a battle, one that was not physical. The first move was to begin circling your opponent. She broke the silence.

"The man who pursues the feud, the Viking called Skar, has taken…" Next step. "He has taken the child." *Boy or maid? How old?*

"When?" She did not dare press too far yet. She kept to the defensive circle, to practicalities, to the surface above the appalling mess, to things a dangerous opponent could, might, answer. "Was it when your father tried to make peace and was killed? Was the child taken then?"

"He disappeared."

A boy, then. "Did you…" She lurched back from the terrible false step. She could not bring up the possibility that his son might be dead like his father. The man would be tortured with the thought. "Were you…" There was no question that did not impinge further into the morass of a hurt she could not imagine.

If it is no longer possible to retreat, attack. He was a bitter fighter. She thought he would find directness easier to deal with.

"Were you there?"

"No."

"Then—" But she broke off, the horror defeating her, cutting her heart, not from a false step in her strategy, but from success. Athelbert's bones. He would not forgive himself for that. Never. "You…" She was lost in someone else's pain. Einhard's.

But there was no one else to ask him. "Were you at sea?"

"Aye. Trading."

You think you are a great merchant, a trader. You have nothing.... Her own voice rose out of memory, her own fine words, so scornful and accusing.

"It happened just before I came back. They took me to see the corpses. They were still unburied. There was no sign of the boy."

"Because Skar had taken him."

"After the killing at the meeting place Skar came back to my home and burned it. No one found my son."

Holy mother. She pushed the thought of death aside, as though he might be able to read it inside her head. He could not deal with that. The only certainty he would accept would come when he found Skar. Whatever happened would have to be dealt with then, not now.

"So you pursued Skar."

"It was a cold trail. Ships can move fast and already there was no trace. I cast around, keeping a base at Dorestad at first, because I could not afford to waste time by moving too far on the wrong trail. Then I thought I had found some information. When I was far enough out to sea, Rorik's ships closed on me."

"For piracy..."

"To exact justice. I had stolen a cargo from Skar's brother and had damaged or sunk his ships and killed most of the crews."

She knew that part of the tale; it was what everyone said. Everyone thought——

"What had you done to offend Rorik? To make him resort to that kind of trickery?"

He made a slight movement, as though he had expected her

to believe the story of piracy to be true, as everyone else did. She had, once. He probably knew that. She watched him.

"I offend Rorik by being Frisian. My kindred is, was, an important force in a valuable merchant city. Nine years ago, Rorik was expelled, and for a while Dorestad was Frisian again. My father was a leading force in that rebellion. When, after a year of freedom, Rorik was able to reestablish his rule, he made a public settlement of peace with those who had rebelled against him."

"But his private thoughts..." Her mind raced. Vengeance. A man with a long memory, an insecure ruler constrained in public, but in secret... "How did the feud start?"

"In small matters that over years became piracy and murder." The burning intelligent eyes met hers and she knew she had guessed right. "Rorik has a taste for intrigue." The lightly accented voice went on. "He also has riches. Skar has, or had, little in the way of wealth except his own skill and his ambition. It is often possible to manipulate a man like that."

Ambition. It had all come about because of ambition and malice. Probably fear. Skar must be hunted by need and Rorik was an insecure ruler who wanted revenge.

And the child was caught up in it. Perhaps dead. She would not speak of that final possibility.

"You say the child, your child, vanished and that—"

"You think he is dead."

The words shocked her, made her breath catch on a savage pain. He had given voice to the nightmare. She had not intended to call that bale out, not when she could sense the crucifying vulnerability that lay just behind the harsh wall of his will.

But it had been in her thoughts and he had known; it was as though he could see inside her head.

The stock words of reassurance rose to her lips, the trite flow of expressions intended to placate, false, without meaning.

It was impossible to say such things to him.

He would see if she was lying. That bright implacable intelligence would know.

Her tongue cleaved to the dryness of her mouth. She tried to force words, any words. Sound.

"I—" Her voice faltered exactly where it should have been strong. She was so far out of her depth, inadequate, struggling with something fundamental that made her heart bleed and yet which she had never experienced. It was worse than a battle. In battle, the question had been only of her own self.

She took a breath. She wanted to be strong in this moment for him. That was what counted. Him. Everything became acutely clear.

"I do not know whether the boy is alive. I cannot know. You will have to guide me in this." Her voice came out so strongly, as though it belonged to another person, someone with faith. "You believe that he lives. That is what matters. It is the only thing that matters. Your belief is enough for me."

She had not meant to say the words that would break the wall of resistance that sustained his will. She no longer wanted to break it. She had thought to help him, but it was too brutally felt. She saw the damage, followed immediately by the uprush of that strong will.

She did not want to take from him, only to offer acceptance, the kind of gift he had given her.

She watched the struggle, unable to move, afraid to touch him.

Acceptance.

She could hear the voices of the past, the reactions to her own loss from people who had not experienced it. People dismissed it because it was impossible to remedy, even the people who wanted to help.

You cannot look back to what is lost. You must put it behind you and go on....

"They have told you he is dead, your son, have they not? They have told you to believe it, to forget, to look forward. They tell you for your own good."

People had said all of those things to her about a defeated land. Quite probably they were right and it was for her own good. But all she knew was that you had to live through what was in your mind first. Only then could you look forward.

Heaven's mercy. She moved. She touched him, still not knowing how he would react, whether he would even want her touch. Her arm slid round the black dangerous shape, the tense muscle.

"You will not forget him."

Her touch was clumsy, awkward, hopelessly inadequate to communicate all that burned against her heart. She had no way to express that, either by word or gesture. But then it did not matter. The harsh wall of muscle moved.

She felt his warmth, the fluid unraveling of his strength, meeting her touch, surrounding her, and the bond was there, like a miracle, like something that could survive. She could not think of that. Neither of them could. There was only the shared warmth, and behind it the unspoken bond. A bond that found its expression in a world beyond words, a world of silence, need, touching. A bond that held and encompassed all the intense unspeakable feelings, that could release them. He had shown her the existence of that spellbound path out of pity and need and the bright dangerous edge of desire.

She led him down it.

Her lips took his and felt the taste of pain and bitterness, hunger and desire. The bright merciless heat of his mouth.

Yet this was different. Every touch was new. What she had seen before had only been a bright-edged shadow, a green untried girl's glimpse of something adult.

This was deeper. She had not realised, that first time, how much had been hidden from her. For her sake. Now, the touch of his hand on her flesh, the glide of his body against hers, the fine heat of his mouth were different. Infinitely and deeply real. Wanted. To a depth she had not known existed in her.

It was the way a man touched a woman.

Her mouth firmed on his. She moved against him, heard the catch in his breath, felt it against her lips. She pushed into him with every defenceless line of her body, driven with the need, his and hers. Open to his closeness, to the raw need expressed through desire because nothing else was possible. She took the desperate, wordless fire and she gave, to the fierce caress of his fingers, the warm blissful pressure of his lips, the hot demand of his mouth and the deep invasion of his tongue.

She held him close, closer. Her hands moved round, moulding his body beneath the cloak, seeking the warmth of heavy muscle, embracing his strength, caressing the wide plane of his back, the solid flesh, feeling the deep muscle tense and flex under her touch. Her breath caught with the intimate feel of him, alien and close. It was the closeness she wanted. There was no price she would not pay. Nothing she would hold back.

Her hand moved lower, down across closely packed muscle, her fingers widening, taking in the unexplored power of his flesh. Her palm opened to curve round the taut dense globes of his buttocks, the movement uninhibited. She felt the reaction, sharp and heated, so primitive that her blood raced with a surge of feeling intense and physical, deep enough to engulf her, bind her in thrall forever. But she only pressed closer, bringing her hips against his, feeling the tightened hardness of him.

Her blood leaped and her mind filled with burning memories, the sight of him, the full shape of male flesh, the heat of his arousal, the touch of smooth skin. The surge of longing was unbearably intense.

Her arms closed, bringing him in tighter, her fingers digging into the smooth springing flesh beneath her hands, the taut masculine curve. His hips ground against hers and the need inside her jumped, flamed. She made a faint sound. Need that was the match of his. He heard it, moved, bearing her down with his weight. She followed. There seemed no barrier. She let the smooth flow of his strength take her and they stayed, cushioned by the cloaks on the mossy ground, close, locked in the hunger of touching, a hunger that was fathomless.

He loosened her dress, found her skin and her body moved for him, boneless. The night air slid over her bared flesh but the outside world had no power against their own world, the spellbound path. She was naked only if he watched her. Her flesh warmed only when he touched her. Her senses kindled, knowing the burning ache of sex only when he woke them to life. She followed his touch, opened under it, more than that, she incited it.

Her body moved, arching towards the hands at her breasts. Her senses swam. Her hunger grew with his, burned. When he took one tight aching peak in his mouth, her fingers moved like a dreamer's, tangling in his hair and drawing his head to her. She pressed towards him, feeling the flick of his tongue. Her fingers caressed the heated lines of his face, traced the small erotic movement as his mouth settled over her, moving, drawing pleasure from her that seemed inexhaustible, laced with fire. Magic.

Deep desire lapped at her consciousness, blossoming under his skilled touch, fed by the raw need underneath. The wanting caught flame and she writhed, the longing a thing past bearing.

His mouth broke the contact for an instant that made her moan. Then his lips brushed her skin, moved lower. He slid down her body. His thighs parted hers, opening her to him. She gasped. He paused at the ungoverned sound of her voice, eyes dark, filled with all the relentless power that drove them both, shared need.

"Touch me." Her voice shivered. Her hands threaded through the bright fall of his hair, sought the heavy width of his shoulders, the warm curve of his neck.

Love me.

She did not dare say that. It had no place in a moment that

was stolen out of time. If it could ever have a place, it was not now. What he wanted was to find his son again. He had a life separated from hers, played out in a world she had not guessed at, a bitter and deadly world. She would not ask for a return he could not give. No more burdens.

There was only what she could give.

Her fingers slid down the supple length of his arm, closed over the solid flesh of his hand. Their hands joined. The heavy fingers parted hers, slid between them, the movement subtly invasive, sensually charged. She was so intensely aware of the intimacy of their position, the weight of him over her, the hot solid feel of his body between her legs. The disarray of her skirts bunched around her thighs.

He moved his hand. The anticipation, the dark urge of desire, stole her breath.

He touched her. Her body jerked in reaction. She heard the harsh sound of his breath, fast in his throat. His gaze locked with hers. Her woman's flesh scorched under his touch, hot and soft against the familiar glide of his fingers.

He parted the folds and slid inside her. She gasped, the sudden ache of hunger so sharp. He watched her eyes, his face shadowed. She saw the limitless measure of her own hunger reflected. His fingers moved rhythmically, withdrew, found the hidden source of her pleasure. He watched her face as she shuddered under his touch. He saw the need she could not hide, the desire his touching brought. The wanting of him. The love. Surely he would see that, even if she could not say it.

But his eyes were dark, filled with a thousand things she could not read. The darkness tore at her heart.

She touched him, her hands digging into his arms, his shoulders. But he moved. He lowered his head, sliding down between her parted thighs. She gasped, her body shuddering on the pitch of desire. She felt the brush of his lips on the thin vulnerable skin of her inner thigh. She tensed. He stilled, but she was caught in the wave of need, in the desire he had created, the headlong path. Even the newness lured her, the sensual promise. But more than that, she would take any step for him to let him see how much she wanted him, without reserve.

She shivered, moving closer, relaxing into the strength of his hold. She arched towards him and his hands slid round framing her hips, holding her still for a breathless instant that was rife with anticipation, latent with uncurbed sexual desire.

He took her in his mouth.

She cried out with the shock of it, with the unrestrained, intensely erotic touch of his lips and his tongue, with the sudden, blinding burst of sensual pleasure.

Her body jerked but he held her, his hands cradling her hips, moving under her to cup her rounded flesh while he fed on her, the kneading pressure of his hands beneath her hips intensifying the sharp rush of feeling. The intense, frantic feeling dived high, the need, the intoxicating madness peaked, and then shattered against the intimate pleasuring of his mouth.

JUDITH WAS THE ONLY THING that existed in the world. Einhard cradled the smooth voluptuous body shivering in the aftermath of frenzied desire. She touched him. Her fingers dug into his flesh though his clothing, the sting welcomed, the small violence of her grip bringing a satisfaction so deep, so primitive, no thoughts matched it. Her response belonged to him. It was like a miracle whose shape he could not contemplate because he had lived in the darkness of hell for too long.

Einhard's arms closed round her. He shifted position so that she lay on top of him. Her light body adjusted to lie close against him, as though she belonged where she could not. He was aware that his breath eased. She stayed. She was the only point of warmth in the dark.

He had schooled himself into the kind of stillness that would govern the black morass inside him, the sharp hunger. But she moved. Even as the tremors still coursed through her body, she sought his mouth. The sensation of her lips teased at senses laid raw, the smooth fullness of her softened by the way he had already touched her. He was still beyond thought, need-driven. His mouth claimed hers again and the bitter control was not in place at all. It did not exist beside the terrible strength of his hunger.

He sought to master it, to place some barrier across the unacceptable power of the feelings locked down inside him for so long. He had denied them, all except the lash of rage that spurred him on to achieve what he must. There was no room for anything else, no weakness that might maim him, drag him down or make him falter in what he had to do. It was not he who would pay the price for failure.

It was Thieto, his son.

The name, the thought of the child, burned his volatile thoughts. He drew back, instinct and the bitter experience of aloneness stronger than the fact that a miracle creature like Judith had tried to step through it.

The kiss broke. His doing. There was no kindness, no grace in his action. Yet she held him, stayed with him, her body close against his.

"Why?" The fierceness of her question demanded an answer he could not give.

He felt her move, the small muscles rearranging themselves with a graceful strength that was part natural to her, part battle-trained. He let go because she would want—

"You are thinking of him, of the little child." He could feel her weight. She still touched him, her hands at his neck, buried in his hair, as though the connection still existed. He sensed the breath she took when she spoke. "You cannot think of anything else."

He could not even hold her. He was not worthy of her. His hands stayed at his sides, his fingers fisted in the grass and the forest's growth. He was aware of the pain strong enough to kill him. He tried to find the words out of the black mess.

"Tell me his name," said Judith.

It was the start.

"Thietmar." He forced speech. "But I called him Thieto because the proper name seemed too large. He has not quite eight winters. He——" Einhard sought control of his voice.

"It is different for a child," he said. "They cannot look after themselves the way an adult can." The vastness of the evening sky wheeled above his eyes, so remote. "He will not know what to do. He will be——" He could not say the word *terrified* because if he did whatever thread of control he had left would break.

"I have to find him."

Her small warm body lay against him. He wanted to take all that warmth and softness and the vital breathing life of her. He did not dare touch her.

"Yes."

It was such a simple word.

But she could not know how he was driven, the demons that ate at him, the things he was capable of.

"You do not understand what— No one does." He had to tell her. "I have broken every friendship I ever had."

"But people would realise—"

"What? Why I will not stop in what I do? That I am right? Right, when they know full well that—" The unspoken mass of pain inside him grew, crippling, threatening to burst through the thin wall that kept it dammed. "The probability is not for life." It was the closest he could get to what everyone told him. "People know—" *That my son is dead.* He could not think it in case the mere thought made it true. He could not speak of Thieto, not to anyone, not even to Judith who possessed magic. He did not deserve her. He tried to explain, but the stunted sound that came out of his throat was not even a word.

"People want you to accept what they see as right," she said, just as though he had spoken like an acceptable human being, not a half-mad hell-spawn.

"They want you to look forward." Her voice swept on, full of her own hidden steel-sharp strength. "They know it is for your own good. They feel sorry for you, particularly at first. But when you cannot do what they want, they cut themselves off from you. They cannot help it. It is like an instinct, how people survive. Perhaps it is the only way survival in the world is possible. But you have stepped outside that truth, outside the shared world. You have cut yourself off from them."

His breath caught. She must hear it. He could not speak, but she said the words for him.

"Such a terrible unbridgeable separation, happens even with those who are dearest to you, even though you do not wish it and neither do they. You have cut everyone off." Her calm voice finished. "Even Tatwin. I have been watching you do it."

No one else had ever said it straight out, not even himself.

"You see what I am."

"I see what I was myself when I came to Wessex, how my heart was still here in my home. I was separated from every-one else even though I walked and talked with them. My thoughts were far away and they knew it. It was loss I would not accept. But with me it was more than that. I was never like you, full in the middle of life, joined with people. I was always outside the circle all of my life, not like the others, running wild, not married, no close companions to share my unsuitable thoughts with, not good at sitting by a hearth. I was so…cold to people."

He could hear the guilt in her voice, something he understood beyond reason.

"But your life was different," she said. "You were never so cold. You are someone who gives, out of your nature, who has always shared, perhaps everything, and only now is cut adrift. You—"

"Judith! I do not— I cannot give."

"You cannot help it. You sent Tatwin away from you for his own good. You saved my life in battle. You gave me understanding when I could bring myself to speak to no one, not even to my own brother. You are looking for your child. I would not stop that."

He could feel the constricted bundle of his breath, deep in his chest, the pain like a caged beast waiting to get out. Her own breath seemed to come hard, something struggled for.

"I wish I had understood," she said. "I tried to take things from you by trickery that I should not."

"No." He cut her off. "Stop."

"But I said things that were—"

"Right." He said it because the truth was there. Nothing changed that. "Everything you said then was right. You wanted to save what is left of this land from the Vikings' power, from destruction. You said that I owed enough to Wessex to give some aid." The vast circle of the stars moved over their heads, relentless. "You are right. It is I who cannot follow what you say."

"But—"

"There is so much you believe." He could feel it now in the quick warmth of her body against his, the kindling of her spirit.

"Do you not believe such things?" Her voice resonated with heat, passion, a belief that was deeply felt and therefore equally vulnerable.

The bitterness cut through him without mercy. "I cannot see." It was the truth. It was like being blinded. Once, he had felt all that she did. He had thought that the future might hold what was no longer possible, peace, that Dorestad might be free again, even if it was only the half freedom under the Frankish Emperor's distant overlordship. He had understood with aching clarity why his father had once been part of a rebellion.

But it was too late now, too late for Dorestad. The change had come. Just as it had here. Even if a hard-won success against Viking invasion was still possible in Wessex, he was not sure she understood how high the price would be or how limited that success. Her hard-pressed king understood. It would take everything he had to hold his land of Wessex. He would not reconquer an open land like East Anglia, so vulnerable to sea invasion. Such an enterprise would take years; it might never happen. Judith's country....

"I have told you. I cannot see a future." His voice sounded brutally hard, colder than he wanted. He stopped. He could not say more. He could not possibly take her hope when he could give nothing in return.

He felt the tightness in her body, the restless movement strong, direct.

"I know I will never have again what I have lost. I will not lie under this sky again and know that the land is mine, just as it was, unchanged. I am not so lost in fantasy. But I...I wanted to defend what is left." Her voice cracked on despair.

"Judith—"

His arms closed round her, faster than thought, taking the warmth and the vulnerable smallness of her body, its bright strength. She turned into his embrace, as though she belonged. It was like trust, so absolute. She moved against him, intimate and unrestrained, edged with need. The unquenched fire flared.

"Stay with me." Her voice was sure, strong as she was. He tried to keep the last threads of sanity.

"I cannot give you all that you wish, what you deserve. I am so blinded I cannot even see what you can. I do not know whether I will live past tomorrow, or if I do what will happen."

"Then stay with me tonight. Just that."

15

THE THREADS OF REASON BROKE, the last possibility of restraint. Einhard's body covered the naked skin, the slender rounded curves. The movement was uncontrolled, base. But Judith's hands tightened on his flesh. Her body responded to his, like a miracle, like an undeserved gift. She stayed with him. He sought control of what he was, of all that was in him, found it, in part.

He held her lightly, easing his weight back, but she took all, as though it were what she wished, the wild heat in his mouth and his skin and the touch of his hands. She had tasted the edge of madness in him, the desperation, all the hidden things shot through with despair that he had no name for.

Her soft flesh filled his hands, warmed for him. She was already half-bared to him, to the coolness of the night. He warmed her skin, the flare of fire hot between them. He drew out the flame until she burned, until her flesh, the delicate curve of her breast, became fire against his mouth and when he touched her intimately the wet scorching heat of her clung to his fingers. Her body tensed, her fingers digging into him. He could read her reactions now as clearly as his own. He had begun to know the particular touch that could heighten her sensations with the greatest intensity, the rhythm of her feelings, what pleased her most. It was like the beginnings of a bond stronger than steel.

Something that had no chance to exist.

He touched her heat and watched her face as the pleasure broke, and thought the long-held pain inside would stop his heart. He felt her move softly against his hand. His lips took hers, the light touch in the aftermath of passion the only possible expression of what he felt for her. But then her body arched hard against him, the touch of her mouth unexpectedly strong, filled with hunger so that he drowned in the kiss, his hand still buried against her warmth. The heat inside him flared, the demand and the power of it driven beyond bounds. But as he shifted their positions, bringing her close beneath him, the last consciousness of rightness held him back.

Her hands dragged at him, seeking to pull him to her when he would have given her space.

"Einhard—" There was so much in her voice, the bright passion, desperation. Fear.

"I will not—"

"You will leave me," she said. "Even now. There will not even be this night."

"I will not take your maidenhead."

Her eyes in the shadows were wide, fixed. "It is my choice. I am betrothed to you, right or wrong. But even if that had not been so, it is my decision, a woman's choice. Or do you think because I am a woman I am not able to make my own choices?"

"No." There was no other answer with her. He had seen her strength. He saw it now.

He bent his head, because it was hard to look on her courage, and touched her flushed skin with his mouth. She shivered but when he looked at her eyes there was no doubt. Her choices were her own. She had already had the courage to risk her life by her own decisions.

No one living could match her.

He claimed her mouth, just as her heat claimed him.

JUDITH'S MOUTH CLEAVED to her lover's. She had what she wanted, his desire and his hidden pain and the madness of trapped feelings. She would release them.

Her body moved at his urging, followed the burning lead of his passion. There were no regrets, only for her lack of knowledge, for the moments she did not know how to match what he felt.

She slid her hands beneath the linen of his tunic, seeking his skin, the smooth heavy feel of his back, the dense subtle play of muscle and the human warmth. The feel of his skin intoxicated her. She felt dizzied by him, by his touch and his closeness. By the heated wildness of the way he wanted her. By the fact that for this single night, outside the terrible grip of the future, he was hers, a bond beyond the grip of time.

The longing for that doomed moment of closeness burned her and her eyes filled with tears she was afraid he would see. Her hands fastened on his flesh, pulling the loosened linen aside with no finesse until their combined hands dragged the tunic over his head and she felt the skin of his body touch hers.

The jolt of desire shocked her, its aching power reborn, as though her hunger for him could never end. She tried to hold herself still beneath the powerful shadow of his body over her, his hips between her parted thighs. But he read her need. His hand slid down between their joined bodies to touch her. She was still hot, wet, aching, and his touch could make her writhe. She moved, bearing against his hand as she had before and he made the desire gather, mount. She felt the smooth circling motion of his finger over her aching flesh, then the tip dipped inside her, deeper, gliding in and out, mimicking what would follow.

She pushed against him, instinct stronger than knowledge. She felt him use two fingers, easing the heated tightness, stretching the narrowness of her sheath. Her breath caught. The smooth movement of his fingers was careful, slow, yet utterly invasive. She should be afraid. She thought perhaps she was. It did not affect her choice. Her body burned. He had built the desire in her so high and the movement of his fingers, for all its care, was intent with desire, primitive and wildly inciting.

She made a faint sound and the fine muscles inside her seemed to pulse to the surge of his touch. The excitement in her grew, transmitted to him, caught from him. Shared. She twisted. She felt him move, free himself of the last restriction of clothing. She felt the fineness and the heat of his skin, the tight dark hair above his sex, the fullness of his desire-hard flesh. The anticipation increased. Her hands reached down to him. She touched the heated, fascinating, carnal shape that would fill her. Another person's flesh, a man's, her lover's.

She heard the harsh sound in his throat, felt the taut power in his body over hers and then he moved. She felt the leashed strength of his body, the tense muscle, the fine sheen of sweat on his skin, the hardness of him pressing inside her. Her own flesh, softened, moistened, fitted to the smooth hardness of him, the achingly slow penetration.

Her body arched under his, her legs curling instinctively higher round his body to take the fullness of him. She felt so tight round him, too tight, and then the restriction gave. The sharp pain made her gasp, but that was done, over. She could feel the power of life renewed, as though it had the strength to conquer anything, even the black wall of the future.

Her body moved against his, the instinct pure, fiercely exultant. More than instinct. Love. She felt the hard powerful surge of his body that seated him fully. The response in her was intense, wildly erotic. He bent his head. She felt the brief touch of his lips on hers, at once fierce and strangely gentle. Even more intimate than the intense feel of his body inside hers. Then he moved, at first slowly and deeply, until the shared desire and the madness were burning out of control. Until they existed only in joined flesh, in the strong fast thrust of Einhard's body, dizzying her senses. Her hips rose instinctively to meet his fierce desire, deep and uncontrolled, the mirror of her own, and there was no restraint. Only the bright-burning flame that tore the blackness and consumed it.

THE SHIPS MOVED at first light. Einhard's barbaric iron-beaked longship crossed into the River Deben before the sun was fully up. They used oars. There was no breath of wind to stir the great red sail. The streamers from the carved weather vane hung down in damp heavy trails like streams of blood. The mist coiled across the water.

Judith hugged the thickness of her cloak close to her body. The coldness seemed to seep from the damp-shrouded land and the flat tidal river, as though the dead cold breath came straight from the burial mounds overshadowing the water into her living flesh.

She had hardly spoken with Einhard since she woke to the eerie greyness. All that they could say had been said last night in the other realm of starlight. Today belonged to the world, to the lost boy and the terrible quest, and the price he paid for it.

She watched her lover. It was impossible to discern the relentless price paid. All that was visible in his face and the heavy grace of his body was the impenetrable determination, the strength of his will like a blank wall. She had misunderstood the power of that wall. Even now it gave her pause, even with the imprint of his warm body still real on her skin. Even though she had had been given one brief glimpse of all that lay trapped beneath the surface.

"What will we do?" began Mildred. "Where are we going? How can they see in this mist? What if…"

"We will not run aground. They have a man to navigate for them, did you not see?"

"Where?"

"He came on board before it was light. They must have already arranged it." She could not say *Einhard* must have already arranged it. She could not say his name into the light of day. It did not seem as though it could possibly encompass the man she had begun to know last night. It was as though that man and the ship's captain giving out his precise, low-voiced orders were two different beings.

The thought frightened her.

"I did not notice," said Mildred. "I was at the camp all night, asleep. Unlike you."

Judith turned the subject and her thoughts. The implications of them were more than she could manage. She knew the intensity that held Einhard. She knew the reason. She had said that his quest was not something she would stop. It was the truth.

"The man they have taken on board knows the river's course. He is a sailor." She did not know how a Frisian stranger had arranged that. The precise and analytical calculation involved in each move of the blood feud chilled her.

"The man is East Anglian," she added to stop Mildred's anxiety.

But that only led to a different kind of dangerous ground. Mildred launched into questions of whether she knew who the man was and where he came from and his kindred. Even Mildred knew the East Anglian royal court had had a palace down river at Rendlesham. Perhaps the man knew who Judith was?

He did. Or he had guessed. She could tell from the wide-eyed glances sent her way when the man thought she did not notice. He knew what he saw, a princess of the martyred blood of King Edmund.

But he did not look at her as though she was a royal *Atheling*, a princess who might return. He looked at her as though she were a spirit from the burial mounds of her royal ancestors, someone already dead, a *shinna* and a ghost, gone from his East Anglian world beyond recall.

The thought ought to crucify her. But its power was nothing compared to this moment, to what Einhard suffered and what he had to do.

She watched Einhard command their progress. Not one point of vulnerability was visible in the blank wall, not even human feeling. Her heart bled.

"You will not come with us."

"But why not?" Judith's reply was low-voiced because of the listening men. She stared at Einhard. She did not feel low-voiced. She felt savage with pent-up force, like a screaming hawk in sight of its target. She had her war-gear ready. The sword was freshly oiled. The helm spilled out of her carrying bag. Its bronze eyebrows and polished nose piece peered over the edge of the leather like a living creature, an occult force. Einhard stepped over the stacked gear.

"It is not fitting."

Not fitting. The words she had heard all her life. Like a slap in the face. She turned her back on the milling crew.

"Do you think I would leave you to face this on your own? Can you think for one moment that I would be afraid?" *Not fitting.* She tried to control her voice, muffle the anger. To be reasonable. He had enough burdens. Perhaps he thought a woman's presence would be another. But he must know. He must understand what she felt for him, what she was quite capable of doing.

"It is my own decision. Can you not see?" She lowered her voice. "After all that…" After what? A lovers' embrace? The heavy air between them was suddenly tight, breathless with the power of sexual attraction, the naked heat of it. *Because of that. Because of an underlying bond that had been shared.*

She took a step towards him before she knew she had done it. But he did not move, no open reaction. There was nothing she could say in such a public place of all that had been between them in the night. All that still existed in the very air that she breathed. In him.

"I want to share what must be done." Her voice scarcely made sound because of the dryness in her throat, because the words were meant for him alone. "It…It is what I wish." They were such lame words for the force that burned through her tingling skin, though the flesh he had touched, marked. But he would understand them.

"It is not what I wish," he said. His voice was distinct, strongly pitched, a captain's voice clear for every man of the crew to hear.

It was like being punched.

"You will not come." He turned away

She stared at the hard-faced stranger, remote, inwardly absorbed, distant. His attention had already gone from her, directed elsewhere. On the search for his child. The way he held himself apart was relentless, unreachable.

She wondered whether it was possible for anyone to break through that focus. For her to break it, to reach *him*.

She plunged away, the movement fast to hide the hurt. Her feet nearly slipped on the moving deck. She righted herself instantly, clutching the ship's side. She regained her balance with ease, warrior's training. But he turned.

She realised the barrier of blank indifference, of control, was wafer-thin. She did not yet know everything that was underneath. No one did.

She would not let one action of hers damage that costly, terrible wall.

"I will stay. You can put me ashore." She bowed her head so that she would not see what was in his face. The errant sun breaking the early mist struck the war-helm at her feet, making the rune glow. *Cen,* the torch. She looked up and saw the barrow downs.

"IT IS UNCANNY," said Mildred. "Can we not go back down and join Einhard's men?"

He had left two guards for her and Mildred, even though it was not necessary. Viking territory or not, she would be able to find those who would give her aid at need, living or dead alike.

Frisian guards served no purpose. It was a waste of men that Einhard would need. But he had ordered it. She would not alter a single thing that he did.

She climbed the slope. Mildred's anxious breathing sounded behind her, then deepened into a gasp.

"It is a *hlæw.*"

"Yes."

Mildred hopped from one foot to the other on the lush grass like a cat unable to tread on hot coals. "There is someone dead in there."

"He will not mind. None of them will." Her skin prickled with the cold awareness of the dead. But it was not fear. "They are my kin. They will help me." *I am supposed to be here. It was meant.* In her mind she could see the pale, dead faces of her ancestors. Macsen's black living eyes.

"Come." She held out her hand to Mildred to pull her up the slope of the *hlæw*.

"There will be spirits, *orc-neas.* The walking dead. They might not mind you," objected Mildred, dragging her hand away and coming to a stop. "But they will mind me." All of a sudden, the West Saxon accent sounded very strong.

"I have to climb up to see as far as I can across the river. You can go back to the guards at the foot of the *hlæw* if you wish."

"I will wait here," said Mildred with commendable resolution. "I will be close. I will hear you."

Mildred's lone figure vanished surprisingly quickly in the tendrils of mist that swirled round the grassy mounds on the riverbank. Judith might have been completely alone. Yet shivers of awareness coursed over her damp skin. Awareness of other presences. Remote and yet at the same time startlingly intense.

She had said the truth to Mildred. The bodies of her forefathers were buried here, with their rich treasures and their wargear arrayed around them to serve them in the afterlife. Perhaps even the man who had once owned her helmet. Her feet might even now touch his last resting place.

What had he thought? Had he known all the feelings that tortured her now? Loved a family and fought to protect them? Her mind filled with the possibilities and then she looked down and saw the river.

There were ships, gliding through the clinging layers of mist across the water. She had hardly time to make sense of what her eyes told her, the black-and-yellow banded sails advancing like a wave, like a swarm of bees. Impossible to count through the obscuring mist. More than Einhard had, surely. More—

She did not hear the footsteps until they were upon her. There was no warning from the dead who saw everything, all that the living could not, only the fast maddened beat of the steps and the figure appearing out of the mist. She heard Mildred's close terrified scream.

"A *shinna...*"

But the fast-moving figure was no ghost. The flushed, sweat-streaked skin, the small harsh rasp of breath, belonged to living flesh, to a human body that felt pain. She held out her hands to him even before she saw his face. Then her gaze took in the wild gold hair two shades lighter with childhood, the terrified eyes that yet held the hint of a force that would one day be unstoppable.

The boy thudded into her, nearly taking her balance. She caught the small warm body, already surprisingly solid for its size. Nearly eight winters old and strong. Her heart turned over.

"Athelbert's bones." Not the most intelligent thing to say. She did not know whether he spoke English like his father, let alone swore. Her hands firmed round the frighteningly tense shoulders.

"It is all right," she said. "Stay still." The solid little body struggled. She thought he did not understand her. She kept speaking, trying to think, work out the next move, making the sound of her voice as calming as she could. "I can help you." She sought in her memory for the name. *I called him Thieto. The proper name seemed too large....* "Thieto. Thieto, listen. You must come with me, quickly. I am with your father. He——" The struggles became convulsive.

"*No*—— They will kill him if he comes. They want him to die." At least, that was what she thought the furious frightened voice said. The words were a mixture of English and sounds that were Frisian. There was also a word of Danish. He kept repeating it as though she were deaf. *Deyr.* Then he said, "Run."

The cold prickling of warning was shivering over her skin. She had been too absorbed in the anxious boy, in the impossible mind-jolting discovery of Einhard's lost child, to heed it. There was no noise. His pursuers emerged out of the clinging mists in a controlled and petrifying silence, like expert hunters on the trail of their frantic quarry.

There were six of them, moving like a wolf pack. They circled her and the child, Einhard's son, and there was nothing she could do. Nothing she could have done even dressed in the helmet and chain mail *byrnie* as she had wanted. She could not shout for Einhard's two warriors, hidden in the mist below. She faced six; they would harm or kill the boy. If only—— They would think she was nothing but some terrified stray Englishwoman.

She was English. She was surrounded by the warrior-shades of her East Anglian ancestors. She was meant to be here. The dead spirits had let her find the living boy. She would keep him.

She put one hand on the boy's arm and extended the other, palm out. The Vikings took it as a gesture of submission. She made it look pathetic so that they understood she was beaten without any more effort on their part than yelling at her in bad English and making threatening gestures.

Since a woman so helpless did not require to be overpowered, they did not search for the knife strapped to her thigh. The *seax* was not hers. She had stolen it from Einhard.

Her main fear was that she would look too useless, so that they would take the boy and leave her behind. Or that Mildred, invisible in the swirling mist would make some betraying sound, or try to come to her out of loyalty.

Go back, she willed silently. *Go back to Einhard's guards, or if they are dead, go back to the shore until he finds you.*

Failing that, stay hidden and you will be safe.

In the end, there was no question. They took her. Her breath had just expelled in silent relief when the child wrenched himself out of her hold.

"She does not have to come," said Einhard's son in his Frisian-Danish. "She is a stranger. She did not know—"

One of the soldiers hit him. The boy did not cry even though she could see how much it hurt. He was not surprised; that was the worst thing.

The Viking spared no more than a glance before turning away, indifferent, goal accomplished.

If she had had her sword in her hand, she would have beheaded him.

"THE LITTLE BRAT tells me you are a stranger."

Thietmar, Thieto, kept talking. There was a dull red mark on his face. Like Einhard, he seemed to have no concept of giving up. He would be a handful. If he ever got out alive.

They were standing before the Viking called Skar on a yellow-and-black-sailed longship with a ring-necked prow carved in a beast's likeness. She watched their captor's thick muscles tighten, as though something was about to combust. But he repeated the question, quiet-voiced as yet, in more or less passable English. The question was directed to her over the boy's head.

The Viking's eyes were slits of carefully contained fury.

"Aye. Lord," she said in broadest native East Anglian. She compounded it by looking dense, a feat her brother had once teased her required little effort on her part.

"You are lying." The fury burst, with a suddenness and an uncontrolled power that shocked an undisguisable reaction out of her.

She forced herself to stillness, watching the man called Skar, Einhard's enemy, and tried to assess in her turn whether the abrupt breaking of control was deliberate or inadvertent. The boy, in spite of his clear courage, had stepped back. He was so small for all his natural toughness. She realized her right hand was clenched, hard, as though she held an invisible hilt. The Viking saw it and yelled at her.

Not inadvertence, but deliberateness. No, both. He had as much trouble containing his temper as the abrupt violence showed. He was a man who knew his own power and how to exercise it. He had brute strength and he had enough men at his command. She thought he must be so used to that kind of power that he saw no reason to school either his reactions or his desires. The man called Skar got what he wanted.

Her heart beat rather fast.

"Lying?" she enquired.

"Like a deceitful slut."

Hang it. She had forgotten to say *lord* and her tone hardly sounded meek. It was a disadvantage sometimes, being of royal kin. She bit her lip.

"Lord," she began subserviently. But it was too late for whatever cajoling untruths her racing brain could have come up with. The huge fist clenched. Sweat stood out on the florid face above the plaited beard, beaded the pelt of brown hair below the thick neck, glistened off the hammer-shaped amulet at his throat. The god Thor's sign, the god of thunder, of unrestrained physical strength.

"Are you so lack-brained that you believe my men did not hear what you said to the boy on the burial mound? They can work out English words just as well as this little brat can. You are Einhard's slut."

She heard the small gasp beside her. She took a step forward, one that placed her half in front of the boy.

"The child did not know me," she said through the blood pounding in her ears. "He spoke the truth." *He would not know such a thing now, but for you, you arrogant swine.* "You can see that." He could. Nothing, no reaction however small, escaped that sharp gaze. A master at intimidation. "Lord," she added, forcing her voice to be even, as calm as she could make it.

The heavy fist moved. She stepped farther, completely block-ing the boy from Skar. But the blow did not fall. Thieto had flinched instinctively and Skar's narrow eyes had marked it. As though he had the reaction desired, he turned on the boy, the swiftness as vi-olent as the threatening fist, disconcerting as it was meant to be.

"So you did not know, little brat, when you ran away to find your father? You did not know how he has been spending his time? Thieving, whoring with this *hor-kona* at his pleasure. He has long forgotten you."

"No!" The word was forced out of her. She could see the stricken look even before the boy's head turned, gaze fixed not on her, not on Skar. "That is not—" she began. But Skar's laugh-ter obliterated her voice.

"Either way, it does not matter. The thief Einhard is close enough now. He will come for one or the other of you two fools and everything will fall out exactly as I planned."

"What will happen?"

Judith had not thought the boy would speak again. Her gaze flew instinctively to the Viking's coiled fist. But it did not strike.

"I shall kill him," said Skar, the adult finality in the statement more frightening than a blow to the boy. The strong voice went on speaking. "…I shall make my own use of the thief's property, just as he has made use of mine." The switch in his attention was so abrupt, Judith did not see it coming. Skar's hand caught her arm, faster than a snake striking. His eyes held fury.

"Come, there is time. You will not take me long. The boy can watch and learn."

The meaning of the words turned her stomach, sent fury

crashing through her veins. She did not stop to think whether the threat was imminent and real, or part of his game of intimidation. The anger simply burst inside her head, limitless, born of her own unhealed rage against the Vikings, the anger on behalf of her lover and his boy. She twisted in his hold. He was strong, but the power of her anger had no fetters, no boundaries, like the driving, consuming madness of the battle rage, yet changed. She could master its power, use it. She would never be quite so uncontrolled again, or so vulnerable. She had finally lived through that first appalling time. Einhard had helped her. She would live through this. So would Einhard's son.

The punishing grip broke. She heard the grunt of shock, pain because she had twisted his shoulder out of alignment. She caught her balance, turned, just as someone else crashed through, foot-tripping her from behind. The unrealness of her strength gave her the power to control the fall. She was not hurt. Skar was yelling. The other hands reaching out for her fell away. By that time she was on her feet again, which stunned him. But it did not abate the malevolence.

"You will pay. You will learn the meaning of that, just as the man who keeps you will learn. He should not have taken what is mine."

"He did not."

"You stupid, witless, lying whore. He stole my cargo. I will—"

"Not him," she yelled with a force that would not have disgraced a fishwife. She was not stupid and witless enough to try and tell him who had. He did not have the capacity to believe it. At this moment, he was too angry for thought. Her mind, working as fast as her body, caught the only chance. Skar had to work it out for himself, if anything could get past the incandescent anger. She watched the wall of fury in the eyes, the hand that would strike.

"If it was not Einhard who robbed you, who do you think betrayed you? Who do you already know is a master at betrayal?" she shouted into the fractured instant of time that was left to her. She thought the inward focus of the eyes flickered, but then she could no longer tell and her voice and his were drowned out by other shouts of the crew.

"The ships—"

Skar turned round. "At last."

She knew enough to follow the switch into Danish.

"Lord! Lord, they are Jarl Guthrum's ships."

"Guthrum's…" Skar swung away, leaving her standing in the middle of the deck to stare after him. There was nothing she could do, after all, one woman in a boatload of warriors.

She knew whose ships were closing on them out of the mist. She had to help him. Now or never. The risk of what he did was appalling. He might still lose the boy.

Something snagged at her skirts.

"Are you all right?" said Thietmar, Einhard's son. He sounded old, like a man.

"Yes. Of course." She thought her breath would choke. "But you—"

"Is it true?" The face was suddenly flushed with color, the

eyes overbright. "What he said. About you...about you and my..."

Whoring with this hor-kona at his pleasure. He has long forgotten you.

"I want to know." The tone was violently unsteady, aggressive, a boy out of his depth with a wholly adult question. She recognised the belligerence that hid terror.

She bent down, sitting on her heels, keeping her eyes on the level of his, the way her long-dead father had done when he had had something important to say to a small girl. The crew streamed past them in a disciplined flood. She made her words come slowly, so that he had the best chance of understanding her English. She wished she spoke Frisian like Mildred.

Let Mildred be safe. Let her have found Einhard's men.

"This is the truth. Your father never forgot you, not for one minute." *It nearly killed him.* She picked her words. "He wanted to come for you as soon as he could. That was all he ever thought of." Thietmar's eyes never left her face. "You were lost. People thought you were dead. Skar took you and hid you. No one knew where you were and your father could not find you. But he will find you. He is coming now. For you. He never gave up."

Over their heads, the black-barred sail dropped. They put out oars. Maneuverability. The best way to meet friend. Or foe. She thought of Skar's shrewd eyes.

"That is the truth."

The boy's gaze slipped away, the way it had before Skar. She did not know what he believed. The ship turned abruptly. She stood.

"What is going to happen?" The question was sudden, desperate, childlike.

I do not know.

"You will be safe. Stand behind me." There was not much time. She could see the other ships so clearly. They were well within arrow range, almost spear range. Her gaze took in the nearest shelter. "Promise you will stay close to me."

The dazzlingly blond head nodded. But she was not sure how much he understood or whether he would obey the directions of a strange woman involved in some threatening way with his father. She did not know him. She might never know him. The thought chillled her heart.

She could see Skar clearly. She moved slightly closer, keeping to the shadow of the mast and the hastily lowered sail.

Skar shouted across the narrowing gap of water. His voice held sharpness, more belligerence than she would have expected directed to the ships of a man who was an earl of the Danes, in effect, a king. She caught the first lash of suspicion. Her heart thudded. Hard. She motioned Thieto back, sparing half a glance over her shoulder. He actually obeyed, even though his eyes were wide. It was the best she could hope for. Now or never.

She recognised the moment Skar realised something was wrong. Too soon. The gap across the water was still too wide and when Skar knew he had been duped, things would happen too fast.

She flipped up the hem of her skirt and unsheathed the knife. She fixed her attention on the back of the creature who had ruined a child's life, and a man's. Who had done feud-killing and was aware of no regret at all.

Behind her, Thietmar gasped. He would be so frightened. The knowledge pierced her, but her own fear was gone.

No one noticed what she did. Their whole attention was on the rapidly approaching ships. She judged her moment. The spirits of her ancestors were behind her, Macsen's *fæg* words that held foresight. But more than that. She held the right knife. Her fingers tightened on the gilded handle.

Skar screamed his war-cry.

16

THE DISTANCE WAS IMPOSSIBLE. It had the power to defeat him, the calm faceless stretch of water and the force of the tide. Einhard shouted. The words meaningless, only the mad edge in his voice driving the men to greater effort with the oars until muscle cracked. Thieto was alive. In Skar's hands. His son lived. His strained mind lurched away from the chaotic power of the thought. Yet the knowing burned through every part of him, deep enough to consume him. He pushed it aside.

Thietmar was not yet his. Skar held him on the dragon-beaked ship. And Judith, Judith who had courage like her sainted namesake.

Judith who had found his son. Judith and Skar.

The Serpent surged forward with each practiced, disciplined stroke, defying the power of the water like something alive.

The swirling mist, once friend, now deadly enemy, obscured the other ships from sight. Just as it obscured Skar's view of him.

But the other man had guessed by now. He must. Only one kind of fool underestimated Skar. A dead fool.

They were within spear range, but he would not give the order to launch the iron rain because Skar had a greater weapon.

Just as he did. He glanced at his prisoner, hidden by mist and distance from Skar.

He leaned forward and bellowed across the gap of water, the sound tearing his throat. The confused din of voices floated back from Skar's ships. They had realised the truth. Spear distance. He yelled louder.

The words shouted in Danish, "I have your brother," echoed off the barrow-mounds on the shore. The mist broke and the distance was gone, swallowed up by the driven, unreal speed of the Serpent.

The view was clear.

The first thing he saw, before his mind could take in the sight of Skar and the set spears, was what the hysterical maidservant Mildred had prepared him for, the woman and the child. Not bound and controlled as his own prisoner was, but loose, ignored. The woman's slender hand held a knife. *God's breath.*

Do not use it. The words were shouted in his mind, as though she knew how to hear the thoughts in the madness of his head. He shoved his own prisoner forward, hard against the Serpent's curving prow. Where he could be seen. *Not now.* There was a grunt of expelled breath.

"Tell him."

There was an inarticulate sound and some spitting. Einhard moved the long knife blade. The carefully braided beard jerked.

"Skar," yelled the prisoner.

The answer was a scream that held pure rage. The raised arm

decorated with looted silver made a violent gesture. But it was one of negation. The poised spear points and the missiles dropped. So did the woman's knife blade.

He was aware of the cutting breath of relief and then Thieto must have seen him because the small blond figure darted forward. His mind slipped control. But the woman's figure caught the childish one, held on to him despite the exercise of all Thieto's precocious strength, spoke to him in some unknown urgent message. *Don't let him go. Judith…*

She stopped him, quietened the frantic, desperate movement. Judith and her matchless courage. She had done it. Saved disaster.

But the danger hung round her, as it did round Thieto. He could not think of that, or the madness inside him would leak out.

He shifted his attention to Skar, wracked with fury, off balance, scrambling to catch up. He gave him time, even though every instinct in his heated blood demanded action. As far as Skar was concerned, Einhard should not have found where his brother Mord's ship had been left in reserve. Mord had been Skar's insurance if things turned sour. Now that was gone. Skar had to readjust. If he could not, if he lost control, they were doomed to a bloodbath. Einhard assessed the positioning of his own men, the weapons open and concealed, the way the Serpent, supposedly held back by the oars, drifted imperceptibly closer to Skar's ship.

He let Mord explain it.

"…he will let me go. You just have to give him back the child and the woman. The child was useless anyway. I always said it was pointless to take him. If you had not—" Brilliant negotiator. At a sign, one of his men shut Mord up with the threat of a knife point.

Skar's venomous words spat back across the narrowing gap of water. But there was little he could do. The vicious cursing resolved itself.

"I want Mord's ship back and all that it holds." It was the first straight demand. The man was thinking again. Einhard watched the narrowed eyes survey the opposition. He did not want Skar thinking too hard. If the mist cleared any more, he would see how few ships there were.

He feigned reluctance over the return of Mord's ship, which increased Skar's temper.

"If you want these returned...." Skar's own prisoners were belatedly hustled forward. He spared one glance. That was all. One glance. Neither appeared hurt. Judith had hold of Thieto's hand. Thieto clung to it like a lifeline, a gift that would lead out of hell. He could never repay that.

He shifted his attention back to Skar; he could not look at his son again. Or at Judith. There had been no sign of the knife he had seen before, but he would swear she still had it. Or she would not be Judith.

Skar yelled, his mind working over the details, following the right path. Mayhap. The gap between the ships closed. He tried praying, as though he still had a soul that was worth something. Tatwin would have been proud.

He let Skar push him over custody of Mord's ship.

The Serpent was so close. They would be able to board....

"You can have them both, your brat...and your vicious little whore."

Judith.Vicious. He refused to contemplate what she might have attempted to do to Skar.

He kept Skar talking as the Serpent scraped alongside.

He capitulated abruptly over the matter of Mord's ship. Skar leaped on the weakness. It possessed his mind. For now. Einhard pressed the negotiations forward at speed. What he really wanted was to keep Mord on the Serpent until he had Judith and Thieto but in the event it was not possible to push Skar that far.

He had prepared for it.

His men had their orders. He could not touch the boy. Not yet. It would break him and all would be lost. The crew knew to get both, woman and child, off the Serpent and on to another of his ships before this finished.

They lifted the boy across. It went without a hitch. Then he made the insane mistake of looking.

He was so close he could see everything, every feature of the childishly rounded face, the bright-blond hair tangled and in need of combing, longer than he remembered it, like a mark of the passage of time. An unfamiliar grey tunic that did not fit. The same shoes, covered in mud as always. He saw the expression in Thieto's eyes.

"Father." Thieto said the word. His gruff voice squeaked with a fear that was new. The sound was naked.

He did not know whether he could do what he had planned. He thought he would do murder. The urge that had lived in him for so long, since the moment his foot had touched the charred ashes of what had once been his home. His head was filled with it, every tight, leashed, blood-gorged muscle in his body. He would kill.

They carried his child away.

"*Soon. I will come.*" The words crossed the small distance to his son, the words he had said over and over in his mind and which only now took shape. A spoken promise. Thieto's wide eyes watched him. *Soon everything will be as it was.* But it hit him for the first time that it would not. Just as he had changed, so had his son. Skar's legacy. He felt the death in his fingers, burning him.

Judith swung over the Serpent's side. He waited. Her feet touched the deck. She looked at him, her hand was outstretched. The rising sun caught the gold ring, the boar shape.

He turned his back on her. Skar was watching him.

JUDITH GASPED. THE MAN WHO HAD taken Thietmar from her arms and helped her off Skar's ship did not let go of her as she expected. He babbled something in incomprehensible Frisian at her. Then he started dragging her across the deck. She wanted to see Einhard. The need was so great it was like a physical pain. But he had turned from her as though there was nothing between them.

Of course, he would want the child, his son... They had taken the boy away, too. Her outstretched hand dropped to her side. Einhard did not even see it. Skar yelled.

"I will see you dead yet," he howled over his brother's back. Judith turned her head.

"Do not think it is ended."

Einhard's shoulders flexed. She dug her heels into the wooden deck.

"You will find no safety from me. Not in Frisia, not if you crawl back to Wessex."

"Wait," she snapped at the dragging hands. The answer was foreign, urgent. It did not contain compromise. She caught Einhard's name amongst the flurry of forceful words and a glance across the ship that clearly read obedience to a commander. Whatever the man was doing was by Einhard's wish. That should have been assurance enough.

Something went cold inside her.

"I will not rest," yelled Skar. "I will find you—"

There was no reply from the foreign-accented voice that could yell as loud as Skar's. She threw her weight back. The move was unexpected both in its force and its skilfulness. She and the sailor stopped.

"I will find you wherever you hide. When I come to Wessex with Guthrum's ships—"

The coldness increased, even though Skar's words were not unexpected. He would join Guthrum who paid so well. The coldness choked her. She tried to quash the fear behind it. It was something that would have to be dealt with later. The fate of foreign Wessex was not Einhard's burden; she did not expect him to take it on. She had scotched that particular demon.

But she refused to move. The crewman became frantic. In a moment, she thought, he would be obliged to resort to ruthless force.

They had Thietmar over the warship's side, on to the next vessel. She would follow. There seemed to be no doubt of that. The crewman had hold of her. Other hands on the next ship were waiting. Einhard was aware of it. She knew without having to turn her head, the moment that Einhard's attention caught her. The potent, double-edged awareness made her breath come fast. It was as though they touched, as though some invisible winged thought passed between them, a thought without words, a feeling, no more.

"No…" *You cannot.*

The crewman thought she was speaking to him. Just as well. It saved time.

Across the deck, Einhard spoke at last, shouted at Skar. "You have no need to wait to find me."

"Then come here——" bellowed Skar.

She produced the hidden knife.

"——Prove your words."

The Frisian sailor was confronted with someone English, female, mad. Armed. As far as he was concerned, it was a disconcerting enough combination to make him believe she would use the blade. There was a fractional pause before he moved. It was all the advantage she needed to shove him aside.

She had to grant him courage for picking himself up again and following as she sprinted across the deck.

"Settle it now," yelled Skar. "Are you ready to sue for peace?" The vicious, spine-chilling sound of his laughter filled the warming air. Einhard would not do it. He had said that the one thing he would never do was sue for peace. He had told her what had happened to his father. He knew what Skar was.

He *knew*.

But Einhard had already moved, as though the violent words, the chilling laughter, were the cue he expected. What he wanted.

His feet landed lightly on the decking of Skar's ship.

She thought she would faint, the dizziness inside her head was so strong, the sick feeling in the pit of her stomach. She dived for the side of the ship. Instinct. Einhard's man grabbed her arm.

Einhard's orders. Einhard's plan.

Skar made a sound like a stabbed boar. There was a general movement of weapons from Einhard's crew.

What Einhard wanted. Her guard held on to her. But it was not his strength that stopped her from leaping over the side in her turn. The knife tingled in her hand.

"What can you offer?" yelled Skar.

"An end to the feud."

Her breath choked.

Skar stood his ground. He had held his men back by the slightest gesture of one hand. The other held his sword. Einhard had no weapon.

"Then persuade me." Skar put the sword down on the wooden decking at his feet. "I may listen." He held his hands in sight, palms out, like a gesture of truce. An agreed peace. Nothing implied in that gesture reached Skar's eyes.

Do you know how it is done? Because you have the promise of safe conduct and witnesses, you leave your weapons and your armour aside.

The sword hilt lay within half a second's reach. Every man around Skar on his ship was armed even though the points of their weapons were lowered.

Einhard took a single step forwards, hands clearly visible in the same way, palms out. Empty. Skar waited for him.

How could he bear it? After he had lost so much, his father, the men he knew. He had almost lost his son. How could he think he would succeed?

Another step.

Why? He had his son. He had what he wanted.

The smooth pacing never hesitated.

Reckless fool. There would always be another chance at Skar's life if vengeance was what he sought. A better chance with less risk. In an endless feud, such chances always came.

Her hand tightened on the *seax* hilt. She had not moved from her place at the ship's side. The Frisian sailor had not tried to take the blade away from her. Together they watched the lone figure take its course. Both of them waited. Every man on Einhard's warship waited. Every man was armed. The damage they could inflict would be almost catastrophic. But they would never be in time to save Einhard's life.

Skar knew all that.

"Why would he do it?" Judith did not know she had spoken the words aloud until Einhard's man turned his head. She got the kind of look that said, *stupid and dangerous foreigner with deranged wits.* It seemed extraordinarily difficult to breathe.

Across the decks, Skar leaned his head back. He smiled. The warming sun caught the feral teeth, the elegantly plaited beard.

"So what," said Skar, "can you offer me?"

Einhard stopped, shoulders set, lethally strong body held lightly, assurance complete.

"More than Jarl Guthrum will."

That was when she realised he had done it for her, for benighted Wessex, for all the things he no longer believed in because he had no reason to.

She watched the perfectly poised back. She might as well have stuck the rune-blade through it.

"I WILL PAY YOU," said the man she had as good as killed.

"You?" The reply held contempt, unabated rage and something else, something Judith could not fathom. It was like knowledge, a superior knowledge of something withheld.

"Consider it a *wergild,*" said Einhard. "A compensation payment for the life of my son."

"And how much is that worth?" The contempt deepened. The volatile anger flared, but it was unexpectedly checked, as though the inward thoughts were focused elsewhere, on whatever was hidden, not on Einhard's words.

"Enough to buy what you want." Skar would kill him. "Enough to set up a landholding in a new colony." The other man's attention suddenly sharpened.

"Somewhere uncontested," said Einhard the Frisian, briefly of war-torn Wessex. He let the pause hang with all the concentrated finesse of a soothsayer producing oracles. "Iceland."

The sharpened attention locked. The difficult control, the protective shield of superiority cracked in two, giving a glimpse of what was inside.

Judith's heart leaped. That was it, the breach so real it drew blood. That was what he wanted, what the greedy dangerous creature Skar truly wanted. His own land in a place that was new.

"So much?" The anger, the violence, simmered under the surface, but the man was caught. Surely?

"Enough to buy what you want. The same price as the profit from a cargo of furs, amber and high-grade silk."

The vicious anger, held back, subsumed by the new desire, ignited. Judith flinched, the instinctive movement of self-preservation too fast to stop. Why had Einhard unleashed that? The spectre of the cargo stolen from Skar's brother. The act of piracy unatoned.

It had not been Einhard's fault, not his action.

The brief change in Skar was obliterated. He spat. Judith thought that it was the nearest he could get at that moment to speaking.

"You thief. You…" The words fell into the kind of Danish that belonged in the gutter. The man beside her gripped his sword.

"I will restore it to you," said Einhard across the flow. "If—"

But Skar was too far gone in rage. The shouting intensified, then became suddenly comprehensible. "…you think you are in a position to offer terms? It is Jarl Guthrum who will give me the payment I want. Do you know what for? For you, for your thieving hide. I fight for Guthrum and I will be compensated. But my first payment is for you. I am to ensure that you and your pirate train do not join the ship-army of Wessex, by whatever means I choose, by reward, or failing that, by destruction. That is my power and my choice."

A violent wave of sickness washed through her, disbelief, cold horror. The blow was not what she had expected. It could not have been foreseen by anyone, not even by the one who had forced that hidden knowledge, that secret power, out into the light. Not by Einhard, surely. She could not see his face.

There was a change in the crew gathered round her, like a signal for readiness. Her heart quickened, the response that she knew, now, would always come before a fight.

"I will not be Guthrum's hireling," said Einhard. "I, at least, am my own master. As you were once. You settled your own disputes."

Skar's eyes flicked so much rage that the air between the two men burned with it. "Why," shouted Skar, "should I settle for the sorry reparation a thief offers when I may take both Guthrum's payment and all that you have?"

"The problem may lie in taking it."

There were so many men behind her, armed like Skar's. Skar knew it. She watched the shrewd eyes assess everything in one glance. Einhard's men could board, fast.

Yet not fast enough for their leader.

She measured the distance between the unarmed man and the sword at Skar's feet, the weapons in the hands of the Vikings ranked behind him. Then she saw Skar's gaze move outward, across the water, taking in the position of the ships round him, suddenly clear to sight now that the fickle mist was lifting. She could see the barrow downs behind the ships and the flat water. Not so many ships, and one not to be risked because it held the boy. Few. Skar, with his seaman's eyes, assessed it.

"I could still destroy you, or let Jarl Guthrum do it because you have dared to refuse him."

She saw the gap of clear water Skar saw. Something that might be taken by speed, with Einhard already on the ship and his men still to try and board it. She saw Skar's hand move.

She knew Einhard had seen the weakness, that he must have calculated and accepted it as unavoidable. He had known when he decided to end the feud and prevent Skar from joining Guthrum's force.

She saw him take the breath to speak and then the dangerous gap of clear water filled with movement. Another ship. She recognised it. It had a patch of light timber on the prow. It had oars.

Tatwin.

"Guthrum is not worth your trouble," said Einhard. His eyes

watched the approaching ship but his voice betrayed nothing of the shock he must have felt. "It is a dubious reward for so much risk. You will have to fight my ships first and the outcome of that is not certain. My offer of an honour payment still stands."

Skar stared at the new ship, fast in the water, at the armed crew. "Honour payment? Is it honour for a crawling thief to return what he has stolen?" He turned his head. "Is it honour to plan an ambush—"

"You tell me." The naked violence in the words stunned.

Treacherous death where peace had been offered. Einhard had the right to exact vengeance, the right to kill. He wanted it with more force than Judith had ever imagined, with a pure intensity the offer to end the feud had sublimated, not extinguished.

She should have understood it. He was as hot-blooded as her, infinitely dangerous. But he had no chance—

The tension between the two strong figures had snapped. Skar moved like a blur. She swallowed a scream. Einhard's men poured over the side of the ship, even though it was too late. Someone tried to hold her back. She wrenched herself free.

"Wait!" The voice was Frisian.

It was not Skar who had reached the sword. She stared, her feet rooted to the deck of the Viking ship among the two groups of men. There was no mercy in the way Einhard held Skar helpless, flat on his back, neither was there any restraint. She looked at the blade held at his throat. She did not know how Einhard had found the moment of time and the power in such desperate fractured seconds to do what he had.

She could see his face. There was a small trail of blood at the corner of his mouth, but otherwise he seemed unmarked. That fair face held no expression, but the force was in it like murder. The low reddened sun of early morning struck fire off the blade. His hand on the gilded hilt was motionless but the same deadly force permeated his fingers. It scorched the air. The power must have been sensed by every fighting man there. Skar must have felt it through every twisted muscle. Through his bones.

Not one of the two groups of armed men dared to move because of what the consequences would be. Judith stared at the poised lethal muscle in Einhard's arm in fascination. It would move. There was no other possibility. No one could deny his right. She watched the intense face with its narrowed eyes, the killing strength. His breathing was fast. The air burned with the power of his fury.

Like a torch flame.

The steel edge drew back slightly.

"You have a single choice."

"What?" The word was a rasp of sound. The dark-haired throat worked under the steel edge. "To ask for my life at your hands?"

The sword stayed still. Judith watched the power of what Einhard had felt, held back for bitter weeks, take its shape.

"It is more of a choice than you gave to those you killed. Or took. Even a child."

Skar's glance flicked to the sword. He had courage, for all his bullying boastfulness. She could not doubt that. Yet the terrible power burned him. His eyes widened and the sweat beaded on his flushed skin, the reaction unstoppable.

"I did not kill the child. I do not take the lives of children. Not even yours."

"If you had killed my child, you would have been dead even before this moment."

It was beyond a threat. Skar knew it. He waited for the next move. He could do nothing else.

"Was it worth the payment from Rorik?"

"The——" The impulse of a dominating man to bluster, to attack in any way possible must have been overwhelming. The venomous gaze meshed with Einhard's, with the power that was remorseless. Judith held her breath. There was nothing, nothing but the clash of bitter will and a time that seemed measureless. Skar's gaze fell away. But the rage-mottled face darkened and the eyes turned into the narrow self-focused slits she had come to recognise.

"I had been wronged. That was the reason. Your father and his men got no more than they deserved. I was in the right. Me——" The sword moved, just fractionally. She did not think that slight movement was controlled. The whites of Skar's eyes showed.

"It is the truth," he said rapidly. "What I did was not dishonour. Rorik paid me to rid Dorestad of a wolf's kindred that had rebelled against his rule. But the feud with your kin had already given me personal reason enough. Rorik does not own me."

Judith's thoughts raced. She could hear her own voice asking questions in the moonlight. *What did you do to offend Rorik? To make him resort to trickery?*

Rorik.

She held the knife hilt tight and watched Einhard's face.

I offend Rorik by being Frisian.

The Viking Skar shifted under the sword blade. "I am not Rorik's man. I am not anyone's man."

"I thought you were Jarl Guthrum's."

"No——" The arrogance of the denial came without thought, without prudence. From a man who did not always choose to exercise control over the passions he felt. Skar's bitter eyes leaked fury. "Guthrum's payment will give me back what I have lost, what you stole, the wealth to cover my stake in a new land. You took that from me. You attacked my brother's ships and you——"

"Not I."

"Liar——" The control was cracked now, impossible to maintain despite the tempered steel's threat. "You stole from me——"

"No. Rorik did. It was his ships that stole your brother's cargo, his men who nearly killed your brother using the cover of my name. You have pursued the blood feud because of that and yet it is no honour deed on your part. You do only Rorik's work, just as you did before——"

"No." The furious creature moved, with a maddened brutality beyond restraint. It was matched. She watched the unstoppable power of Einhard's body and thought, *he will kill him.* The steel blade flickered. She cried out, beyond thought, too fast for it, not knowing that she had moved until her shadow loomed over the convulsed figures.

She must have been allowed to make those half-dozen steps across the deck only because she was a woman, not a warrior, a creature outside the hard, tightly packed intensity that belonged to the bitter playing out of masculine honour. But even as she ran, Skar went still. She saw the line of blood where the sword blade lay against skin. She saw what even the slightest increase in pressure could do.

No one else had moved, and yet she could see the hands readied on weapons on either side of Skar and Einhard. They waited only for that slight increase of weight on the blade. The demands of a feud knew no mercy. On one side there would be a living leader to protect, on the other a dead one to avenge. They would fight because they must.

Her voice shaped the words to the bitter heavens.

"You will kill him."

17

AT THE SOUND OF HER VOICE, Einhard glanced up. He had not
once looked round during the whole of the contest of wills
with Skar. Yet there was no surprise in his eyes. It was as though
he had known, always, that she was there, that she had not left
the ship as he had arranged, that she had stayed. Their gazes met
and she could see plainly all that before she had only guessed at.
She understood the power of that living force, the brutal depth
that cried out for atonement.

She held his gaze. Whatever he did, she would not leave him,
nor would any of his men while they lived. Loyalty. She had been
trained all her life to know how much that required. More than
that, she was his, whatever happened. She tried to convey the
meaning of that pledge through that bright contact of sight, in
a moment too dangerous and fleeting for words. She tried to
tell him she understood. She held her ground. Her hand tightened competently on the hilt of the *seax*. The bright crucible of

his gaze seemed to fix on the movement of her hand in the light. The glittering handle dug against the gold boar ring on her finger. East Anglia. She could feel the power of her dead ancestors at her back. The blank fury of Skar's gaze flicked to the knife.

She expected the bright sword blade in Einhard's hand to move in its turn. It held still and in that fractured moment, Skar's gaze locked on the knife in her hand, changed, tightened. It was recognition, an instant so powerful it caught him, even in the moment that must hold his death. It was his knife, the knife that had been used by his own hired assassin. But the recognition was different.

The knife moved in her hand and the sun, reflected clear along the shape of the great *hlæw,* glanced off the fine handle, off the blade, the straightness of it, the Danish-carved rune. *Cen*—the torch. The creative force that shaped and reshaped people and deeds.

The assassin who had wielded the knife had been Frisian, not Danish. Skar might use a Frisian, but so might—

"Rorik." Her mouth shaped the word even before her thoughts had time to form. "It is not your knife."

The bale-filled eyes of the Viking flickered, ignited with the same insane anger that had made him attack the man who held him. Einhard's body flexed, cutting off the movement before it could be made.

But that ruthless, savage movement did not cut off the words. Her fingers slid more firmly round the gilded hilt of the assassin's knife, a trained warrior's grip.

"It is my knife," yelled Skar who could not govern his fury.

Her breath caught. The sword in Einhard's fast competent hand would strike. The knife vibrated in her bloodless fingers. "I gave it to Rorik. It sealed the bargain on my part, a token of honour. And now you have it. Where did you get it?"

Einhard's voice broke the silence before she could speak. "From the assassin sent to kill me." His gaze turned to Skar, assessing the trapped man's eyes. But Skar was too far gone in fury for the complexity of lying.

"An assassin? A secret killer? It was not of my contriving. My deeds are my own, done by my own hand. If the knife was in Rorik's possession, then it was Rorik's man who used it. It was not only your father he wanted me to clear out of his way. I should have killed you."

"But you did not manage it."

The furious, self-absorbed gaze flickered. "I did not much care. It was your father my quarrel lay with. His death closed it. It was over, paid. And my brother had charge of the payment, the cargo. It would have fetched enough to set both of us up in Iceland. I would have gone there, left you to rot except—"

"You had not finished Rorik's work for him because I was still alive. You turned out to be unsatisfactory to him, not worth his payment."

"I am not Rorik's man," yelled Skar.

Judith nearly stepped back. Skar's eyes were glazed with fury, wild with it. But the bitter intensity of the reaction, the uncivilised power, changed nothing in Einhard. He drew it on, provoked it. *He understands it,* she thought. *He knows.* In some way it was what he felt, like some appalling mirrored reflection. *That is why they can talk, why they can hold each other on the edge of death. They understand what to say. At least, Einhard does....*

"You acted at Rorik's direction," said Einhard. "You worked for his payment, the wages in silks and furs and amber. But because you failed to complete the work, he took it from you and you did not even understand what he had done."

"He betrayed me, the——" The spit flew. The furious frustrated passion found its way out. Einhard made no move to stop the wild outburst. Then Skar said, "...I acted in my own honour."

Honour. She thought of the dead men betrayed at the peacemaking, the stolen, terrified child, and her own rage flared, so easy to give in to, even while the sane part of her brain could see that to his own incensed mind Skar spoke the truth.

"Rorik played you for what he could gain," said Einhard across the headlong, self-willed flow. "He will do that still if you let him, just as Guthrum will use you on the promise of plunder you may never get. You pursue this feud even now at this minute, in this place, because of what someone else would have you do."

The sword rested against the exposed skin. The remorseless voice went on. "I have said you have one choice left to make — whether you end your life by a blood feud pursued for someone else's gain, or whether you end the feud now, abandon Earl Guthrum, take your cargo and find your place in Iceland and stay there. Because I tell you this, if you move from your new land with the intent to harm my son, or this woman, or anyone connected with me, I will not stop until I have killed you and your brother and every man who has ever had a hand in anything you have done."

Judith watched the man sprawled on the deck, Einhard. *This woman.* He did not glance at her but the thread of awareness between them burned like flame.

"What do you choose?"

Life or death. Future or past.

"It is over," said Skar.

She watched Einhard move back.

"Where is he?" Mildred ran the carved bone comb through her mistress's hair.

Judith stared at a pot of lip salve.

"Halfway to Iceland by now, with his honour payment."

The comb snagged in the windblown mess. Mildred disengaged the teeth. Her hands were not entirely steady. Judith watched her own fingers round the salve pot, steady as a rock. Her shaking was on the inside.

Mildred began combing again.

"Then it has all turned out well."

"Yes. Very well." And Einhard had all but taken death ensuring it was so—Thieto safe, the volatile feud ended, Skar dealt with. She herself could go back to Wessex, to Hunferth, with the danger averted, with Guthrum's burgeoning fleet left all the smaller. Back to the king.

She thought about what the news meant to Alfred, to her brother, to every man who waited across the border and planned and hoped and worked at the great deadly game, the relentless bitter struggle for survival. Her eyes filled with tears. Stupid, when everything had worked out well. She undid the rouge pot.

"I was not asking about Skar," said Mildred. "I was asking about Einhard."

"About Einhard?" Her fingers, enviably steady, discarded the lid. The scent of ripe cherries. It filled her mind, her senses, she could feel the lingering smoothness of the salve on her skin, the sweet taste on her mouth crushed and released by Einhard's lips, by the first mad kiss of passion. A creation of spell-craft, recognised as magic even by one who had no experience of the game of loving, one who had been mead-glad and besotted not just by drink, but by a man, by the first wild, rapturous tasting of him. There had been such magic she had not understood.

"Where is he?" said Mildred.

She took a breath. "With Thietmar."

The comb moved slowly. The cool breeze whispered through the shadows of the East Anglian trees. It would soon be too dark to see. Tomorrow they would sail for Wessex.

"Well, that is as it should be," said Mildred. "The child will want his father and the father…"

The father had nearly gone mad with grief and longing for the child. She knew that. Mildred doubtless guessed it.

The comb never faltered.

"Are you going to use that salve?"

"The lip colour? No." She could never go back. Never. The soft East Anglian air whispered over her skin. She thought of the girl she had been on that first day at Stathwic, shocked, dislocated, so bitter. Haunted by the need to do some deed that would set things right, driven by it until she had found herself in a stranger's bedchamber, mad and desperate and obsessed by what she wanted. So single-minded, even though she had striven to do what was right. As she still did.

Einhard had understood that single-mindedness. He had also understood the desperation and he had met it with a sense of honour she could never repay. Not the ordinary kind of honour, the narrow dogmatic kind she had accused him of betraying, but with something deeper, something she had not truly understood until it was over.

"Finished?" There could not be a single hair left uncombed by Mildred's gamely diligent fingers.

"Just this bit." Mildred fussed at random. "It is only natural, you know, for him to be with the child just now."

"Yes. Of course it is." She was not so base as to begrudge that. She had witnessed, almost from the start and by accident, all that was involved. What she had seen of Einhard on that first night when he had thought himself alone was something she could never forget.

She thought of Thieto running out of the mist on the barrow downs, his smallness, his face full of fear and distress and the terrible traces of determination that were his father's legacy. She could still feel the warmth of his hand in hers, the anger at watching Skar torment him. Then she thought of the way his eyes had looked when he had seen that his father had found him at last.

She could not quite find the words. "It...it is right."

Mildred fluffed out her hair. Their hands touched, briefly. Nothing to say. Except, perhaps there was.

"I am glad you stayed with me through all this."

"Duty," sniffed Mildred. It was hardly convincing.

"Friendship." Judith tested out the brand-new word on her tongue. Mildred, with rather heightened colour, made no objection. Their eyes met. It was actually rather comforting to have it out in the open. No crippling distance, no holding back. She would never have said anything so risky as that miracle word except for the influence of—

What he must feel for his son in this moment. She could scarcely imagine it. She concentrated on her hair.

"That looks better," said her friend. "Do you want the kohl for your eyes? A little of the rose-scented oil, perhaps?"

"No." No seduction. The time for that was gone. She had seen that much truth, so very late.

"Nothing?" asked Mildred.

Best to admit what you truly were. "Would you help me with the knife belt?"

"So?"

"Just as you would expect. Sailing well," said Tatwin. "Easy enough run to Iceland in this weather."

"Aye." Einhard stared at the darkening water.

"Believe it. The only thing you can say for Skar is that he is not a fool. He not going to hang around East Anglia after disappointing Guthrum, nor is he going to risk what you gave him anywhere near greedy hands in Dorestad. He has no ties elsewhere. He might send for anything he has left behind in Frisia, but he will be lucky to get it out of Rorik's clutches. He knows that."

"Yes." All that he hoped, nay, wanted to hear before he could go back again to Thietmar.

"What you did back there," began Tatwin. "How you could have—" But Einhard could not talk of what he had done, or of reasons. "When I got there," pursued Tatwin into the silence. "And there was just you on that ship and Skar with clear water in front of him. If I had not come back—"

"But you did come back." It still seemed unlikely. He looked at Tatwin. "Why?"

Tatwin carefully inspected the sheet of water that was now far too dark to make out. "Because I had made new oars by then. What? Did you think I was too feeble to sail with the damage you had caused?"

"Yes."

"Bastard." Tatwin unclenched his fist. Perhaps violence was unmonkly. "I believed you were wrong," said his friend. "I—I was sure the child was dead and I blamed you for what you were doing. It was so...so relentless. I thought you were the next thing to mad. But you knew that."

"Yes." He thought of the torchlit chamber and the dead assassin. He could still feel the coldness of the black air on his skin. How could anyone blame Tatwin for what he had thought?

"Then I changed my mind, so that meant I had got it wrong. I thought I had better put things right," said Tatwin with what he obviously considered was logic.

That simple. Bloody hell.

He decided to sit down.

Tatwin obligingly sprawled his length on the damp ground, as though the movement Einhard had made had been one of voluntary ease and not the next thing to collapsing.

"I saw through what you were doing," said his friend, apparently still motivated by a helpful spirit. "You wanted me out of the way so you could spare me the gory ending to the most comprehensive feud ever to come out of Dorestad. Not your best attempt."

Einhard laughed. It seemed the only thing left. "It should have worked." Then he said, "I was mad. I think I still am." He could feel it inside, under the relief that was so strong it was edged with violence and still unreal. The hideous oppression still burned. It had been there so long, black and bitterly consuming. Hell's bond.

"But you were still right, all the time."

"What changed your mind?"

"The girl," said Tatwin. "The East Anglian princess. It was what she saw. She does not know how to give up. She is like you."

It was as well that the other man was looking at the black sheet of the river once more. He wondered what would happen if everything held inside broke at last. The disaster seemed interestingly close.

"She made me acknowledge the truth," said Tatwin.

Einhard stood up, even though everything in his body protested. His thigh muscle ached where Skar had kicked it. The pain in his abused left arm was like fire. He forced each muscle to work. He had to go on.

"She believed that things could be different."

The East Anglian princess. Some things stayed the same. He made himself walk toward the dark bulk of the Serpent without limping.

"She has her own course to follow." It was true. It was enough. Tatwin did not know—

"What will you do about her?"

THEY HAD LEFT A LAMP burning on the Serpent at his orders. The guards were competent, still watchful. It was quiet, only the calm of the river and the restful movement of the water. He ducked into the small enclosure made from sailcloth. The small figure under its fur coverings might have been asleep.

He lowered himself down onto the deck.

"What is it?"

Thietmar lay still. The boy he had left in Dorestad would not have been able to keep quiet for more than two seconds when offered a question that related to what he thought. The new silence stretched out. He found the pathetically small hand. It lay against his without moving. It seemed cold despite the heaped coverings.

Silence and the lamp-flame burning.

He was not free of the bitter madness, the terrible rage. It burned brighter. It wanted escape.

"Thieto?" He used the familiar name. He kept the madness out of his voice. He would swear it. But the small hand jerked in his.

"You are angry with me."

"No. That is not true. What would make you think so?"

"I did not mean it to happen. Everything."

"*You?* Of course not." He controlled his voice, blocked everything out except the reassurance. "Thietmar, nothing that happened was your fault. We both understand that. Remember what we said." They had been through what had happened, explained—

"It is what Skar said."

The flames inside turned murderous. It was not just the

physical hardship Thieto had suffered, it was so much that was harder to reach, perhaps impossible. He tamped down the rage, turned his mind from the sickening, elemental fear. Thieto had only him. He had to find the way through this.

"What did Skar say?"

The small shape moved convulsively. "That I was too much trouble, that you would not want to come after me. He said it all the time."

"You know that is not so." But he did not think his son could hear him. The tormented body thrashed in the fur covers. "Thieto, come here—" But the small hand snatched itself out of his.

"Today he said you didn't want me because of her, the lady Judith. He said were spending your time…" There was a small deliberately collected pause. "Whoring for pleasure," said Thieto.

Einhard stared at his son across two feet of lamplight. He tried to think past the rage and the pain that were clawing at him like the greedy fingers of the sea taking a drowning man. Thietmar's eyes were huge, haunted and childlike, yet the compact figure was already shaping with the promise of future strength. Just now, it was taut as a wild animal's.

"Was that what you wanted?" asked the changeling who had been his son. "Whoring for pleasure?"

The words chosen, the question, were vicious, adult, nothing that should have sprung from Thieto's mind. Less than half understood, part of the new and terrifying world he had been pitched into with no defence.

Einhard sat back. "Skar has a foul mouth," he said with the

firmness of the old world. "You do not."

He saw Thietmar's colour rise because he had been taught what was right, but the angry, terrified gaze accused him.

"Is it true?"

He held the bitter wildness in the changeling's eyes. *Listen to me. For mercy's sake believe me. Don't slip away from me the way your mother did.* He took a breath that scored pain through his lungs. "I looked for you from the hour I learned you were missing. I looked for you until I thought I would go mad with it." The wide gaze that had been fixed on his wavered. He tried to find the words that were true and not frightening, simple and true enough for Thieto to understand.

"I had looked for you for a long time before I met the lady Judith and I never stopped looking." The bitter gaze dropped away. He kept speaking, hoping that the right words would come, the words that would stop the hurt, repair the damage.

"When you went missing, everyone thought you were dead, that you had died when Skar burned the house. There was no sign that you had survived and even I was afraid that it might be true, that you were dead."

He could not see Thieto's face now, only the averted head in shadow. The need to touch that small figure was visceral, but he could not. Whatever was held in that sharply turned head had to come out.

"When I looked for you," he said, "people thought I was crazy. Everyone did." He forced his voice to go on, steady. "I was on my own. Everyone believed I was wrong. The lady Judith was the only person I met who wanted to help me. When I kept looking, she followed." He swallowed down what he felt, the thought of Judith and her trueness and her courage, the sight of her with Skar. And with Thieto. "She found you. She stayed with you." He watched the shadowed form and said the truth. "She wanted to protect you from Skar. Can you understand that?"

He did not know whether the truth was strong enough, whether it was possible to reach through what Skar had done in his anger. The untidy head bent.

"She did not want Skar to hurt me."

"No." He felt his pent-up breath choke.

"I did know that," said Thieto, his mumbled words scarcely distinguishable. "I did like her. I just... I did not want you to want her more than me."

"It is not like that. One kind of liking does not cancel out another. I am still your father. I always wanted you and I always will. That is what fathers do."

There was a small choked sound, not a word, but it was enough, more than enough for whatever fragile control he had left. He moved, closing the narrow, light-filled gap.

It was not enough. The terrible power of the guilt that he had not been able to protect Thietmar from this, the brutal elemental fear that the loss was irreversible, swamped him, mingling with the black exhaustion in his mind. All that he had done in the savage struggle to find his son, everything he had said, made no difference. Thieto's tense shoulders jerked away from his touch. The price of every moment of bitterness since the day he had returned to Dorestad found its place. Not in his pain but in his son's tense body. There was no way out.

He thought of the black moment of despair in the borrowed chamber at Stathwic. He had still kept going, but the moment had held him, like a foretaste of this, hell's torment, living death.

"There is nothing wrong," said Thieto. The boat twisted on the moving water of the Deben and the lamplight struck his eyes. His mind snapped into focus.

Nothing wrong.

There is nothing for you here, he had said to Judith in the bright room. But she had ignored that. She had just waited, the stranger who had turned everything round, who had had such unconquerable belief. Faith.

"You can go away now," said Thieto.

*I am staying…*said Judith.

"I am going to stay."

"That's stupid," said Thietmar.

"Aye." His voice was like a rock, immeasurably steady. "Did you know that stupidity is inherited?"

Thietmar choked.

"Passed on from father to son," said Einhard.

The choking sound worsened. He might have been stupid, desperate, blind with pain, but he was not stupid enough to stop this. He let the furious violent tears come out. Then his hand lighted on one bony shoulder. The resistance vanished, as though it had never been, as though it were wiped out and the promise of a future was possible, like a miracle undeserved, a matter of faith.

The storm of weeping that followed was bitter but the grubby hands with their broken nails clung to him and he waited on the swaying deck of the ship, holding his son in his arms and fixing his gaze on the lamplight. Thieto wept and he willed the fierce heat that could have been his own tears out of his eyes because his son needed him. He did not know what he said, words that made no sense, as though Thieto were still three winters old and afraid of the dark. But the words did not need sense, not between them. The love was understood.

"...They did not know how well I could understand Danish," said Thieto what seemed like a lifetime later. "I used to listen to them when they talked at night. That is how I knew to escape. I did not want Skar to harm you when you came for me. He kept saying he would."

God's breath. There seemed no end to the disaster. He ran a hand through his hair.

"Aye, well." He kept his voice complacent. "In the end Skar was not up to that. You should have known it. It was easier for me to find you with Skar. But—" He watched the anxious fleeting expressions on Thieto's face. "I can see there will be no fooling you from now on."

"No," said Thieto. He yawned. All of a sudden he sounded smug. His solid compact weight lay still under the fur coverings, warm now. "I know how to speak some English, too. English is hard, though."

"Yes."

"Do you really like her?"

The question was so unexpected it threw the exhausted remains of his thoughts off track.

"I do not really mind," said Thieto. "Only..." *Only what?* "Do you know she walks around with a knife strapped to her thigh?"

A... He shut his eyes against the vision.

"She wanted to stab Skar. Do you think she would...would often use it?"

Judith.

"You mean would she use it on you if you were bad?" He choked on laughter that came out of nowhere. "I...I think it is probably safer to do what she says."

Thieto started giggling. "Like I always do with you?"

"More so," he came back promptly, knowing precisely what *always* was worth.

Thieto digested the *more.* "Why?"

"Because she is a lady."

Fortunately Thieto was still of an age to accept one of life's incontrovertible truths without asking for an impossible explanation.

"I could be good," offered Thieto, who despite high spirits and occasional stubbornness had always had a core of kindness. "If I tried." He sounded as blithely confident as an ale-sick man swearing off the mead, more than that, he sounded earnest. Einhard felt his heart contract.

There was nothing to say, even though Thietmar expected some sort of answer. He stared at the moving deck of the ship and thought how far relief and exhaustion and vulnerability had brought him. Beyond bounds.

"If..." began Thieto, but his voice trailed off, half slurred with sleep.

"The lady Judith is a princess," Einhard said. "We are merchants, you and I. Only that."

326   FEARLESS

"Rich pirates?" countered Thieto on a vague note of hope.

"Go to sleep."

"Will you…"

"I will stay until you sleep."

The lamp burned steadily. He waited it out, longer just to be sure. Then he stood, the movement forced through stiffened limbs, the clumsy unsteadiness that came with exhaustion. He moved away. The crew would have spoken to him then, the Serpent's captain would have followed. But it was impossible to stay, to form even a word of command. Tatwin held them back. Einhard slid over the ship's side and kept walking. He realised that his feet had taken him back across the eastern shore, into the burial mounds. It did not matter. Even dead spirits did not matter. The dead inhabited their own world, removed at last from cares. He thought of Geva, his dead wife, the frail spirit who had had no time to live, who had hardly known Thieto, but who had given him life.

Geva who had been given so little time, with Thietmar or with him.

I got your son back. I found him. At least I did that much. You can be happy about that.

The breeze rising up from the river stirred the night air, cool and remote as the stars, as the dead spirits. The air streamed past him. It was like saying farewell, with a finality never achieved through the bitter ending of physical suffering in this world. The loss of Geva had been too unexpected, too sudden for the measure of his grief. Too harsh, so hard on the heels of the gift of Thieto's life.

The breeze stilled and there was nothing, only the remoteness and the sense of a distance that could not be bridged. He knew it was right. What he wanted for Geva was peace.

It was impossible to walk any farther, even to stand. There were no longer any stars, only the darkness and the emptiness. Enough emptiness to take all that had been locked inside him since the moment he had returned to Dorestad and learned what Rorik and Skar between them had wrought.

THE FLARE OF LIGHT first stung his closed eyelids and when he opened them he could see the torch flame moving, carried high. Then the slender form advancing silently like a spirit. But no spirit at all, blessedly real.

Judith.

She stopped, as though afraid to come near him, doubtless because of how he appeared.

For all he knew, she had heard him. The sound he had made had been black and irredeemably violent, like a savage beast's.

Then she came closer, as no one else on God's earth would have done. He turned and the light struck his face. It was remorseless. She would see all there was to see, what had happened, the barbaric release of the fierce rage and the madness, the bitter traces of moisture on his skin. There was no disguise. No point. If anyone deserved to see the truth, she did.

"It is where we began." His voice sounded strange, hoarse, not his, but quite steady. He took a breath. She must have felt pity for him on that first night in his room when he had thought himself alone. Pity for the mad creature he was amongst all her desperate plans. She need not this time. It was over.

"It is a good place for an ending," he said.

"The only place." She stuck the torch into the soft East Anglian ground and the circle of light surrounded them, held them fast.

She knelt down and touched him.

18

⮀

JUDITH DID NOT KNOW whether he would accept her touch. It was over, whatever the connection between her and the dangerous Frisian merchant called Einhard had been. He had said so. She could go back to Wessex with one more threat averted. Skar and his ships were gone. The king's fleet had the precious gift of time. Einhard had risked his life for it.

The fragile light flickered over them in the sea of darkness. It streamed out over the ground, caught both of them, touching, joined and not joined.

Einhard had his son back, his whole world, entire and complete. It was not a world she had a place in. She had never felt the isolation of that more keenly, now that she had had her own brief glimpse of what closeness meant.

Her hand rested along the curve of his neck, her palm against his firelit skin, her fingertips deep in the shadowed hollow under the smooth weight of his hair. His skin was warm despite the night air, the muscles under her hand firmly strong, living. Living and therefore vulnerable. She closed her mind on Skar and death. Skar could not harm any of them. Einhard's doing. Like a gift, one of many he had given, gifts that had changed her.

She took a breath.

It is a good place for an ending.

She had to be worthy of the gift, at least. She had to speak. There were a thousand things she wanted to say. She wanted to thank him. She wanted him to know that she realised the danger he had been in and the sacrifice he had made. But only one thing mattered at that moment.

"I am glad you found your son."

Her hand curved round the fine line of his neck. She did not dare touch his face, with all the grief in it. She did not dare even to look on that.

Her inadequate words hung in the flickering air. But he would know, perhaps, how much lay behind them.

"It is a good place for an ending," she said. *Just as they had begun.* "I always seem to be where I should not be. But I promise I will leave you, this time." *I just had to know that you were all right, that the grief, at last, was over.* "I will not stay. I should not—" She started to move, as she ought.

He touched her hand. One moment there was nothing, just her leaning over him where he lay on the ground with her fingertips scarcely brushing the edge of his skin. And then the solid feel of his hand. The strong fingers, the wide palm closed over hers, moved her unsteady fingertips upwards to the flame-lit line of his face. She felt the harsh familiar shape, the rough edge of his jaw, the hot skin, the faintest remaining trace of moisture, and she was not alone anymore. Neither of them were.

She knew it was because of his courage, the same way he had not turned away from her when she had hidden in his chamber for her own ends and seen the black edge of his grief. That time there had still been secrets; this time he held no reserve, and this time she could meet him. Equal.

He was moving, pulling her down and she met him. Her body covered his. Their mouths touched, melded, entwining in human warmth, shared, until there was only one sensation, fierce, bright and filled with deep desire. Such wanting of him. She was lost in it, bathed in feelings she could not name. She let the kiss deepen, sweep her forward, carry them both like a tide in flood.

She took his hunger, his fierceness and the gentleness of his touch. She took everything, the familiar shape of lips and tongue, the difference in the way he kissed her, the way the strong hands caressed her body, the mysterious, overpowering difference in him.

Her response leaped, intensified, caught in his attraction, in the touch of masculine hands, the movement of his body. The intensity of feeling multiplied, increased a thousandfold. Her hands fisted in the linen of his tunic, spread out across his shoulders, felt the ridged muscles of his back. She heard his breath tighten. The fierce urgency, like pain, could have been in her own lungs. Her fingers speared through the smooth cascade of his hair, shaped the curve of his skull, held his head close to hers while his mouth worked insane magic on her.

The kiss dizzied her senses, her need so deep that the smooth glide of his lips, the invasion of his tongue brought wild pleasure, intense and full, edged with the desire for him that was depthless and would be as long as she lived. Her mouth cleaved to his. Her body moved at his urging, at the touch of his hands on her clothes, on her skin. His hunger for her was real, so strong, a need with depths and power beyond mortal measure. She was not frightened by it. The power made it only the more possible to respond. Because nothing had to be held back, nothing hidden for the sake of pride or defence or self-protection. There was nothing that would not be accepted. No barrier of distance. Only the longed-for closeness to another person. All that her heart had desired with such pain, a complete abandonment, the sharing of one self with another. There was only now. Only him and the edge of desperation and grief.

Her arms closed round him, the feelings deep. Her hands moved to his face. She touched his damp skin. She closed her eyes on her own tears. Her senses swam in heat, her flesh burned like fire under his fingers, under the smooth caress of his mouth. Her body twined with his, locked in the need, taking in the feel of his weight over her, the shape of his hips between her thighs, the sweet hot torture of his lips at her breast, her tight swollen nipple.

She arched her back, thrusting her hips against his, moving softened aching flesh against his hardness until she felt what she wanted, the glide of his hand under her bunched skirts. He adjusted their positions. She moved. Anticipation coursed through her veins. She sensed his gaze on her face. He would see her desire in the flickering firelight, measureless, just as he must feel it through her skin.

When he touched her, her gaze locked with his even as her body thrust against his hand, the response unstoppable, the pleasure so blinding, so deep, she had no control. His gaze held hers as his broad palm, his smoothly skilled fingers moved. She watched the intense brilliant lines of his face in the shadowed light, the brightness of his eyes until she could see nothing, until there was only the pleasure and the depthless consuming need and the closeness of him, until the gift that he gave, the slightest movement of his fingertips against the heat of her flesh, was all that was needed to take her soul.

She clung to him afterwards. No separation this time. Her lips and her hands and her body told him all that lived in her heart, in her heightened senses, in her desire-heated flesh. No restraint. She held on to the closeness until the fierce grief-edged hunger that filled him flared bright. Until his need had as little control as hers.

They moved together, their hands stripping away the last barrier of clothing. His touch possessed her, just as she courted his desire in each inciting brush of skin, in the hard touch of heated aroused male flesh against her exposed softness, in mingled breath and wordless sound and shared movement. Her flesh was aching and wet with desire and the madness of pleasure. She opened to the urging of his body, widened to sheathe the fullness of him. No pain this time, only the wild abandoned joy of feeling him inside her, the hot tightness of her made for pleasuring, for the smooth taut thrust of his body. Her hips arched against him and there was no control for either of them, only the edge of bright emotion, the deep need and the release of it. Matched souls.

JUDITH LAY STILL, her head on Einhard's skin. She could feel the wild beating of his heart, like the echo of her own. She could have lain there forever, touching him, as though the world did not exist.

The sense of closeness was still there. Like a miracle, complete, a place apart. A world within a world. Its power was intense.

Her hand twined round his neck. The faint breeze touched her exposed flesh, slid over skin still damp and heated with sex. With loving. She could not think of that. She felt him move, dragging the crushed mess of her cloak close across them for warmth. She did not care about the night; the only possible warmth could come from him. Yet her hand moved instinctively with his, reached down, brushing his fingers, the crumpled cloak, the tight curving muscle of his thigh. The torchlight, the accidental touch of her fingers, showed her the dark mass of bruising, the swollen flesh.

The coldness touched inside her.

"I thought you would die." Her voice choked on unsteadiness. "I was so afraid, watching you and what you did. I thought Skar would kill you."

"Nay." His voice was steady, the way it always was. "I was afraid it was you who would kill Skar too soon." The steady voice became pained. "You are the dangerous one."

"Me?" she said incensed. "Because of that *seax* blade? It was you who had planned everything, what you would do, how you

would confront Skar with no weapons, when all he had to do was slice off your head with a sword, or sail away with you on board the ship and let Guthrum do whatever he wanted. You are the one who is dangerous. Stupid—"

"I had a knife in my boot," he said indignantly.

"You…you did not? You…you *pirate*."

"So you say." He gave a melancholy sigh. The warm edge of his breath tickled her cheekbone. It was all designed to distract her. She took one fast glance at his face; it was impassive. But she saw the faintest trace of blood now at his lips, from the damage to his mouth that Skar had caused, exacerbated anew by the way they had kissed. He wiped it away when he thought she was not looking. She stared at the light. His slightest movement made the smooth swell of his skin press against her naked flesh and shivers of awareness raced through her, the response immediate, deep. And now savagely possessive.

"Yet you did not use the blade," she said. "You confronted him with nothing." *Nothing except the force of your will. And honour. And high-hearted recklessness.* "You did not—"

"But I wanted to." The carefully achieved lightness dropped from his voice. "Did you not see that?" he asked. "Did you not understand the black force that was inside me, all through everything I did, right or wrong? I wanted to use the knife. Or the sword, his sword. It did not matter which. That was what I wanted. There was no honour in it, no decency. It was like insanity."

She held on to the viciously tight muscle. Her heart pounded. She kept still, poised at the edge of the blackness, the hidden pain. "There were two people who understood that." She took a step where there was no safe ground. "One was Skar."

He moved as though she had used the *seax* blade. She caught hold of him, lunging like a wildcat. She caught his arm, terrified that he would draw back even then, even after what they had shared. "The other was me." He became still. Just that, but it was enough. Perhaps. *For the sake of pity,* she thought, *it has to be enough.* Her arms tightened round him, as though she would never let him go, as though they were one. He forced himself to speak.

"Skar and I could sometimes see through each other. We..." The bloodied mouth paused. "We can recognise things in each other because they are the same." She felt the harsh push of his rib cage, like someone unable to breathe. "As you said, the other one who can recognise such things is you." The strained muscle stayed in her touch. "Because only you have seen what is inside me."

"Yes. I have seen what there is in you." Her throat was so tight. "More than you seem to know." She held him, her flesh against his. "It was you who stopped the feud. You did what Skar could not. You made a choice he was not capable of making."

She raised her head and said as though it was the most obvious thing in the world, "I never had the chance to thank you for what you did—"

But his voice cut her off, hard as tempered steel. "I did nothing that deserved thanks. Tatwin did." There was a pause, the movement of his skin against hers. "You did."

"No—"

"You helped Thieto. It was you who found him. You stayed with him." She felt the shudder that passed through strong muscle. In her mind, she heard his voice in the dark, the violent, wordless sound of grief and anger and rage, of horrifying pain. "I can never repay that."

The torchlight blotted out the stars, made fire out of his dark gold hair. She felt him breathe. He was whole and alive when he might be dead, after he had come so close to death's power. He had Thieto.

"I do not want payment." She paused. "Not this time." She remembered all that she had once said, her harsh words about what she thought he owed to a country that could mean nothing to him. Now, out of the recognition he had credited her with, the recognition that had come too late, she understood the bitterness that had been in his eyes, the eyes of someone hunted, driven beyond what it was possible to endure and yet who still forced himself on. The stars hovered far above, beyond sight. The flame hurt her eyes.

"You acted for love. If there is a way to fault that I do not know it." She felt the sharpness of his breath. "Thieto is your future. I want nothing."

"Nothing." He moved, the fine, tautly-held living muscle close, touching her body. "What will you do?" he said in his accented English

The East Anglian night closed over her. "I cannot stay here. Not now. My time in this land is over—it may never come again." She sensed the closeness of the secret mounds hemming them in, surrounding the hollowed ground where they lay. Filled with sleeping spirits outside time, who had had life and a fair country lent to them for a little while and now were dust, their great empty treasures heaped round them in the earth. Life and death, wealth and loss, joy and sorrow in endless change.

"I will go back to Wessex." The cool breeze, the breath of her ancestors, touched her, caught in change as she was. They had helped her. They understood, those fierce warriors in their tombs. She breathed the air into her lungs. "Wessex is where the battle lies. I cannot give up." Einhard of all people would understand that, Einhard who could look into her soul but who had his own life and his own path.

"I will go back." *But I will never be the same, not now that I have known you. Even if you are a thousand miles away, you will always be in my heart.*

"Besides—" the pain settled in its place round her heart "—an oath is an oath."

"Sworn in blood to the king of the West Saxons? From a woman?"

Her body stiffened. "No. The king would not take such an oath from a woman."

"Then he should. I think he already has."

She caught her breath and her heart beat fast. "I know you think he is wrong, that he will lose this struggle."

"I did."

"Did?"

"I had not met him."

"And now?" She watched him in the fire and the shadows.

"I do not know. I cannot see as far as you can. Or I could not."

Her heart caught. She watched his face, now controlled, its

strength deep in the bones, in his mind. She thought of all that had been hidden. His voice touched her.

"I do not know how to see the future. Perhaps we are not alike in that. Perhaps I can never be what you want, or give you what you want. You have such faith in the future. I lost that. And now——"

"Now?" Her heart beat so fast she thought it would choke her. She moved round. Their skin touched, like something shared. She wanted that touch more than she had wanted anything in her life. Closeness to someone else. Her fingers sought his face, just as her gaze, blinded, sought his eyes.

"You have given more to me than I have ever known or deserved." Her voice stammered. She watched his eyes, the depthlessness of them, and her heart beat with fear and hope and everything held down inside her. Love.

The words came, all the things she would never have dared or known how to say but for him.

"You give without ceasing, all that you have. You did all that had to be done to find your son, everything, and you never counted the cost. When you faced Skar, you would have sacrificed your life for that future you say you cannot see, for a foreign land in need. To give me what I wanted. I never knew how to give, even though I tried. It was as though something in me had died in that battle at Hoxne. It was you who brought it back to life. You who showed me what life was, and how…how other people should be loved."

She thought the pressure in her heart would kill her. The

light flared in the night breeze. She could see nothing but Ein-hard's eyes.

"If I could make one half of the return to you of what you have given, if I could give you the happiness you should have, I would do it. I would love you if that was what you wanted." The pressure choked her. "I already do."

She felt the touch of his body, the way his arm closed tightly round her, and the rest was oblivion.

Her breath came in appalling gasps like his. Her hand was fisted in his hair. He removed it carefully. Her fingers were like an animal's claws.

"I am sorry," she said.

He held her hand. The gesture seemed to cover everything, passion and insanity and simple care.

"I think I am mad," she added.

"Just as well."

She heard his laughter. The first time, quite free, like a miracle. "We will match. I have been telling everyone I am mad for some time now." His breath was not steady. Her heart leaped. They were tangled together on the ground. More than that, he still had hold of her hand, like a troth-plight, a betrothal gesture. The touch of his hand was real. She spoke, out of the terrifying hope of that gesture, out of faith.

"Just as long as you are insane enough to love me." Her voice shook.

"Aye." There was no longer a disguise. Truth. "I was always that mad."

Her breath trembled. "Always?"

"It was only the future I could not see. I did not think I could give you what you wanted, deserved." He moved his arms, settling her against warmth. She was lying on him. "But I always loved you. Yes."

She thought her heart would burst. Her head dizzied. He was all that she wanted and more. And he loved her, had loved her...*always*. "But from when? How could you love me? I was appalling. I tried to seduce you for my own advantage, tried to bribe you. I nearly got you killed in battle and then there was Skar—"

Her heart beat so hard, not just from the bright fire of passion but from what might be, from the miraculous possibilities. From him. She felt his quick breath.

"When you put it like that, it becomes hard to pick the moment. I am spoilt for choice. You missed out the assassin—that was good." His other hand moved wickedly across her hips. "But I did enjoy the seduction. Just like now."

Now had been... She felt her face burn, all of her body where she lay on top of him, her skin melded to his in heat. "Now—" Her hand gripped his.

"But there was one disappointment this evening." His arms tightened.

"What?"

"I was looking forward to the knife strapped to your thigh."

"The..."

She glanced across the firelit ground to the discarded knife belt, the glittering hilt of the *seax* with its hidden rune.

"It seemed unfair to leave that for Skar. Thieto, by the way, was particularly impressed." His fingers glided across naked skin. "Although not for the reason I would have been."

"Frisian idiot," she said. The fingers of her free hand touched his face, careful to avoid the damaged mouth. "Fool of a flat-lander. Swamp dweller."

"Next you will be criticising my webbed feet. Is not that the order of things?"

"Oh. Yes, that was always it. People always had to say that to me as though it was something new, just because one of our es-tates was on the edge of the fen country." She felt her own laughter, like something long unused, free as his had been. "It was enough that I was East Anglian," she said and like a mira-cle, the laughter held.

He sighed. She felt the delicious rippling movement of his chest beneath her. "The trials of having been born in an open land." They considered the unfairness of those living in a country full of hills.

"Mayhap we should make the best of it," he said, "and stay in Wessex."

She thought of the word *we*. She thought of what it might mean and her heart beat madly, like a lark's wings before flight.

"But…it is not your home and you love the sea."

"I cannot go back to what was my home, just as you cannot." The laughter faded on the night air, gone like smoke, like the ephemeral spirit of a lost kingdom. But there was something else there, something in its place. Something new. She did not feel the cold. Only the shared warmth. She pressed closer to him, so that he would know she was there, with him, and let him speak.

"I have spent half my life at sea. Because I was brought up to, because when my father rebelled against Rorik we lost nearly all we owned and I had to. Sometimes because it was the only place left in which to feel free of Rorik and the Danes. But it had a price."

She felt the small signs of tension she knew well how to recognise. She waited, holding him.

"I had less than a year with my wife."

She held her breath. But she had given her love. Nothing changed that. She held him close.

"Tell me."

"We had no time. We——" He broke off. She held him in the silence and then he said, "When the marriage was arranged we were both eighteen. We were strangers. Geva wanted children. It was her whole desire. I did not realise then how much having a child meant, how that changes everything."

She thought about having someone as small as Thieto to look after, the appalling moment facing Skar with a helpless child behind her. But she did not want to pull away. She pressed closer.

"Thieto came just before the end of that first year and she was so happy. I had never seen anyone so happy. All had seemed well at the birth, and then within days she had a fever and she was dead."

"I am sorry."

"It was so sudden. We had less than a year and even for part of that time I was not there with her. I had lost her almost before I knew her. She slipped away from me and I could not stop it. All I could do was promise her that I would look after the child, keep him safe. And Thieto—" He stopped speaking. Her hands slid across his body, over the strong tense muscle. But what she saw was the shocked, grief-struck, eighteen-year-old he must have been, stunned with pain, faced by all that responsibility. He had not turned away from it. Never.

"You brought your son back. He is safe. You kept your promise. You will always look after him."

"Geva died when her life was just beginning and part of the time she did not have a husband, just as Thieto did not have a father. After she died, it was my own father who brought Thieto up just as much as I did, and I almost lost him."

She held him in the darkness and the light.

"You love him. No father could love him more. He knows that. I could see it in his face and hear it in his voice. Just as he loves you. You were all that he thought of."

"I do not want to be away from him for half my life. I want to see him grow up. I do not want half a marriage that might end at any time before it has properly begun. If you are asking whether I want to spend long periods of time at sea, I do not. It costs too much. I won't pay that price again. I want a family."

A family. Close. Her heart filled with a longing that was savage, that she had never known could have such power, had never let herself know because she had turned away. She would never turn away from such ties again. They were what created life. She could feel the hot prickle of unshed tears at the back of her eyes.

"But what does Thieto think?"

She sensed the last thing she expected, a sudden lightening. He did not laugh. It was almost impossible to surprise that sound from him. "He has given me his permission."

"His...his permission?"

"Yes. He has also promised to be good. Or at least—" she could feel the smile now "—to make a heroic attempt in that direction. Remember, he saw the knife."

"Athelbert's bones. He wants to be good because I have a *seax?*"

"Aye." The laughter almost formed. "For pity's sake don't feel sorry for him. Never let an advantage go past when you are dealing with Thieto. Besides, he likes you."

The unshed tears suddenly choked her. "Really?"

"Really. The little hound has also worked out that I really like you. He wants to have a mother. He can scent an arrangement."

"Athelbert's—"

"—much abused bones. He sees a promising arrangement from his point of view. He is a merchant's son after all."

"A pirate's son. It must run in the blood."

"Yes."

She thought of what it would be like to live with Thieto, with his courage and his determination and his ready tongue. To share the responsibility for bringing him up. It was a frightening thought, but it was also immeasurably exciting.

"Perhaps I could practice sword fighting with him."

The answer was decidedly Frisian. She stored away the word for future use.

"Thieto would be your slave forever if you did. But I am not sure I fancy my chances in this household."

"Nithing."

"Yes. Do you mind that?"

"What do you mean?"

"That I am only a merchant. You wanted a prince, someone who could spout sweet words."

"Instead of witless Frisian remarks. So I did. I think I was a maid of thirteen winters when I made that decision." She slid her hand across bare skin like heated silk. She stopped suggestively at the top of his thigh. "Something changed my mind since."

"You are a Jezebel. I should have listened to Hunferth."

She said something uncomplimentary about Hunferth in East Anglian.

"Aye. But one thing is true," he said. The light tone over the hidden depths dropped. "I am not your equal."

"You are better. No, let me say what I think. It is the truth. You have shown it in courage and honour. Besides," she said across what he would have denied. "Do you know nothing of English customs? A merchant who has thrice crossed the sea in his own ship is worthy to be called a thane, a nobleman. Surely you do not mean to tell me you have not crossed the sea three times."

"I—I believe I qualify."

"Well, then. Besides, you know how to trade in fish blubber, which I do not. Only consider the usefulness of that."

"I am considering," he said with fitting humility.

Her lips twitched. "Good." Then she said, "Did you really

think that, about being a merchant and not— And then I said things that—"

"Yes." His heavy finger touched the boar-shaped gold ring on her right hand.

"I never meant—" Her hand tightened against his skin. "I only said such things because you were so difficult."

"Difficult? Me?"

She resisted the temptation to hit him. "Yes, and so…" Her fingers spread out over living warmth. "So attractive. It was self-defence. Anyway, as for me, I am princess of nothing. I have no kingdom and no king."

"Except the one in Wessex. I suppose in between cargoes of fish blubber I will end up swearing some blood oath to the West Saxons, like the prince your brother and that British bastard who can see things nobody in their right mind can."

"Macsen? You noticed that? He will be mortified. I think visions are the bane of his life. Except he thought—"

"What?"

"In the end, after he had told me what an appalling pirate and first-rate bastard you were, he…he seemed to think it would work out."

"He thought…"

"He mentioned the burial mounds and…light."

"Torchlight." It flickered off the rune blade, *Cen, Kenaz,* the torch, the sign of the power to reshape people and deeds, the sign of a child. "It was the torch and the blade that led me to you," he said. "That led you to Thieto."

"Aye. That and—"

"What?"

She held him close. "Your courage. The power of your love."

"You are going to marry us then, pirate and pirate's brat?"

She looked at the sky. Stars. Torchlight. "Hunferth is expecting it. And you were going to make a settlement with my brother whom you could buy and sell. I expect a really expensive morning-gift."

"Fish oil?"

"Perfect."

Her arms tightened round him. Close.

Epilogue

THE BRIDE-GIVING WAS A notable event. It was also a celebration. The West Saxon king had put his new ships to the test and had destroyed Guthrum's reconnaissance fleet in a battle at sea. Between them, the Sea-wylf and the Serpent had captured one of the Viking ships.

It was a victory. No one pretended it was permanent or that the threat in the northeast would not grow again. But it was a step. No one looked further than that. It was the way the West Saxons dealt with the future, a way that worked.

Einhard had lost count of the numbers of Saxon and Anglian thanes present at the wedding, not to mention the victorious king. Somehow Einhard had ended up swearing his oath to Alfred on the eve of the sea battle, as he had known he would. By doing so, he seemed to have acquired an entire brotherhood. The list included Macsen the Briton who saw uncanny visions, an English thane known as Ash who had spent most of his life as a Viking, the king's own cousin, who-knew-who-else and, of course, his brother-in-law.

Judith's brother, the prince he could buy and sell, was unexpected, much in the way Alfred the king had been unexpected. The marriage settlement had been arranged without fuss; he had made sure of it. It was only Judith who had thought the wealth in solid silver of her morning-gift too much. It was enough to buy a good piece of Wessex land, a new home.

Einhard and his brother-in-law had reached a wary understanding. After the sea battle, it had become complete.

Judith and Berg were close—

"Do you think she has the knife?" asked Thieto, breaking his thoughts.

Einhard eyed the erotic fall of his wife's gold silk skirts. "I hope so."

Thieto's eyes widened. "Why?" But fortunately his son's rapidly working brain had leaped elsewhere. "Why did Uncle Berg bring a swineherd with him to the wedding?"

Uncle— The disconcerting prince. "I have no idea. Perhaps it is an ancient East Anglian royal custom." The swineherd had apparently been rescued by Berg's wife. There was much to discover about his new kindred. At that moment, Judith turned round. Her hair, under a daringly small veil, was loose, deeper gold than the silk dress. He knew what it felt like to touch.

"Oh," said Thieto in the voice of a child unconvinced. He kept talking. The silence that had dogged him in the days after Skar was fading, particularly when Judith was around. Thieto was fascinated. "I like Aunt Elene, too."

Berg's wife had developed something of an affinity with Thieto. She had once been a Viking captive herself. No one ever spoke of such a thing in her presence or in Berg's. But she chose to talk to Thieto. Einhard had no words to express gratitude. He thought she knew.

Thieto grasped his hand, as though it were quite an ordinary thing to do. Einhard met Judith's gaze across the noisy celebrating hall packed with people and it was as though there were only the three of them in the world. There was everything in his wife's eyes, promise, trust, blatant invitation and the courage that moved mountains. Faith.

It might not be so bad being English.

Historical Note

EINHARD'S HOME, the fabulously named city of Dorestad, had a tragic history. Dorestad, near the mouth of the River Rhine, was the principal trading port of the flatlands known as Frisia (now divided between The Netherlands and Germany).

Frisians had a reputation for strength. They were great traders, skillful seafarers and sometimes pirates. But Frisia, conquered by the great Frankish emperor Charlemagne, was left fatally weakened to Viking attack. Unable to defend Dorestad, Charlemagne's successor Lothar "set a thief to catch a thief," handing the city over to the Viking Rorik. Rorik fared no better. Continued raiding and changes to the River Rhine eventually lost Dorestad its riches and its trading value.

In England, King Alfred of Wessex commanded the only land still free. His struggle against the invading Vikings included naval warfare. King Alfred, like many men, was fascinated by boats. He built a navy, and in 875 the *Anglo Saxon Chronicles* proudly record the king winning a battle against seven Viking ships—one was captured and the rest put to flight. Being a canny ruler, Alfred knew when to import expertise. Some of the courageous shipmasters so briefly mentioned elsewhere in the *Chronicles* bear a tantalising addition to their names: "the Frisian."

Turn the page for a haunting preview of Helen Kirkman's next dramatic novel UNTAMED. The stirring tale of an outcast healer and the dark warrior who haunts her dreams...

coming December 2006

From HQN Books

Wytch Heath, near Wareham, the South Coast of England, A.D. 876

THIS TIME THE DREAM of him was different. The man who had invaded her dreams was closer. Aurinia caught the sense of danger from him and her breath sharpened, even in the bands of sleep.

She saw his face first, only that, the strong lines and the night-black hair, the eyes dark as ripe sloe berries, and her heart tightened on the familiar dizzying ache.

Light and shadow from her empty hall flickered over her closed eyelids and the dream pulled her down, overmastering her senses, making them catch fire. He called to her, her dark warrior with the costly armour and the eight strands of gold at his neck. His presence and the potent sense of his vitality overwhelmed her. But this time the shadowy bond was fierce, intensified by the danger. Pain.

She smelled the blood. It was all around him, terrifying and death-filled, like the shouting.

He saw her, had sensed her, five miles away on the battlefield.

The brilliant eyes locked for one burning instant with hers and the unspoken bond snapped tight, frightening and deep. Then the contact broke. She saw him swing round, the swift sudden movement of the leaf-bladed spear in his hand, its flight like lightning through the dark, a bright curving arc of terror.

Aurinia's fist clenched, hard against the patched linen of her dress. The shouts all around him were in Danish, Viking words. He was not Danish, with his dark eyes and his fine high-bridged nose and his bronzed skin that spoke of southern climes.

Then even as she watched, caught in the dreaming, the sharp arrow points ripped through the air, a death rain hissing towards him, and the slighter, unarmoured figure next to him fell. The screaming voices, the fast feet of the Vikings, rushed forward like a wave.

He had kept his feet, but he would have to turn, run.

Run. Her heart spoke to him across distance and time that had no meaning, as though they were one, she and the dark warrior who fought so bitterly against odds that were desperate. As though he could feel her touch and the desperation in her own heart, as though his unmatched strength had the power to penetrate the frozen isolation that held her trapped in this empty hall, to shatter it with his heat. As though they could touch.

Run.... She watched him unsheathe the glittering line of a broad-bladed sword. She could smell death, death and wounds.

He did not turn back. He stepped in front of the fallen man. The wave broke over him.

And she— The desperation flooded her heart, terrible, matched by a raw will.

"Lady!"

The sharp sound of Huda's voice shocked through her, real, close, the sense of dislocation intense. The grip of her steward's hand on her shoulder shook her awake in the quiet hall at Wytch Heath. His breath rasped with his fear.

She was shivering. The dream dissipated, impossible to hold on to, lost like the hot vital grace of the dark-haired man.

Not lost—

"Lady. Aurinia…" Huda's voice, anxious, demanding, cut through, breaking the sleep that had come over her as she sat beside the window. The only retainer who had remained faithful to her had come to tell her what she already knew. That the invading Vikings and the troops of King Alfred of Wessex were fighting at Wareham, not five miles from here.

"…there is battle. Men fleeing from the army may force their way through here."

"They cannot." Aurinia sat up, forcing movement through her stiffened body, every muscle wound tight with tension. One thing in this world was certain. No stranger had ever reached the hall at Wytch Heath. The pure isolation of her home stood unbroken.

It had the strength of a curse—

"No Viking will get through."

"No," answered Huda, the heaviness deliberate. "Nor Saxon." He paused and then said, "Not even a king's man."

A king's man. Aurinia had glimpsed him, the stranger of her dream, in a hall greater than this, cloaked in shadow and rich light, the weight of the golden dragon pouring down his shoulder like fire. The Saxon king's sign.

"Are we not on the same side as the king's men?"

Huda's hand tightened for an instant on her shoulder. "No one is on our side."

She looked away. Huda was the nearest thing she had to a father. She had to protect him as she had to protect herself. The isolation at Wytch Heath existed for a reason. Her fists were still clenched, as though the battle five miles away, as though the terrible life-and-death struggle of the stranger touched her even now. Five miles.

No one ever found the path through the treacherous ground to her hall. It was wolf-ridden.

Unless— She stood. The white cloth and the rune staves at her feet scattered. She had already read those angular shapes carved on wood, at once an ancient alphabet and signs filled with hidden meaning. She did not look at how they fell. She had seen the portents.

They had spoken of death.

The red glow of sunset filled the chamber, stinging her eyes, staining the pale cloth like the blood she had smelled, tasted. She could feel pain, heat, despair. How could she turn away from that? From *him*.

Sudden sound made her gasp, and Muninn's winged shape sliced through the sunlit air in a flurry of disturbed plumage. The raven perched on her windowsill. Muninn, bird of memory, sacred in the old days to Woden, chief of the sky gods who was supposed to have found the wisdom of the runes. A raven was a messenger.

Huda crossed himself, even though every living creature who visited her was familiar to him. Ravens were double messengers, they might bring bliss, or they might come to feed on the battle-dead. The sun struck the bird's blue-shadowed wing as it settled. It was the same colour as the night-dark hair of the king's man.

She could feel the power of his will across the distance that separated them. It reached inside her. Her heart seemed to stop, suspended between one beat and the next.

He would bring the outside world and the scent of blood if he fought his way here. If she let him. If he lived.

Her life would change.

She did not meet Huda's eyes. Her decisions were her own. They always had been. She watched the raven.

He would come.